THE *ex* FILES SERIES

EXPOSED

LISA RYAN CAMPBELL

GET YOUR FREE BOOK!

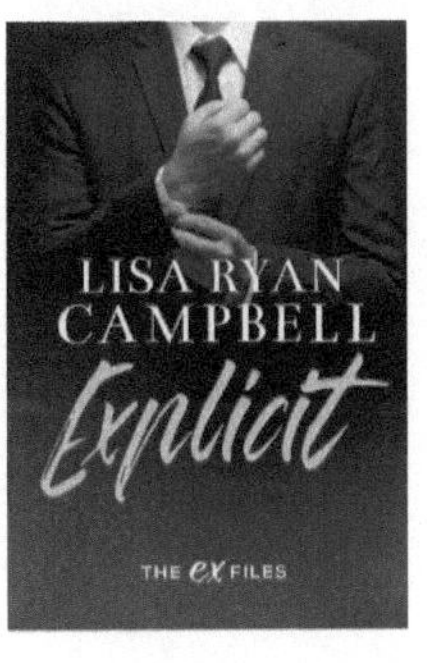

When you have a one-night stand with your next-door neighbor, and he turns out to be your boss.

Click here for your free copy of EXPLICIT!

For Larry,

I miss you and will always love you.

PROLOGUE

From inside her car, Havilland gazed up at the ten-thousand-square-foot mansion in the Pacific Heights district Terrence shared with his wife. Even under the night sky, she could see it was stately and majestic. It made her think of her own three-bedroom Victorian in Walnut Creek, which paled in comparison to this one, with its stunning views of San Francisco Bay and Alcatraz. But she didn't regard the home before her with envy. She looked at it with scorn, particularly for the man who waited inside for her. It was because of him that she'd crossed a line she never thought she'd ever cross in all her years with law enforcement. She looked over to the passenger seat and stared with dismay at the plastic evidence bag she'd stolen two days ago and realized she didn't just despise Terrence; she hated herself for what she'd become and the lengths she'd gone.

She was jeopardizing everything for a man who'd left her years before for so-called greener pastures. Only he hadn't left her completely, because he was still pulling her by the strings, forcing her to do his bidding for him and not giving a damn about the consequences she faced.

She should call Carl. She should call him before this goes any further and tell him she was done. But if she called Carl, he'd only convince her to continue on with the plan, reminding her that she was the one who organized this partnership in the first place. That was true. She'd entered this deal to protect her family but was now sorely regretting it.

She'd become a puppet. Once she met Terrence and gave him the stolen ledger, what was stopping him from calling her again for the next favor? Would there ever come a day when she could refuse him, or would he always have this ridiculous hold on her? She just wanted it to stop.

She was starting to think she was losing her mind because her thoughts were once again returning to the idea of getting rid of him permanently. The man had enemies, and it would be simple enough to make it look as if one of them took him out, and she would finally be free.

Havilland looked up at the darkened house again and felt the weight of her gun holstered to her hip. It would be so easy to go in there and just erase him from her life completely, especially since no one knew she was there. Terrence mentioned in his text that Devon would have left for the airport by now, and the staff had been dismissed that afternoon, giving them the privacy they needed to make the transaction. She could use this to her advantage. Her time as a police officer with the Atlanta PD and now as a CBI agent taught her all about crime scenes, so she knew how to cover her tracks.

With her mind made up, she pulled her gun from her waist, checked the clip, and returned it back to its holster. She then grabbed the evidence bag with the accountant's ledger, tucked it inside a crossover bag, and climbed from the car. She was only bringing it along to get him to trust that she was on the level, but she sure as hell was taking it along with her when she left and he was dead. She'd have to arrive at the office early tomorrow morning in order to return it to the evidence locker before anyone else saw her. That is, before Eric saw her and discovered she'd gotten herself into one hell of a mess—again. He already mistrusted her, but this, what she was about to do, would have him turn his back on her forever.

She bypassed the front door and crept around to the rear of the home, just as Terrence had instructed her. She came to the back patio, and there, just like he'd said were a pair of French doors, which would be left unlocked for her. What he hadn't told her was that the doors would be wide open with one of the glass panels shattered.

Instinct and training instantly brought Havilland's gun from her holster to her hands along with her flashlight. She turned in a full circle, searching her surroundings and straining her eyes and ears for any sign of movement, but she only saw the trees in the backyard and beyond those were the darkened waters of the bay and the now shadowed structure of Alcatraz.

She braced herself against the outside wall of the home and used only her head to quickly peek around the corner and then shined her flashlight into the room that led directly from the patio.

"This is Special Agent Sawyer with the CBI," she called. "Is there anyone inside?"

Silence.

She stepped one sneakered foot inside the room, wincing at the sound of crushed and broken glass beneath her shoe. She stepped another foot inside and swung the flashlight from corner to corner. Judging from the desk placed in the center of the room and the bookshelves that lined the walls, she could see she was in the den. She reached for a desk lamp and yanked the chain over and over, but only the insistent clicking sound returned with no light to fill the room.

Where was Terrence?

Havilland moved through the room with her gun and flashlight leading the way, all the while keeping her back close to the wall for cover. She didn't get too far because as soon as she rounded the other side of the desk, her foot kicked something heavy and immovable. She shined her flashlight down and trailed it along a body lying motionless and then immediately backed away in shock as familiar and now dead, sightless eyes stared up at her.

No. It can't be.

She took several deep breaths to compose herself and then knelt down and checked for a pulse. When she didn't find one, panic seized her, and somewhere in her head a voice was screaming at her to get out of there. Fast. No one could know she had been there. She could hurry back to her car, drive a few blocks down the street, and make an anonymous 911 call. But that plan was swept away the moment she heard something that told her she was not alone in this big house.

Havilland looked up from the body on full alert, absolutely certain her ears weren't deceiving her and that what she'd heard was the slightest creak of a heavy footstep on a wooden floorboard. She stood to her feet, and her arm came up again as she aimed for the darkness from where the noise had come.

"Come out now, and show me your hands."

Her heart was beating fast as adrenaline coursed through her. Add to that, she was fearful, not because of the danger she may be in but the possibility that she was going to have to subdue and arrest whoever this was and then later explain how she happened to be in Terrence and Devon Miller's home.

The sound of movement grew louder and more distinct. Whoever was there was slowly following her instructions, and she held her breath, keeping her gun aimed in the direction of their footsteps. When they finally came into view, their body was cast in shadow, but she could see the outline of a tall man with his arms extended and aiming something right back at her.

"Drop it!" she commanded as her finger slightly brushed the trigger. "I said drop it now!"

Just as she was about to shoot, the man spoke, and the instant familiarity of his voice sent a renewed dose of fear straight up her spine.

"No, Hav. You drop it."

She stared wide-eyed and mouth agape as the man stepped forward, shedding the darkness around him. Her husband came into full view.

"Eric?"

"Yeah," he said, his voice level and cold. He stepped closer with his gun still trained on her. "Now, slowly put down your weapon and face the wall. You're under arrest."

CHAPTER ONE

ive weeks earlier...

The large conference room was abuzz with jovial excitement as everyone gathered together to celebrate Agent Eric Sawyer's recent promotion to Special Agent in Charge of the Controlled Chemical Substance Program. They all politely laughed at his jokes, cheered him when appropriate, and gave him slaps on the back for more congratulations. As the evening wore on, the party began to wind down, and those who came out of some sense of obligation started to leave. Others, who were close friends of Eric, invited him to a second party they had planned for him. He happily accepted the invite to a neighborhood bar close by that the agents frequented and then searched the room until his eyes landed on her.

Havilland had been waiting for him to finally notice her, and when he did, he politely excused himself from his colleagues and joined her where she stood by a table covered with half-filled to near-empty plates of mini subs, chips, veggie platters, and dip that was now room temperature. He reached into a cooler of melted ice, pulled out a soda, and unclasped it. He took a long swig, looking at her over the rim of the can and then lowered it.

"We're all headed over to Kelly's after this."

She nodded and smiled while nibbling on a Dorito. "The after party."

He smiled weakly and shrugged. She then waited for him to ask her.

"Do you want to come?"

It was purely out of spite that she made him wait for her response. She knew he didn't want to ask her. This entire night had been awkward as hell with the two of them walking around, barely saying a word to each other, and on the occasion they did converse, it was only just enough to keep the others from wondering if their marriage was nothing else but blissful.

At long last, she shook her head, and the visible relief that came over him made her heart break for the both of them.

"No, I'm pretty tired, and I'm sure Jeanetta could use a break."

They both smiled, and it was the first genuinely intimate moment they shared all night. Then the moment was gone, and they were left staring at each other as an invisible space filled up between them with all the things they wouldn't say to each other.

"Hey, boss, the guys are getting impatient and asked me to come get you."

The two of them looked over to find Maya Landon looking sexy yet professional in the same black pantsuit she'd worn that afternoon. She'd removed the blazer and was now in a pink blush cami top, and her long brunette waves cascaded over her shoulders. Even in six-inch peep-toe heels, she had to slightly look up at Eric as she gave him a dazzling smile. Havilland was glad she'd changed into her brown over-the-knee boots with heels, or Maya would've dwarfed her five-foot-three frame. She looked down at her own attire of skinny jeans with an oversized beige sweater and suddenly felt underdressed standing next to the woman.

"I'll be right there," Eric said and then turned to Havilland. "I won't be out too late."

Maya turned to her with a curious frown. "Aren't you coming, Hav?"

Havilland gave her the crestfallen look she'd practiced. "No, but you guys have a drink for me."

"After the day I've had, you can count on it," Maya said with a gleeful smile and then looked at Eric. "Say good night to your wife, so we can go and get you back home at a decent hour."

She had the grace to then walk away and give them some privacy, but it hadn't been necessary. Eric wasn't about to kiss her good night in front of these agents. So, Havilland stepped back and grabbed her jacket from behind a fold-up chair.

"You have to be up early for your flight tomorrow," she reminded him.

He downed the rest of the soda and tossed it into a nearby trash can. "I'll make it," he said with confidence.

As part of his promotion to SAC of the department, Eric was ordered to attend a weekend leadership training in Los Angeles before he officially began his duties on Monday.

"Then, I'll see you in the morning," she said. "Good night."

"Good night," he replied and walked away from her to join the others, who were laughing and talking animatedly about the rest of the night's events. Together, they all filed out of the conference room that had served as the makeshift party room, calling good night to her. Havilland waved and watched as Eric shrugged on his own jacket and took up the rear to walk beside a laughing Maya.

CHAPTER TWO

Eric stood in solitude on Pier 30, staring at the imposing Oakland Bay Bridge, the brightly lit skyline of the financial district at his back. At this hour, the pier was deserted, and he welcomed the peace and tranquility while he killed time.

He'd left Kelly's early, growing tired of the camaraderie and Maya's subtle flirting. He looked at his watch and figured now would be a good time to cross the bridge and head home. Havilland should be asleep by now, and not for the first time, he thought about how ridiculous it was that he was standing on this pier waiting for the moment he could enter his home without having to face her. But he knew her nightly rituals before bed, and some nights it used to include making love to him—that is until he put a stop to it. By now, she was curled under the covers with her iPad next to her, since she more than likely fell asleep scrolling through her social media feed or browsing realtor websites, looking at homes they couldn't afford.

An unexpected pang of sadness and then anger at that sadness came over him. He missed her. He missed the way things were. But rather than let the past consume him, he turned and made the trek back to his car and drove in the direction toward home. There was a certain girl who owed him a good-night kiss.

* * *

Havilland scrolled through her social media feed on the tablet, looking at pictures of celebrities, celebrities and their babies, her friends' vacation photos, status posts, and million-dollar homes. All of it was a way to keep her mind off the fact that Eric was still not home. She looked at the time on her tablet and saw it was nearly ten thirty.

How long would they all be at Kelly's?

She thought of how happy he looked when the department surprised him with a mini celebration for his promotion. He deserved it. He'd been an excellent Agent for the CBI for years—long before she was recruited, but he'd be able to really show off his skills as head of the CCSP. She wondered how it would be between them now that he was her superior. No doubt the rumors of potential favoritism were already swirling. She thought about putting in for a transfer to another department, but she loved the work she did in CCSP and would've also put in for the SAC position herself if she hadn't known Eric wanted it. Wryly, she thought to herself that he'd only gone for the job to keep an eye on her.

How much longer would it be this way between them?

They'd grown apart so much it was destroying her. She held back the self-pitying tears that threatened to fall and instead swiped through the online articles of the *San Francisco Chronicle*. She sat straight up in bed and stared in disbelief when she saw a colored photograph of a man and woman from her past with a headline that read:

Foxworth Pharmaceuticals Brings Thousands of Jobs to the Bay Area

Havilland stared at the grinning couple and could feel her grip on the tablet tightening until her hands began to ache. He'd really done it. She shouldn't be surprised, because he'd warned her he was moving out there, but she'd hoped against hope that those plans had fallen through. *Damn.*

Downstairs, the front door opened and closed, and she turned the device off, reached over, and shut off the bedside lamp and burrowed under the covers to pretend to be asleep. As she'd done every night for the past month, she prayed he'd come into the bedroom and sleep next to her. But even as she prayed, she knew it was a fool's wish. He would stop in Kimmy's room first and then continue on past their bedroom to the upstairs den.

But maybe…just maybe…

CHAPTER THREE

*E*ric trudged softly up the stairs and opened the door to Kimmy's room. He crossed over to the small bed surrounded by stars circulating overhead from the night light on the table. He knelt down beside the bed, reached out, and brushed one soft, puffy cheek with the back of his hand. He smiled to himself as he noticed how small her face looked with the large satin bonnet Havilland made her wear at night to protect her natural curls.

At the feeling of his touch, the child's eyes slowly opened, and her lips formed a sleepy smile.

"Hi, Daddy."

"Hi, honey. I didn't mean to wake you."

"Yes, you did."

He chuckled. It was a ritual of theirs. If he got in from work late, he'd come in and say good night to her, and as much as Havilland disapproved of him waking her up, he couldn't go to bed without speaking to his little girl. Kimmy came to see it as a game and also looked forward to their nightly talks.

"Did you have fun at your party?"

He wrinkled his nose in mock disgust. "Too many grownups."

She giggled. "I had pizza for dinner."

"You did?" he asked with exaggerated enthusiasm.

"Yeah, and Netta let me watch two movies tonight."

Netta was their regular nanny, Jeanetta, who picked Kimmy up from school and whom they called when both he and Havilland had to work late. If she wasn't available, they also had Lola, Havilland's mom, who never passed up a chance to see her grandchild.

"That sounds like a lot more fun than my party. Next time I'm staying home, and you can go to work." He smiled when she giggled some more. "Did Netta read you a story?"

"No, Mommy came home and read me one. How come you didn't come home with her?"

Good question.

He shrugged. "Some of the guys I work with wanted to spend a little more time with me. I'm their boss now, so come Monday, they won't be able to have as much fun with me."

"Mommy says you'll be her boss, too."

"Only at work." He winked. "We both know who the boss is at home."

They laughed together some more before he finally let her go back to sleep. After he tucked her back in and kissed her good night, he quietly left her room and made his way to the opposite end of the hall. He slowed his steps and then came to a full stop in front of the closed double doors that led to the master suite. No light came from underneath the door, but it didn't mean she was sleeping. Maybe she was waiting for him like she used to when he worked late, with her soft curves curled under the warm down cover. He almost reached for the handle to open the door and personally thank her for organizing the surprise party for him. The guys told him at Kelly's she'd been in charge of the celebration. At the very least, he owed her a good-night kiss for that. But he knew all too well how those full lips of hers tasted, and if he kissed her, he wouldn't be able to stop. He wouldn't want to stop. He'd take all of her.

He backed away from the door and continued down the hall to the guestroom.

CHAPTER FOUR

The next morning…

Terrence strode past the master suite to see Devon unpacking with the help of the staff. After two days of living in a hotel suite, they were finally moving into a mansion he'd rented that was well over ten thousand square feet and nestled in the heart of Pacific Heights. Devon had live-in help, who were obediently following her instructions as they hung all of her designer shoes, clothes, and handbags. Later on, she was meeting some of her friends for lunch who had made the trip out there from Atlanta to be with her as she settled into her new home. It was enough to ease any ordinary person's moving stress; however, since their arrival in San Francisco three days ago, she had yet to wipe the disappointed frown from her face.

Terrence shook his head, not understanding it. He grew up with nothing, he came from nothing, so this life of wealth that came from marrying her was something his mind was still trying to assimilate. He absolutely enjoyed the benefits of it with his own designer clothes, jewelry, and cars, but somewhere deep inside of him, it all still felt like a dream that he'd yet to wake from.

He looked again at his wife, who was dressed casually in designer skinny jeans, high heels, and a cream-colored blouse that looked great against her light-brown skin. Her hair was tied back in a ponytail, giving her the appearance of a young coed, and he admired her curves as she inspected the items of each carefully labeled box. He couldn't deny she was a lovely woman, and five years after their wedding day, he still couldn't see himself married to anyone else but her. That didn't stop him from entertaining the occasional mistress every now and then, but no matter how many women he chose to be with outside of his marriage, he wasn't foolish enough to leave Devon or the lifestyle she introduced him to, and she knew that. However, there was one person who didn't want him to get used to this life of luxury he'd married into, and that was his father-in-law.

He'd been admiring her, lost in thought for so long that he realized she'd paused in her inspection of the boxes and ordering the staff around to look at him hovering outside the bedroom's double doors.

"What is it, Terrence?"

"I'm just wondering when you're going to start smiling again. This is a great city, and you're going to love it here."

She looked over at him with a not-so-amused stare.

"What's there to smile about? You drag me out here away from my family and friends and for what? To fulfill your never-ending dream of impressing my dad? You do realize that we're married now, and you're vice-president of the company. What more do you need?"

"I'm not doing it to impress your father. I'm doing it for the increased responsibility. I told you I was bored out of my mind in Atlanta. With this move, I feel like I have a real purpose now."

"Yeah, whatever. Sounds to me like you're being ungrateful."

He narrowed his eyes, but before he laid into her, he took several breaths. He wasn't about to let her spoil his good mood.

"I need to go down to the construction site and do a final walk-through with the contractor. I'll be home later."

She groaned in exasperation. "Dammit, Terrence! We didn't have to come up here to oversee this new plant. Dad has plenty of other management staff who are capable of babysitting."

"Well, maybe I got sick and tired of someone babysitting *me*."

She was clutching a few items of clothing and was heading into the grand walk-in closet to hang them up. But when he spoke, she stopped and handed them to one of the maids, who was already carrying more than she could handle, and turned to face him with her hands on her hips.

"What's that supposed to mean?"

"Tell me what's bothering you more: our move to San Francisco or the fact that Daddy Dearest isn't around to watch me?"

She fell silent but her narrowed eyes told him he'd struck a chord.

"Dad has always looked out for me. When my mom left years ago, it was just the two of us. He can't help it if he's a little overprotective of me."

He'd heard this same speech from her before, and it still irked him. All he heard was that she was a spoiled daddy's girl, and the two of them would always be a united front against him. The times where she'd sided with her father over him and vice versa were too numerous to count. They never missed a chance to show him he was an outsider and would always be an outsider. She may have taken his last name, but he could see now it was only a formality. She may be his wife—a Miller, but she would always be Robert Foxworth's daughter, and there was no guessing which name carried more weight.

Nevertheless, he was determined to make this a smooth transition for the both of them, and getting into an argument with her was the opposite of what he had planned. He needed to keep her at ease, because Devon at ease meant Robert wouldn't be interfering, and he could continue on with his plans to beat the man at his own game.

He put on a mask of humility and approached her, took her hands into his, and softly caressed them as he spoke to her.

"I apologize. I know you and your father are close and that you miss him and your friends, but this is a new beginning for the both of us. I want your father to see that I'm capable of eventually running this company when he retires, and overseeing this plant opening is the opportunity I was looking for. I want to make a life and a future for us and our children. You can understand that, right?"

That finally brought a smile to her face, which he knew it would. He'd been promising her a baby since the day they were married. Five years later, he was still promising her, and she was still believing him.

Terrence left her to finish unpacking and when he descended the stairs, he headed toward a room he'd already designated as his personal office. It was in a secluded wing of the house and gave him the most spectacular view of Alcatraz prison. The house staff were busy cleaning and unpacking, but at his instructions, they left this room alone. He closed the door, went to his desk, and unlocked the top drawer. He mentally sighed with relief at the sight of the ledger still tucked inside, but he needed to get it somewhere much safer.

He pulled out his cell phone and made a call to the contractor.

"Mr. Miller, it's good to hear from you. Are we still on for the final walk-through?"

"I'm leaving the house in a few minutes," Terrence confirmed. "But before I get there, I want to confirm that last addition came through with no problems."

"Yes, sir. A state-of-the-art fire and waterproof wall safe. It arrived yesterday morning, and the men have already installed it. You can test it out when you get here."

"Good," he said, now clutching the ledger in his hands. "I'm going to need to put something very important in there, today."

CHAPTER FIVE

*H*avilland played the role of the helpful wife by doing the laundry and laying out several outfits for Eric to pack for his trip, all the while, trying not to succumb to the pang of sadness that he would not be near her. Even though they were hardly speaking, his presence had always been a comfort to her, and without him around for the next two days, she felt out of sorts. However, there was a tiny part of her that also felt relief for the mere fact that she had an appointment to meet someone while he was gone, and it would be much better if he wasn't privy to her movements.

Despite his late night at *Kelly's*, as promised, Eric woke early in time to have breakfast with her and Kimmy and say goodbye. Kimmy, obviously not feeling as sad to see her dad leave, was more interested to know what gift he'd bring her back from L.A. By the time they'd finished eating and he was donning his coat and grabbing for his set of car keys, Kimmy was still on the same subject.

"Kimberly," Havilland said in a scolding tone, "stop asking about presents and wish your dad a safe trip."

"It's all right," Eric said, kneeling down in front of his daughter. "You know I'll bring you something, but presents cost hugs and kisses. So, where's mine?"

In answer, Kimmy threw herself into his embrace, wrapped her small arms around his neck, and gave him a big kiss on the cheek. Eric held her tightly, returned the kiss, and then stood and barely looked at Havilland over his shoulder as he spoke.

"I'll be back Sunday evening."

"Are you sure you don't want to take an Uber?"

He shook his head. "No, I'll keep my car in the airport lot. It'll save time getting home. See you later."

"Have a safe flight," Havilland said.

"Aren't you going to kiss Mommy?" Kimmy asked, just as he reached the front door.

Havilland cringed. They'd gotten good at keeping their strained relationship hidden from her, so she shouldn't be surprised her daughter would think everything was still normal. From the way Eric turned to look at her and then Havilland, she could tell he was feeling the discomfort too.

He finally forced a smile. "Of course, I'll give Mommy a kiss."

He trailed his wheeled luggage behind him in one hand, reached Havilland in two strides, and quickly took her chin in his other hand just like he used to. Havilland closed her eyes and tilted her head up to meet his lips, anticipating the feel of their fullness brushing across her own. She could sense his slight hesitation as his mouth hovered over hers, but when she didn't feel anything, she slowly opened her eyes to find him staring at her. They were so close she could see her reflection in the blue tinge of his eyes. He was saying so much to her right then, but she couldn't begin to read it all. Time lapsed even further, and she realized their daughter was standing there, looking at them and waiting. Rather than continue on with this torture, she started to step away, but Eric tightened his grip on her chin, lowered his head, and kissed her. It had been so long and his lips felt so good that she couldn't help herself when she emitted a tiny moan, and then she felt embarrassed because Kimmy was still an audience.

Before she got lost in the moment and surrendered to the urge to wrap her arms around his neck and press herself into him, she broke the kiss and stepped away from him. Eric was looking at her as if he knew what she was feeling and wanted to continue it too. But Kimmy was now giggling at seeing her parents kissing, and that was enough for the two of them to gather themselves.

"I'll see you Sunday night," he said once again, turned, and waved goodbye to Kimmy and then was gone.

Havilland continued to stare at the front door for a moment longer.

"Where's Los Angeles?" Kimmy asked in her soft voice, teeming with curiosity.

"Oh, it's several hundred miles south of us," Havilland said, still staring at the screen door.

"Will it take Daddy long to get there?"

She then turned to smile at Kimmy. "Not by airplane. He'll be there and back in no time."

Havilland continued to smile at her and then looked beyond her at the foyer table where she saw Eric's cell phone.

"Honey, get your shoes and jacket on. I need to catch your dad before he leaves."

She crossed to the table, snatched up the cell phone, and hurried out of the house. She stepped out onto the wrap-around porch and immediately looked to her left toward the two-car driveway, half-expecting to find only her car sitting there but was relieved to find Eric's Jeep Cherokee in the same spot it had been last night when he came home. She waved to get his attention, assuming he was inside, but before she could take one step off the porch, her arm was grabbed from behind. She turned around and was completely shocked when Eric pulled her into the corner of the porch and up against him. The next thing she knew, he was kissing her, and his arms around her was the most natural and yet sensual feeling in her world.

Havilland put her hands to his face, returning the kiss and feeling the very slight stubble just beginning to form from his shave that morning.

"Eric," she said, pausing the kiss and moaning in delight with her eyes closed. "Eric…"

She could feel him watching her, enjoying her pleasure, and she knew he wanted to increase it. She indulged herself by doing what she'd wanted to do earlier and that was to push herself into him, feeling every hard inch of his body and reminiscing on how wonderful things used to be.

"I left my cell phone on purpose, hoping you'd come out here. Hav?"

He waited until she opened her eyes and was looking directly at him. Now his eyes had grown hard.

Is there anything I need to know?" he asked.

"What?"

"Whatever is going on, you can tell me." He removed one hand from her waist and lifted her chin with his forefinger to ensure she was looking directly at him. "You can always come to me. You know that right?"

"I know."

"So, again, is there anything I need to know?"

"Would it change anything between us?"

He looked away in frustration. "It's not about us."

"But it is. We may be close to each other physically right now, but emotionally, you're still so far away from me."

"Stop. Let's worry about that later. Is there anything—"

"No," she said, mentally reconstructing her own wall and pretending to not notice the disappointment in his eyes.

She put his cell phone in his hands and stepped out of his arms. "I need to get Kimmy to school. Have a good trip."

He gripped the phone in his hands but refused to take his eyes off her. Even as she turned around and headed back into the house, she could feel him still watching her, trying his damnedest to decipher her secrets.

CHAPTER SIX

"Agent Sawyer? You can go on in. He'll see you now."

Havilland stood, smiled her thanks at the assistant, and adjusted her blazer and knee-length skirt before heading inside the large office in the downtown San Francisco Federal building. She opened the door and spied David Holladay on the phone. He waved for her to come inside while he continued his conversation.

"Parker, I have a meeting right now, but I'll see you tonight for dinner. You can tell me all about the interview then. All right, give Lily a kiss for me. I love you."

He hung up the phone and Havilland wanted to giggle at the slightly embarrassed look on his face but settled for a smile.

David smiled sheepishly. "My wife is interviewing for a TV anchor position and add to that we just had a baby and…"

"So, in other words, life is good."

His smile broadened and Havilland kept her envious feelings at bay. She remembered when life was good between her and her husband too.

"Yeah, I guess you could say that," he said and then shook his head, stood from his desk, and gestured her to a sofa in a corner of the office. "Can I get you something to drink?"

"No, nothing for me," she said, unbuttoning her blazer and sitting down. "I won't be here long. I just wanted to know if you'd heard about this."

By the time, he grabbed a bottle of water from a small refrigerator and joined her on the sofa, she had pulled her tablet from her purse, powered it on, and was scrolling to the news article she'd read last night about Terrence and Devon Miller moving to the bay area.

"I'm sorry for the short notice, but this is the reason I wanted to see you."

He took a swig of water, replaced the cap on the bottle, and took the tablet from her. He skimmed the news article and then after a moment, slowly handed the tablet back to her. He looked to an opposite wall of the office and was quiet for a long time, seemingly lost in thought.

"This must've happened quickly," he finally said.

"The last time I saw him in Atlanta, he told me he was planning to move to California to help his father-in-law with the new plant opening," she said. "I was hoping he'd have changed his mind."

"Why?" David asked with a frown. "With Terrence here in San Francisco, it'll be easier to keep an eye on things."

"I was doing that just fine while he was in Atlanta," Havil-land said and immediately regretted the note of desperation in her voice.

She was worried. Terrence being there, in her city, was the last thing she wanted or needed, and she had a sinking feeling that his presence would only cause a lot of disruption in her life.

But David had obviously heard the tremor in her voice

because he was regarding her with all seriousness now. "Does your husband know you're here?"

"No, and that's another thing. Eric was just promoted to SAC of the department, which means he's my boss now. How am I going to—"

"You don't have to do anything," he said. "You can pull out anytime."

She appreciated the out he was giving her, and his voice had a gift of making her feel so calm she nearly took the offer to step aside like a lifeline. But at the end of the day, she was still an agent, and she had come too far.

"No. It's all right. I can handle it, and I can handle Terrence."

"You're sure?"

"Yes."

"You can do this," David promised.

She nodded her thanks, thinking of a way to put this entire situation to rest without it erupting in her face.

CHAPTER SEVEN

*M*onday morning…

Both Eric and Eric's boss, Carl Hewitt, stood as Robert Foxworth was escorted into the conference room with his attorney.

"Mr. Foxworth, it's a pleasure to meet you," Carl said, doing the honors by introducing himself and Eric.

"Thank you, gentlemen, for seeing me," Robert said, and all four men took a seat at the rectangular conference table in Eric's new office.

Eric took his seat and noticed the tie Robert was wearing went well with the expensive tailored suit he wore. It was dark navy; the same color suit Havilland had picked out for herself this morning. It was laid out across the bed, and as Eric walked by the bedroom on his way downstairs, he couldn't help but stop to admire it. She was in the shower and didn't see as he stepped into their bedroom and eyed the blazer and skirt. She didn't wear pants to work often, which always made him crazy because the skirts accented her great legs and the heels made her small height appear statuesque. He'd run his fingers along the satin white blouse she'd chosen to wear with the blazer and pictured her full breasts cupped inside the black lace bra and her firm plump ass cradled in the matching panties.

"Eric?"

He snapped himself free of the erotic images and focused on the other men in the room, who were now regarding him oddly. It was enough to tamp down the erection in his pants as he sat up straight and cleared his throat.

"Sorry, about that. Please, Mr. Foxworth, continue."

Robert Foxworth smirked as if he knew Eric had been thinking about his wife, but continued with his statement.

"I came here today because as much as it pains me to say this, I have reason to believe my son-in-law, Terrence Miller, is stealing from me."

"Stealing what? Money?" Eric asked.

"No. This is why I chose to make an appointment with this department in particular. You investigate the theft of narcotic substances, correct? Terrence is stealing the raw materials we use to make the narcotics and is selling them on the black market."

Robert looked around the room as though he expected more of a reaction to that news, but when no one uttered a word, he continued. "He pushed hard for me to send him here to San Francisco to open the new plant and to stay on as overseeing manager. Terrence is vice-president of the company. His job doesn't entail plant management. I have people for that. But he insisted, and my daughter has been hounding me to give him more responsibility, so I agreed. But his true reason for wanting to come out here is to have the freedom to continue his schemes without me looking over his shoulder."

Carl leaned forward in his chair, resting his elbows on the table, and looked at Robert with all sincerity.

"How do you suspect he's getting the materials out of the building?"

"I don't suspect anything," Robert replied, indignantly. "I have proof of his crimes, and it's not him, directly. He has a network of employees working for him."

Eric sat up straighter, willing himself to not get too excited. Robert Foxworth had actually walked into the CBI building and was handing Terrence Miller over to him on a platter. For a long time, he knew the man was dirty, especially after he convinced Havilland to feed him information about confidential cases. He'd jeopardized her career all for his own selfish gain and add to that, his presence had created friction in their marriage. For months following that bullshit in Atlanta, Eric had been hoping and praying for the day he could get his payback. But since Terrence resided in Georgia, he and whatever he was involved in were the GBI's problem. But lo and behold, Terrence's greed had brought him to California and right into Eric's territory. The bastard was all his, but he still had to do his due diligence. If he was going to make an arrest, he was going to do this by the book and make sure no technicality existed to give Terrence a "Get out of jail free" card.

"I have to ask, Mr. Foxworth," Eric said. "How is it you came to hear about Mr. Miller's dealings? Is this something you, yourself are involved in?"

"All right, just a minute," Robert's lawyer began, objecting.

"No, it's all right," Robert said, patting his arm. "I expected this question, and I know you have to ask. But the answer is no, Agent Sawyer. I'm not a drug dealer. I have no involvement whatsoever in my son-in-law's schemes. He's acting on his own. And to answer your first question, three years ago I hired a private investigation firm to follow him. I never trusted him, and I was hoping they'd find something out about him that I could take to my daughter, Devon, and convince her to finally leave him. But when they came to me about his illegal operations, I decided to keep it to myself, get more evidence, and get him arrested. They were also able to give me the name of someone who works closely with Terrence when he makes his deals. He's one of the chemists I employ."

"All right, Mr. Foxworth," Carl said. "We'll see what can be done, on the contingency that you have evidence to back up these claims against your son-in-law."

Robert turned to his attorney and gave a brief nod, to which the slightly younger and distinguished man withdrew a USB flash drive from his briefcase and handed it to Carl.

"Keith is my attorney. Unless there's anything I need to discuss with either of you, personally, he will be your contact from here on out. Given the circumstances, I don't think it's a good idea if Terrence or even my daughter get wind that I'm in contact with your office."

Carl nodded and handed the flash drive over to Eric. "Agent Sawyer is in charge of the Controlled Chemical Substance Program. If we feel there is sufficient evidence to go after Terrence Miller, his department will be leading the investigation."

Robert Foxworth barely glanced in Eric's direction before speaking again. "Then I'll leave everything to you, gentlemen."

He and his attorney began to rise, and Eric quickly put a stop to it.

"Just a moment. As Agent Hewitt said, my team and I may very well be leading this investigation, so I'd like an idea of what I'm getting into here."

This time, Robert gave him his full attention. "What would you like to know, Agent Sawyer?"

"First, you said this all started about three years ago. Why did you wait so long to bring this to our attention?"

"I started an investigation with the GBI, but for reasons I can't explain, the case went nowhere. So, when Terrence agreed to come out here to California, I let him, hoping he would continue operations and create enough rope to hang himself with."

Eric swallowed, knowing exactly what happened to the failed GBI case. Havilland is what happened. But instead of risking going down that road, he took a pen from his shirt pocket, ripped a sheet of paper from a blank legal pad, and took a moment to write down several names. When he'd finished, he hit the intercom button and called for his assistant, Elena.

"One more thing," Eric said, "I'd like the name of the chemist you say is working directly with Miller."

Before Robert could answer, Elena entered the conference room. "May I help you, Agent Sawyer?"

"Yes, I need you to send out a confidential department memo, announcing that a task force is being established," he said and then handed her the sheet of paper. "These are the agents in the task force. These agents only."

"Right away, sir," she said and exited the conference room as quickly as she'd entered.

Eric turned back to Robert. "The name of the chemist?"

When Robert told him, Eric stilled in his seat. This case just kept getting more and more personal for him.

CHAPTER EIGHT

*A*s Kimmy chatted incessantly that morning on the way to pre-school, Havilland mentally prepared herself for the first day of her husband being her superior. He had always held more rank than her since he'd come into the agency several years before she did, but now it was official. She would be reporting to him. It wouldn't bother her so much if things were better between them, but she feared this promotion would only heighten their problems—well, actually, *problem*. There was only one problem, one issue they had yet to resolve, and it had been all her doing. He'd gotten in late last night from L.A., but she still stayed up, waiting for him, only to once again be disappointed that he didn't join her in their bedroom. This morning, however, he was up before her and Kimmy and off to work.

As soon as she stepped into the wing of the CCSP department, she looked to the rear where Eric's new office was and noticed he was having a meeting with his boss, Carl Hewitt, and…

She froze in her steps at the sight of Robert Foxworth, the CEO and founder of Foxworth Pharmaceuticals. Her mind immediately went back to her conversation last Friday with Deputy Director Holladay and wondered what he would think of this development. Terrence showing up in San Francisco was one thing, but his father-in-law being here was something else entirely and didn't bode well at all.

She set her coat and purse down at her cubicle, caught the eye of Jerry Hicks, another agent in the department, and walked over to him.

"What's going on?" she asked, folding her arms atop the wall of his cubicle and nodding her head toward Eric's office.

Jerry swiveled in his desk chair toward her, with a worried frown.

"It looks like your hubby is getting his first big case straight out of the gate."

"What case?"

"I'm not sure, but whatever it is, it has something to do with Foxworth's company, and it's important enough for Hewitt to be present."

Havilland had to agree with him, but she wondered what Robert Foxworth could be saying in there and why it was suddenly being thrust onto Eric and not his predecessor. Jerry must have been reading her thoughts because in the next second, she had her answer.

"This is Hewitt's chance to get Eric out."

She'd been looking at the glass windows of the office, wishing she could read lips, and then shot her gaze back to Jerry. "What?"

He shrugged. "You heard the stories. Excuse my French, but Hewitt has a real hard-on for your man. He's been dying for an excuse to kick him out of the agency for years or at the very least, demote him ever since his daughter decided to resign. This case, whatever it is, is a test. If Eric fails, I'll bet he's either demoted or transferred out."

Havilland could now feel herself wearing the same

worried frown he was. She knew about the friction between Eric and Carl. It was apparent whenever the two saw each other. Eric used to tell her that Carl would love nothing more than to see him resign, transferred to another agency, or outright fired. It all stemmed from the time Eric dated Carl's daughter, Christina Hewitt, a few years before Havilland joined the agency. The relationship was getting serious, but slowly things fizzled between them and to Carl's disappointment, Christina resigned. Carl held Eric responsible for not only his daughter's broken heart but also for the sudden end to her career.

Jerry's notification on his computer went off, signaling he had an incoming email message. Havilland looked away to give him privacy but turned right back toward him when he let out a low whistle.

"That didn't take long," he said and gestured toward his screen. "This is going to be big."

She leaned over him, read the email, and held in the gasp when she read the names *Terrence Miller* and *Foxworth Pharmaceuticals*, but she kept going until she came to the words *suspected selling and trafficking of a controlled chemical substance.* Her eyes shot up again and saw that Eric was just now escorting Robert Foxworth, a younger man who was likely his attorney, and Carl Hewitt out of the office. She tried desperately to catch Carl's eye, but he ignored her as he chatted congenially with Robert Foxworth. When he passed by without even an acknowledgement in her direction, she tamped down her anger and lowered her eyes back to the email.

"Did everyone in the department receive this?" she asked, already looking toward the top of the email message to find the names of the recipients.

"I don't think so," Jerry said. "It looks like he's setting up a task force."

She read through the short list of names. Jerry's name was one of the first, followed by Maya and several others, but no Havilland Sawyer. Jerry must have noticed her name wasn't listed the same time she did because he awkwardly cleared his throat.

"You have another case on the books or something?" he asked. "Otherwise, I'm sure it was an oversight that he didn't include you."

She decided to spare him any further awkwardness and sighed dramatically. "Yeah, I have another case."

"Damn the bad luck," he said, smiling and winking at her.

She smiled back and turned toward the direction of her desk. But she didn't stop there and instead bypassed it while keeping a pleasant expression as she walked by cubicles, passing agents who were already whispering excitedly about the new task force and the trafficking case against Terrence Miller. She took advantage of the current distraction and detoured to Eric's office, where he was now alone. She knocked once but didn't wait for a response before she slipped inside and closed the door behind her. Only then did she finally let her pleasant expression transform to outrage.

"Not here," he said, not bothering to look at her but continuing to stare into his computer screen.

"Yes, here. This is work, and I have a work-related complaint."

He hesitated a moment, and then slowly moved his eyes from the monitor to look at her. He then gestured with a hand for her to take a seat. Havilland did so, and their eyes locked hard on each other.

He spoke first. "I know this is about the task force."

"I want in."

He leaned back in his chair to study her and for the moment, he let his silence speak for him.

"I can help you."

Silence.

"My past relationship with him can be an asset."

Eric finally spoke. "I already have a much more valuable asset."

Havilland wanted to scream. This can't be happening. "You mean a CI?"

"That's all I'm giving you," he said.

"Eric, listen. I know how he thinks. We used to be partners."

"I know more than enough," he said, his jaw turning to iron. "Don't bring it up to me again."

"That's not fair." Her voice began to rise and tremble with outrage. "You're using your personal feelings against me to keep me from this task force."

She didn't expect him to either confirm or deny it. "It doesn't have to be this way between us. You could put an end to this at any time if you would just stop being so stubborn and try to understand that I never meant for you—"

He sat up. "That's enough. This is no longer a work-related complaint. This is about us and our marriage, so the meeting is officially over."

"Eric—"

"I said I'm done discussing it."

"But I'm not."

"Get back to work, Hav!"

Her back stiffened at the command and icy tenor of his voice. She stood in a flash, turned to open the door, and made sure to slam it closed behind her, not giving a damn about the curious eyes of her colleagues now watching her.

CHAPTER NINE

*E*ric sat fuming at his desk and staring at the closed door for a long time. He hated it when she slammed doors, and she knew it. He had to count to ten and then count ten more because it was taking everything in him not to get up, go after her, and really give the other agents a show. But when he caught up to her and was gripping her in his arms, he wasn't so sure if he'd shout at her or take her home and rip off that navy-blue suit. Only he himself knew just how much it turned him on when she stood her ground, but too much had happened for him to surrender to those basic sexual urges. He couldn't just wipe away the past; it was still too raw.

Didn't she know this was killing him too?

What was going on between them was really fucking with him. His inability to trust her was not the way things were supposed to be, but it was, and he couldn't rewind the days and weeks to change it all.

He returned his attention to his computer and continued to review the evidence Robert Foxworth had managed to gather against Terrence Miller. Eric was going through with this case. An arrest like this would cement his position as head of the CCSP and Carl's bosses would begin to pay attention. His career with the CBI would advance even further, giving him a nice bump in salary, which would be good for his family. He and Havilland could buy a new home, put Kimmy in a better school district, and…

He looked up from the computer again and searched for his wife at her cubicle, but she wasn't there. Most likely, she'd stormed out, looking to get some air and calm down. Here he was, planning a future with her and things between them were going to shit. She wanted so badly to be involved in this case, and he'd known once she saw that she hadn't been included in the task force, she'd blow a fuse. It only confirmed for him that his decision was correct. There was no way in hell he was allowing her within fifteen feet of this case, and not because of her history with Terrence but because of Eric's history with his immediate superior.

Carl Hewitt never wanted him to get this promotion, but he had no choice but to award it to him once Carl's bosses saw Eric's performance record and dedicated years of service. Now, with this high-profile case, there was no doubt in his mind that Carl would be scrutinizing his every move, praying that he failed in order to give him an excuse to be rid of Eric.

The last thing he needed was Havilland helping Carl plant the knife even deeper.

* * *

February 2018

She'd been working in his unit for nearly a year, and he had only managed to quickly introduce himself as well as give her a "good morning" and a "good night" every day since. That was the extent of their conversations. He hadn't grown big enough balls to go any further than that, even during moments when he'd walk by her cubicle and catch her staring at him. Interestingly enough, when he returned her stare, she bashfully looked away with a smile. Yet, instead of taking it as a cue to talk to her, he'd ignored it and pretended that the feeling in his chest wasn't an ache to get to know her, but a subtle warning that he needed to stay as far away from her as possible. In fact, it would be good if he just stopped conversing with any new female agents who joined the division. It was safer that way. However, Havilland and his staring game hadn't gone unnoticed. He'd already been approached by other guys in the department, telling him to stop being a pussy and just ask her out. So finally, on a chilly February morning, he walked into the office, saw that she was already there and seized his chance before everyone else began to arrive for the day.

She was folding her coat over the back of her chair and then leaning over her desk to turn on her computer. Eric was walking up behind her just as she leaned over, and lucky him, he got a nice view of her very round ass in her knee-length skirt. He had to stop and gather himself before he spoke, but he also didn't want to risk her turning around and catching him staring. He got one last good look and then cleared his throat.

"Good morning, Hav."

She must not have heard him come in, because she jumped at the sound of his voice, gave a cute little squeak, and turned around with her whiskey-colored eyes wide from surprise.

"Eric," she said, putting a hand to her chest. She wore a light pink sweater that fit snugly over her deliciously round breasts. "You scared me."

"Sorry about that," he said, needing to hurry this up before he embarrassed himself. She had flawless golden brown skin, chin-length curly hair that perfectly framed her attractive face, and a body that he could fantasize about for years. He wanted her and couldn't at all explain why she affected him so strongly. It hadn't been that long since he'd been with a woman. But God knew, he'd been tiptoeing around this one for too long.

"Is there something you needed?" she asked.

"Yeah," he said, clearing his throat again. "Would you like to have dinner with me sometime?"

She opened and closed her mouth without saying a word and then she smiled. "Well, yeah, I would love to. I—um…I didn't know…" She stopped and seemed to be sorting out her thoughts.

Eric hid a smile. Thank God he wasn't the only one flustered.

"Are we allowed to do that?" she asked. "I mean, it's not against department policy, is it?"

He shrugged. "I'm sure it won't be a problem. It's just dinner."

She smiled again. "Okay. Great. I'm free this Saturday."

"Saturday, it is. Give me your address, and I can pick you up. How's six-thirty?"

He saw the briefest look of panic come over her face. "Actually, I'd rather meet you. Let me give you my number, and you can text me with the details."

He frowned but then shrugged it off and gave her his number, assuming she was just being cautious. Aside from seeing each other at the office, she didn't really know him that well and probably felt safer having her own car in case their date went left.

The other agents were beginning to come in for the day, and Matt, one of his buddies, must have seen them exchange numbers because as soon as Eric returned to his cubicle, Matt was right there with a cocky smirk on his face.

Eric shrugged off his own jacket, sat down to turn on his computer, and then finally gave Matt his attention.

"What are you smiling at?" Eric asked.

"You finally closed the deal."

Eric gave him a withering look and then pulled out his cell phone to plug in this Saturday's date into his calendar.

"I'm happy for you, man. It's been a long time since you've put yourself out there."

He was right. Eric hadn't been on a date in over a year. He'd been so focused on getting his career moving again after it had stalled when he'd made that huge mistake with Christina.

Matt must have been reading his mind because he leaned over the partition of the cubicle with all seriousness now. "Just be careful this time."

Eric looked up at him and nodded. "I will. As far as I know, Havilland isn't the boss's daughter."

CHAPTER TEN

"Agent Hewitt's office, how may I help you?"

"Denise, it's Havilland Sawyer. I really need to speak with him."

"Just a moment, Agent Sawyer. I'll see if he's available."

For the few minutes she was on that brief hold, Havilland already knew what the answer was going to be before his assistant returned to the phone.

"I'm sorry, Agent Sawyer. He'll have to return your call."

She sighed, not at all pleased to have her suspicions confirmed.

"Okay, thanks," Havilland said, and as soon as she ended the call, she scrolled to Carl Hewitt's private cell number.

He'd given it to her when he was serving as Acting Special Agent in Charge for the CCSP while interviews were being held for a permanent SAC. When she told him what she was involved in, he gave her the number with the instruction that she use it for emergencies only. This definitely qualified because she needed advice on how to proceed. She dialed his number and cursed when it rang a few times and then went to voicemail. Was he avoiding her?

She tore her eyes away from her phone and spotted her daughter running around the school's playground during recess. Despite the inner turmoil she was dealing with, Kimmy's laughter mixed with the other children's brought a smile to her face. Every now and then, especially when her caseload was light, she'd drive by Kimmy's pre-school during her recess time and park across the street to watch her play. It was just what she needed to get her heart to stop racing.

Her argument with Eric had only succeeded in pulling him further away from her. Now that he knew how much she wanted in on the investigation of Terrence Miller, he'd make double sure she was kept out of the loop as much as possible. A hot surge of jealousy shot up her spine as she thought of the alluring Maya working in close contact with her husband. Oh, yes, he'd made damn sure to include *her* in the task force.

Havilland closed her eyes, breathed in and then out several times before opening her eyes again. Eric would never betray her like that. No matter what they went through, he was loyal to a fault, even when she didn't deserve it. And Maya was a good agent. In a profession dominated by men, Havilland tried her best to get along with the only other female in the department. Still, Havilland noticed the way she would look at Eric and only another woman knew what those looks meant.

She glanced over at the schoolyard and found her daughter on the swings with one of her friends. They were trying to swing as high as they could and laughing with so much joy and innocence that Havilland found herself envying them both.

Her phone began to vibrate in her hands, and she looked down to find that she'd received a text from Carl Hewitt.

Carl: *I know you were blindsided. I was, too, but we can't meet.*

It would draw too much attention. Just proceed as normal. Nothing changes.

Havilland: *Eric didn't assign me to the task force. How am I supposed to stay informed?*

Carl: *If I speak to him about it, he'll know something is up. Just find a way, Hav.*

Suddenly, her phone began to ring and the display read it was Eric. She immediately answered it, wondering if he could sense she was talking about him.

"Hello."

"Where are you?"

She paused at the brusqueness of his tone and then guessed he was still smarting from their argument earlier.

"I'm at Kimmy's school."

"Is she all right?" In an instant, his hard tone was gone and replaced by worry.

In spite of herself, Havilland couldn't help but smile. He loved that little girl more than life itself, and these days, she seemed to be the only thing in their lives that kept the two of them connected.

"She's fine. She's at recess right now."

He chuckled, probably thinking about her running around like crazy, trying to play on every piece of equipment before the bell rang: the slide, the monkey bars, the swings, and whatever else she could get her small hands on. It was what she did whenever they took her to the playground on their days off. These days, however, it was either him or her who took Kimmy. They didn't go as a family anymore.

"I was calling to let you know that I'm meeting with the task force tonight to go over our agenda, so don't hold dinner for me."

"Yeah, sure no problem. I'll save you a plate."

A long pause ensued.

"Are you all right, Hav?"

"Yeah, why wouldn't I be?"

A little chime came from the inside pocket of her purse. Havilland reached over, dug into the pocket, and pulled out the burner phone. She knew who it was without having to look because he was the only one who called her on this phone. She'd bought it specifically for him.

"I don't like arguing with you at work," Eric said.

But Havilland was only half-listening as she read the text message:

If you haven't heard, I'm in San Francisco. We need to meet. Now.

"Hav?"

"I'm here," she said, quickly. "And I'm fine. In the future, I'll be sure to compose myself while at work."

He sighed with irritation. "That's not what I meant."

"I have to go. I'll be back this afternoon."

She hung up before he sensed something was wrong. She took one last look at her daughter and saw the teacher was blowing the whistle to end recess. As Kimmy got in line with the rest of her classmates to go back inside the school, Havilland turned the ignition and pulled away from the curb to go meet Terrence Miller.

CHAPTER ELEVEN

*D*evon stood at the second-story window in her bedroom and looked down the street, watching Terrence drive away. She eyed the taillights of his Denali all the way down Vallejo Street until she couldn't see them anymore. Even when he was no longer in sight, she continued to stand, watching and waiting but more like hoping he'd turn around and come back.

After five minutes of standing there, it became evident he wasn't returning. She smacked the curtains with frustration and turned away from the window. He knew damn well that he was supposed to have lunch with her, but twenty minutes ago, while she was getting ready, he strode into their bedroom, so cocksure of himself to tell her their lunch plans had been canceled because he had a previous engagement.

"Why would you make a previous engagement at this time when we have a standing lunch date?" she'd asked, her eyes squinting with malice.

"Because it couldn't be helped," he said. "I'll make it up to you and take you out to dinner tonight instead."

But that small consolation wasn't good enough. She could

sense he was feeling entirely too free, because God knew he wouldn't have dared broken their lunch date back in Atlanta. And she'd reminded him of that, which only led to a screaming match between them that no doubt gave the house staff something to talk about.

She looked toward the double doors of the bedroom and saw that Irene was just finishing up sweeping shards of the broken vase Devon had thrown at Terrence's head. He'd ducked, but instead of succumbing to her tantrum, he simply shook his head at her and walked out the door. Now she was left with nothing but feelings of embarrassment.

As far back as she could remember, Devon had never like being told no, which had only served to spoil her. Her mother left when she was very young, and she became her father's focus. He'd raised her to eventually take over the business, but along the way, he didn't miss a chance to show her how much she meant to him, as well as soothe the pain of her mother's absence in the way of gifts. At first, it was every toy a little girl could ever want, and as she grew older and matured into a woman, so did the gifts. It went from Barbies and baking ovens to designer clothes and European trips. Her education began in the finest private schools, and she ultimately finished her studies at Spelman College with Bachelor's and Master's degrees in both Business and Finance. She was no dummy, but in recent years, Terrence made her feel just like that. He didn't cater to her wishes as much as he did when they first met. Back then, he practically fell over himself trying to get her to notice him. But he needn't have tried so hard. She never told him, but one look at him, and Devon had been determined to make him hers. He'd been seeing someone else at the time, but that fizzled out really fast, especially when she gave him a taste of the future that could be his if he had her on his arm. To a man who came from nothing, her promise of foreign cars, luxurious homes, and international travel was enough to seal the deal. Six months after she received her Master's degree, they were married in front of all of Atlanta's elite. Devon had been over the moon, but her father had been against the marriage from the beginning.

"You're too good for him," he said. "He's an opportunist. Can't you see that? You dangled a life of money in his face, and he took the bait. Where did I go wrong with you, Devon? You're a beautiful, educated, and strong black woman. Why do you feel the need to buy a husband?"

Those words still made her wince whenever she thought of them. That had been the biggest argument she'd ever had with her father, and ever since she married Terrence, it seemed all of her arguments with her father centered around her husband. But despite his misgivings, Robert Foxworth did everything he could to ensure Terrence never stepped one toe out of line. At Devon's request, he gave his new son-in-law a high-level executive position in the company, but with not much power. Devon wanted him to feel important but not so important that he gained enough experience to walk away from the company. Only half of his salary went into his personal account, while Devon kept the rest in a joint investment account. She wanted him to feel independent but not so independent that he raised enough money to walk away from her. Her dad made sure to keep him buried in paperwork, and his social calendar was only filled with lunches with her, dinner meetings with the other C-suite executives, and weekends spent at the family's second home in Savannah. She did agree to him having a day off to himself on days when she met her college friends for lunch, but he was always to be home in time for dinner at 7:30 p.m. The entire arrangement made Devon feel secure. That is, until her father made plans to open another plant there in San Francisco, and approved Terrence's request to oversee its opening and management. Terrence, of course, was thrilled with the idea and Devon cursed her father.

"He will have too much free time," she said. *"What am I supposed to do?"*

"Let him have his fun," Robert said. *"You won't have to worry about him and his shenanigans much longer."*

"What are you talking about?" Devon asked.

"Just trust me. I'll handle everything."

Devon grabbed her purse, left the bedroom, and hurried down the grand spiral staircase to the first floor. She didn't say a word to the staff as she left the house and climbed into her white Range Rover parked in front of the home. She input the address of the investigative firm she'd been researching into her GPS. She hadn't wanted to play this card just yet, but they hadn't been in California for even a week, and Terrence was already trying to pull away from her. She backed out of the driveway and headed toward her destination. She didn't like that her father was once again, being so secretive, and she wasn't about to trust him to do anything but find a way to get Terrence out of her life. But, she didn't want Terrence to leave. She wanted him to remain her husband, come back to Atlanta with her, and continue to follow the life plan she'd so thoroughly laid out for the both of them.

CHAPTER TWELVE

It was October. Fall had arrived, and school was back in session, which also meant it was the off-season for San Francisco's tourism industry. Because of this, Havilland had been able to find parking pretty easily and found herself walking along the Embarcadero without having to battle the usual crowds. Normally, she'd avoid this part of the city, but this was where he wanted to meet, and she wasn't going to waste time arguing about secret meeting spots when they had more important things to talk about. Even at midday, Havilland had to keep her jacket closed against the chill coming in off the waters of the bay. But she kept up her trek, until she arrived at infamous Pier 39, the popular destination of Fisherman's Wharf. But gone were the throngs of people that normally populated the area, and what was left were only a few tourists who chose to brave the colder weather in exchange for less crowds and cheaper hotel bills.

She walked toward a wooden railing and stared out at the bay to watch a carrier vessel slowly make its way across the waters and under the Golden Gate bridge. She thought of

Eric whenever she saw those ships. He'd been in the Navy and loved to retell stories of his time at sea including the times he'd sailed under the infamous bridge and how he could never get used to the sight.

She felt a tug on the sleeve of her jacket and turned to meet the man with smooth ebony skin and piercing dark eyes. He'd grown his beard out. It was full and luscious and only added to his handsome, mysterious, and hard exterior. She once believed she was in love with him, but looking at him now, she could see they never had a chance.

"Special Agent Sawyer," he greeted, only it sounded as if he were mocking her title. "Long time no see."

"Hello, Terrence."

He paused and then his smirk disappeared into a frown. "That's it? That's all I get?"

She shrugged. "What else do you want?"

His answer was to snake an arm around her waist so quickly it startled Havilland to suddenly feel him touching her. He jerked her up close to his body and tried to lean in and kiss her. Havilland turned her head to the side to avert his kiss and pushed against his chest with everything in her.

"Get off of me!" she hissed.

He kept up his efforts until he must have sensed they were causing a scene and then finally let her go, laughing. Havilland backed away from him, disgusted and wishing she had the nerve to slap his face.

"All right, all right," he said, raising his hands and still chuckling. "I was just playing around."

"Don't ever touch me again."

His tone turned somber, but she knew he was mocking her again. "Forgive me."

He then turned away and braced his elbows against the wooden railing and looked out at the water as she'd been doing. "So, tell me what's new?"

She hesitated, still seething from his audacity and then slowly moved to stand beside him. Instead of facing forward, she braced one arm on the railing and looked directly into his profile.

"Why are you here?"

"Don't you read the paper? I'm overseeing the opening of the new Foxworth plant. My father-in-law says I'm a big boy now and can handle it."

"Your father-in-law is also in San Francisco and paid a visit to the CBI this morning."

He kept his face straight ahead, but the playfulness in his eyes was now gone. "What did he say?"

"I wasn't in the room, but soon after the meeting, Eric set up a task force to begin an investigation on you."

"To investigate what?"

"Theft, trafficking, and selling raw substances."

Terrence closed his eyes, and Havilland watched as his hands gripped the railing, and she guessed he was fantasizing having his hands around Robert's neck. After a moment, his muscles relaxed, and he calmly pulled a stick of gum from inside his jacket pocket, unwrapped it, and popped it into his mouth.

"You were supposed to stay as far away from California as possible," she said.

"Sometimes plans change."

She clutched his arm. "Listen to me. You need to leave here. Now!"

He slowly turned his head from the blue waters of the bay and looked down at her hand clutching his arm. Then he raised his eyes to meet hers and she saw nothing in them. No compassion for anything or anyone but himself.

"Now why would I want to leave?"

But she continued on, desperate to appeal to him. "You being here is too close. If this investigation doesn't go away, everything we've accomplished, all these months of work will be wiped away."

He didn't say anything for a long time, but just stared at her as if he were assimilating every word she'd said and replaying it in his mind. He then shrugged his arm from her grasp.

"That's why you're there. To make sure any case against me goes away."

"I tried to get on the task force, but Eric, he...he doesn't trust me anymore."

"Smart man."

Havilland felt her temper rising. "That's not funny. His feelings for me are all your fault! I should just let him and the other agents take your ass down. Maybe then I won't ever have to see your face again."

"Oh yeah?" he asked, pushing away from the railing and invading her space so she had to back away from him. "You do that, and I take your brother right down with me. You want that? Then again, prison might do him some good. He can't blow all of his money on chips in there."

Havilland grew furious as she felt herself becoming trapped by him all over again.

Terrence pointed a finger at her chest. "I left Atlanta, because I had no other choice. It was going nowhere. You were supposed to be my eyes and ears, but it all stopped and I was left in the dark. So, yeah, when the opportunity came to move to California, I took it, figuring I could keep an eye on you and ensure you do your part to make sure this shit goes away—once and for all!"

"I've done everything you've asked of me," she said. "At great risk to myself. If anything ever went wrong, my career would be over. My boss may be in the know, but he would protect himself before protecting me."

He shrugged. "You don't seem to be doing too bad for

yourself. I hear your husband just got a new promotion, you're happily married, complete with a child and a picket fence."

He paused to laugh. "Good for you, Hav. You ended up with everything you asked for." He leaned in toward her face, and the spearmint scent of his gum tickled her nostrils. "Everything you asked *me* for."

She started to back away, but he grabbed for her arm, halting her. "Meet me here, same time next week."

She shook her head. "That's too risky."

"I don't care. I get a little antsy when I don't hear from you. I want to look you in the eye every time you keep me updated on this case."

"I'm not involved with the investigation—"

"Then figure out a way to get involved," he said. "You find out everything you can and make sure you don't miss one single detail. I didn't come this far only to be stopped by your Super-Agent husband."

He roughly let her go and walked away. Havilland looked around, satisfied no one was paying them any attention, and then turned around to walk in the opposite direction. Fear and anguish gripped her, but she had no choice. If she was ever going to be free of Terrence, she had to get answers for him. She'd have to do everything in her power to sabotage Eric's case.

* * *

Even though Terrence had walked away, he only made it a few feet before he turned around and watched with amusement as she went in the opposite direction. It was really too bad that things had ended between them the way they did. He'd always had a soft spot for Havilland, only these days he didn't show it. But the fact remained, he missed being with her. She reminded him of when times were simpler, when his only responsibilities were issuing traffic tickets and working long hours with zero respect. But despite that, he'd enjoyed being a cop, and he'd enjoyed being her partner. Still, even with Havilland as a sexy distraction, he wanted more for himself. And when she invited him to an alumni dinner at Spelman College, he accepted and his fortunes changed by way of Devon Foxworth.

Yes, he and Havilland were technically dating, and things between them were growing serious. But with Havilland, he saw the same thing day in and day out, and his future didn't look too exciting. Devon, however, with her beauty, society connections, and her father's wealth had him dreaming about the possibilities. So, he left Havilland, married Devon, the heiress to the Foxworth fortune, and said hello to a new life of luxury.

But he soon came to find out that the life he'd chosen over Havilland came with a price. In exchange for an executive-level career, designer labels, and foreign cars, he had to give up his independence. Because of Devon's insecurities and fears, it was mandated that he remained chained by her side whenever possible. His own salary from Foxworth Pharmaceuticals wasn't his to keep. He was given an allowance, but just enough to keep him dependent upon Devon and her father. After a year of that, Terrence grew tired of the charade, but he couldn't leave her. There was no prenup. A divorce would only leave him with the clothes on his back. So, he began to look for other ways to have his own money, and he'd found it, or more accurately, it had found him. It wasn't exactly legal, but for years, he'd gotten a semblance of his freedom back, and that was enough for him. Then one day, he'd discovered something he wasn't meant to, and just like that, his money train was in danger of coming to an end.

He kept his eyes on Havilland as she retraced her steps

along the Embarcadero back to where he assumed she'd parked her car and then pulled out his cell phone to make a call. When the other line picked up, he didn't waste time with greetings.

"I made contact with Havilland—yeah I know I'm not supposed to call you, but she told me my father-in-law is in town and running his mouth about my operation. I've got an investigation on me, again, and I'm not sure if I can trust her anymore to handle this. If the CBI doesn't back off, you're going to have to step in."

He paused to listen to the other caller.

"My part of the deal is almost fulfilled. You just be sure to do your part and while you're at it, find a way to keep tabs on Agent Eric Sawyer. He and I have an adversarial history, and I know he's salivating at the chance to see me go down."

CHAPTER THIRTEEN

Later that evening, Eric sat at the table nestled in the breakfast nook just off the kitchen and put a forkful of steak and mashed potatoes into his mouth. He'd skipped lunch and the task force meeting had run late, but he'd turned down invites to dinner and made his way home, instead. When he got there, he'd made a beeline for the kitchen and found a foil-wrapped plate in the refrigerator for him to heat up. Now he was eating his dinner alone and listening to the girlish laughter coming from upstairs.

Soon, he heard footsteps coming down the stairs, and in a few seconds, Havilland appeared in the doorway that connected both the kitchen and family room. She stopped when she saw him and then continued into the kitchen to take a glass from one of the cabinets.

"Is Kimmy in bed, yet?" he asked.

"She's upstairs with Jeanetta, taking her bath."

He nodded.

"I didn't expect you until later," she said, taking fruit juice from the refrigerator and pouring it into the glass.

She was still wearing her work clothes, which meant it must've been a busy night with Kimmy, because normally by the time he came home, she was showered and changed into more comfortable clothes.

"Tonight was about assigning everyone a particular task. The next few weeks is when things will get interesting." He finished up the vegetables on his plate and then reached for his glass of wine. As he tipped the rim to his lips, he stared at her and found she was watching him too.

He put the wine glass down and sighed heavily. "Are we going to argue about this again?"

"You're shutting me out. I'm just as good as those other agents."

"Setting aside recent events, it's a conflict of interest for you to be anywhere near this case. Once we get an arrest, he'll tell his lawyers about you."

"He doesn't have to know that I'm involved at all. Let me help you."

"I'm a pretty damn good agent too, Hav, and I've been working these cases long before you joined the bureau. I can handle it."

"And what happens when he tells his lawyers about *you*?" she asked. "You're the one leading the case. Let's talk about these recent events, because from what I can see, this is very personal for you."

He got up from the table with his plate and glass, and she didn't move as he came to stand next to her by the sink.

"You're taking a big risk. If I can't be on this case, then you shouldn't be either."

He turned to her and spoke in a deep and ominous tone that warned her to back off. "I told you I've got this."

He grabbed for the sponge and detergent and began washing the plate vigorously. He didn't look at her again but could feel her staring up at him, her eyes following his movements.

"How long, Eric?"

He ran warm water and soap over his plate, fork, and glass and then rinsed them, watching the suds swirl down the drain.

"How much longer are we going to do this?" she asked.

He set the dishes on the drying rack and grabbed the dish towel to dry his hands. She was so close to him he could feel his right forearm brushing lightly against her breasts. It used to excite them both when he did that. On some nights, before things changed between them, when he washed dishes and she dried, he would accidentally on purpose rub his arm against her breasts until he felt her nipples harden through her bra. Each time he handed her a dish to dry, he'd make a light brush against each nipple and they'd look at each other, silently communicating their erotic thoughts. By the time Kimmy was tucked into bed, they were racing each other to the bedroom, hot and ready for each other.

"Please, say something," she said, "because I can't keep living like this. There's got to be an end date."

Eric squeezed the dish towel tightly between his hands, watching the blood rush through them until they were red fists.

"Tell me when you're going to start trusting me again."

Tighter.

"Do I really need to ask you to point it out on a calendar?"

His hands were now aching.

Havilland put her face dangerously close to his and lowered her voice. "Exactly what day are you going to start fucking me again?"

He threw the towel to the side and instead of cotton fabric, his hands were now touching soft flesh as he gripped the back of her neck and held her in place.

"This doesn't end until I'm satisfied he's out of our lives," he hissed. "I don't know what you're planning when it comes to Miller, but just know that I've got plans of my own. He's in my city now, and I'm taking his ass down. You tell him that the next time you see him."

He expected to see defiance or maybe even guilt in her eyes, but she was giving him nothing but a look of surrender, and that crumbled his defenses, making him long for her. She didn't say anything, but her lips slowly parted as if to welcome him, and he leaned closer unable to hold back anymore. He had to taste her.

"Mommy! I'm ready to get out!"

"Mrs. Sawyer, she's clean and ready for her bedtime story," Jeanetta also called with mirth in her voice.

Eric released his hand from the back of her neck and immediately put distance between them at the sound of his daughter's delighted shout from upstairs. It was just the distraction he needed. A half a second longer, and he would've drove his tongue into Havilland's mouth and ultimately, anywhere else she asked him to.

Havilland started to leave the kitchen, but he gently took her arm.

"I'll read her a story," he said. "With this case, I may not get many more early nights like this with her."

She nodded and he walked by her, careful not to touch her in the slightest. She'd felt so damned good crushed up against him, and it had been a testament to his willpower not to snatch her clothes off, lift her thick ass onto the island, and take her right there. By the look of regret in her eyes and the sound of her shallow breathing, she'd wanted the same thing. But as much as he desired his wife, he was still a prisoner of the fury and jealousy she'd made him feel. Even as he climbed the stairs to help Jeanetta get Kimmy ready for bed, he knew that he and Havilland still had a long road to go before they could ever come together again. Because she hadn't changed out of her work clothes, he could smell her usual fragrant perfume. Only now, it was mixed with the scent of strong and expensive cologne.

CHAPTER FOURTEEN

Havilland got comfortable underneath the down comforter and settled in for another night of restless sleep. After Eric read Kimmy a bed-time story, he tucked her in for the night and left the house with no explanation to Havilland other than he was going to take a drive and wouldn't be gone long.

She could see it in his eyes that he wanted her, but there was someone standing between them, and she couldn't get rid of him without hurting someone she loved.

She put down the tablet she'd been mindlessly browsing through and picked up her cell phone on the nightstand, pulled up her contacts, and scrolled to a name. His picture was saved next to his name, and she smiled at the way he grinned in such a carefree way toward the camera. He always made her smile and yet, at the same time, he always managed to break her heart.

She tapped the dial button and put the phone to her ear. After three rings, he picked up and from the sound of his voice, he was just as happy to hear from her as she was to be calling him.

"Big sis! What took you so long to call me?"

She chuckled. "The phone works both ways, you brat. Why haven't you called me?"

"Yeah, you're right," he said. "I've been busy with packing up my things in Atlanta and getting settled here for my new job."

"At the Foxworth plant?"

"Where else?" he asked with a snort.

She sighed. "I don't know, Stephen. I thought maybe this time when I called, you'd tell me you found another job. Maybe working in a hospital?"

"Hospital hours are just as long, and the pay is nowhere near what I'm making with Foxworth."

"Is the money really so worth it that you have to work for *him?*"

By him, she meant Terrence.

"Hey, I'm just trying to live and Foxworth Pharmaceuticals gives me a good living. Your past with that man has nothing to do with me."

Havilland wasn't so sure of that. Stephen's employment at the company was a big part of the problems she continued to face with Terrence. She loved her brother dearly, and Terrence used that love against her every chance he could get.

There was a long pause on the other end of the line before he spoke again.

"Go ahead and ask me."

Tears came to her eyes because he knew her so well, and it saddened her that this topic was always at the center of their conversations. Maybe it always would be.

"Are you back at the tables?"

"No."

The answer came too fast for her.

"Stephen—"

"You asked. I answered. Now are you going to insult me by asking me again?"

"Only if the first answer was a lie."

"Good night, Hav."

"No, wait! Please don't hang up."

Another long pause.

"I'm sorry," she said. "You did answer me and part of your recovery is having my trust. I believe you."

He was silent for a while longer, and she knew he was struggling to let go of his anger. Finally, he released a long and heavy sigh, and she knew they were back on steady ground. For now.

"Tell me about my niece."

She began to smile as she filled him in on all of Kimmy's latest antics, and they were soon laughing hysterically.

"Now, that I'm living here, I can come see you guys more often," he said. "I miss you."

"We miss you, too, and I know for sure Mom is glad you're close by."

"I found an apartment in the city. I'll take her with me to see it. She'll like that," he promised. "So, what else is going on? How's Eric?"

The lingering smile melted from her mouth. "He's fine."

"That's it?"

He seemed to be waiting for her to elaborate, but there was nothing else more she could say.

Stephen cleared his throat. "I know it's none of my business, but nowadays, whenever I ask about him, it's always a few one-word answers. It never used to be like that. You used to sing that man's praises so much, I thought maybe he wore an invisible Superman cape."

She laughed. "Was I that bad?"

"Yeah, you were, but it felt good to know you were so

happy." He paused. "You're not at odds with him because of me, are you?"

"No, of course not."

"You sure? The last time I got myself in trouble, you really helped me out, and I know he wasn't too happy about it. Taking from your retirement to clear my debt would cause conflict in any relationship."

"That was over a year ago, and it wasn't the last time you got into trouble," she corrected.

"You're right. But the last time, it was your ex that bailed me out." He paused again. "I'm really sorry, Hav. For everything."

It was a year ago in Atlanta that Terrence had stopped two men from beating Stephen for a significant amount of money he owed them. Terrence had even paid the debt Stephen owed, and a few days later, Havilland's arrangement with him began.

"You've already apologized, and it's not you, Stephen," she said. "Yes, Eric and I are going through some things, but it's just typical marriage stuff. We'll get through it."

Even as she said the words, she wasn't so sure she believed them. But the alternative scared her.

She quickly changed the subject. "You'll call me when you have any urges or temptations, right?"

He groaned. "I have meetings and a sponsor for that. Trust me, Hav. You don't want me calling you every time I have an urge or need to gamble. You'll never get any sleep. Worry about yourself. You have a family to think about."

Tears began to trickle down her cheeks. "You are my family."

He sighed. "Fine. Let's just end it there. I love you, big sis."

She bit down on her bottom lip hard before speaking. "I love you more."

"Yeah, that's the problem," he said, chuckling sadly and then ended the call.

Havilland put the phone aside and grabbed for the pillow on Eric's side of the bed and let out the sobs she'd been holding back. She knew Stephen was still gambling, but he would never admit it to her. He saw it as a way to protect her and keep their relationship from being destroyed. She also knew the illegal shit he was involved in with Terrence, but Stephen figured she was ignorant to all of it. She would do what she could to keep him from going to prison, but as far as the gambling, she had to trust he would somehow find his way out of it. Until that day came, she had to live with this helpless feeling and seek comfort wherever she could find it, like in this pillow that still carried Eric's familiar scent.

CHAPTER FIFTEEN

As soon as Stephen disconnected his call with Havilland, he tossed his cell onto the bed. He then went to rejoin the man waiting in his living room, who'd rang his doorbell only five minutes before.

"Sorry about that."

"No problem. Was that her?" Eric asked, sitting patiently on the couch.

"Yeah. She was worried and just wanted to see how I was."

"She won't know about any of this," Eric said. "She's not on the task force, so she won't be privy to any of our witnesses or CIs."

Stephen snorted derisively. "You've known Hav long enough to know she finds a way to get answers."

"I'll take care of Hav. I just need your agreement to give me what I need. You cooperate, and I can assure you receive immunity in exchange for your testimony against Terrence."

Stephen let out a breath he didn't know he'd been holding, along with the pent-up fear of having to go to prison. "That's very generous, but I don't know anything about the details on how the drugs are transported. I'm just the chemist. I know how the product is made and what ingredients are needed to get top dollar. But as far as the business side, I'm not going to be much help without Terrence."

"He brings you with him when he meets the buyers, doesn't he?"

"Yeah, but—"

"Then don't worry about it. You just tell me what you know, and my surveillance team will get the rest of the details. Hell, Terrence himself will give me all the information I want for a reduced prison sentence."

Stephen went silent at that last word, and Eric must have sensed his apprehension.

"Look, I know you two go back. He hired you right out of college, and you feel like you're betraying him when he gave you a chance."

Yes, getting a job at Foxworth Pharmaceuticals right after receiving his PhD in Chemistry had done wonders for his ego and bank account. However, instead of using the generous salary to pay down his overwhelming student loan debt, Stephen had discovered more excitement at the gaming tables. But no matter how he squandered his money, he was still grateful to Terrence for giving him a chance, even though in the back of his mind, the only reason Terrence called him was because he was feeling guilt over the way things ended with Havilland. If he couldn't make amends with her, maybe he believed he could make things right with her family.

Eric pressed on. "Listen to me. Terrence will always look out for himself. He's not loyal to you, so protect your own future."

"It's all right, Eric. you don't have to sell me," Stephen said. "I know how he is, and I'll do what's necessary."

"See that you do."

Stephen cursed himself for the mess he'd gotten himself

into. For months, he'd been thinking about cutting his losses and moving on. He was convinced that what he and Terrence were doing was no longer just between them. They were being watched, and it was only a matter of time before they were caught. He was risking his license, his good salary and benefits, and even more precious, his freedom. But the arrangement he had with Terrence was very lucrative, and over the past three years, they'd built something very sweet that had kept both of their pockets padded nicely. But more money only kept Stephen at the underground gambling dens. The more he played, the bigger his losses and the deeper in debt he got. So as much as that fear had urged him to walk away, the prospect of more money kept him on Terrence's leash. Now, it was too late. He was in the middle of an investigation that meant lengthy prison time if he didn't cooperate.

His thoughts trailed to Havilland. She sounded so sad whenever he talked to her, and he knew it was the weight of worry she carried on her shoulders for him. He wanted to see his sister smile and laugh more. He didn't want to be the cause of her sadness, but with the case being turned over to the CBI and Eric conducting the investigation, it was only a matter of time before she discovered how deeply he was involved.

* * *

August 2017

"You're working late tonight."

Stephen was locking up the lab and turned at the sound of the voice behind him. "Mr. Miller," he said, surprised to see Robert Foxworth's son-in-law standing there. He came forward and reached out his hand to shake Terrence's. "It's good to see you. I had some work to catch up on."

"All finished?"

"Yeah, but now, I've got to get going. I have an appointment."

Terrence looked down at the platinum watch on his wrist. "This late? It must be a date."

Stephen shrugged. "Not exactly, but it's a commitment I can't miss."

"Do you mind if I walk you to your car then? I have something I'd like to talk to you about."

Stephen nodded and the two walked through the corridors until they came to the lobby of elevators that led to the employee parking garage.

"I know you think I'm out of touch up there on the executive floor, but I've been hearing that you do good work here in the lab," Terrence said. "Your supervisor tells me you're one of his best chemists."

Stephen punched the button for the elevator and looked around, thankful that they were alone. Most of the employees had gone for the day, and he wasn't too keen on people noticing that the boss was singling him out and paying him compliments. That was all it would take for rumors to start spreading that he was some kind of company man or corporate snitch.

"I'm glad to hear it, Mr. Miller."

"Come on, Stephen, call me Terrence. I dated your sister for Christ's sake, and I'd like you to know I recommended to your supervisor to give you a raise."

Stephen had been keeping his eyes on each floor number as it lit up, indicating the elevator's descent, but at the prospect of more money, he instantly turned to Terrence and didn't move when the elevator arrived at the lobby floor and the doors slid open.

"Wow. That's very generous of you, Mr.—I mean, Terrence. You've already done enough for me by getting me this job in the first place."

Terrence waved away the gratitude, motioned for Stephen to proceed him into the elevator, and then punched the level for the parking garage.

"I do have some power, and I like to recognize our employees for their hard work." He paused. "I'm sure the extra bump in pay will come in handy."

"Yes, it will. Thank you again."

"But it won't be enough."

Stephen frowned. "What do you mean?"

"That little bit of raise won't ever be enough to keep the loan sharks at bay, will it?"

The elevator doors once again slid open, but this time, Stephen's feet were on the move. He now barely looked at Terrence as he headed toward his car. "Again, I appreciate the raise, but what I do outside of work is my personal business. Good night."

"Stephen, wait."

He could hear the heels of Terrence's wing-tipped shoes against the asphalt as he hurried close behind him.

"Listen, I didn't mean to put you on the spot like that. You're right. Whatever you do after work is your business. I just wanted you to know that I understand. I understand more than you know."

Stephen pulled his car keys from his pocket and chirped the alarm off. He then tossed his messenger bag into the backseat, shut the door, and then turned to look at Terrence.

"I doubt that. You're the owner's son-in-law with a cushy VP position, and you and your wife live comfortably in his Buckhead mansion. I find it hard to believe you'd ever be short of funds."

"Well, believe it. I may have married into money and may enjoy the benefits of it, but my wife keeps all the accounts in her name and doles out an allowance like she would to a teenager. And my father-in-law is just as bad because after he deducts half my paycheck and invests it for his daughter, my salary more resembles the guys who work in the warehouse than that of a vice-president. My job is purely for the title."

Stephen tried to keep his mouth from falling open in surprise. He couldn't decide what shocked him more—Terrence's predicament or the fact that he'd openly shared it with him.

"I'm sorry. I didn't know that."

"Look, I didn't keep you just to unburden myself," Terrence said and dropped his briefcase beside Stephen's car. "I just wanted you to know that we're more alike than you think. We both want money. We both want our own thing. I want to be my own boss and make my own decisions, and I can see that in you too."

Stephen gave a slight shrug. "So, what if I do? Maybe someday, but right now I can't afford to just up and quit this job to go and start a business."

"That's the last thing I want you to do." Terrence stepped forward and lowered his voice. "What if I told you that I have connections who are willing to pay you handsomely for your expertise?"

"What does that mean?"

He eyed Stephen's car. "Give the gambling hall a rest for tonight. Let me take you to dinner, and I'll tell you how we can make even more money."

CHAPTER SIXTEEN

"Hav, I don't mind filling you in on the investigation. I owe you one for when you helped me way back on that Baxter case. I just have one question."

Here it comes, Havilland thought to herself. She figured taking him out to lunch coupled with the fact that he owed her a favor would've curtailed any questioning but apparently not.

"Why don't you just ask Eric?"

She sighed. "I can't go to Eric with this."

Jerry chuckled and popped a french fry into his mouth. "Okay, not to sound like an asshole, but don't you two live near each other?"

"Ha, ha," she said dryly and figured she could make up something closely resembling the truth without revealing her husband's distrust for her.

"He's a stickler for the rules. You know that. If I'm not on the task force, he doesn't want to share the information. It's too important of a case to him, and he doesn't want to leave anything to chance."

Jerry frowned. "Are you talking about leaks? Does he think you're going to run and tell whatever you hear?"

He thinks I'm going to run and tell Terrence.

"Not me, personally. It's just a general rule he has, and even though I'm his wife, he doesn't want to get caught bending the rules just for me."

Jerry shrugged. "All right, I get it. When I get back to the office, I'll forward you the case notes. But this is between us, right? I don't want Eric coming down on me for sharing information. I trust you to keep this to yourself."

Havilland nodded gratefully. "He won't know, I promise, and this is purely for my own curiosity."

He smiled, grabbed ahold of his club sandwich, and took a bite. She smiled back, taking a sip of her iced tea, and felt terrible for lying to not only her coworker but her friend. She didn't want to bring him into her deception. She didn't want to do any of this, but her back was against the wall. She'd agreed to this and was now in too deep to just walk away. Plus, if she pulled out now, Terrence would follow through on his threat to implicate Stephen in everything, and she couldn't let her brother go down for Terrence's dealings.

But as Jerry changed the subject, she thought about the first time she risked her job for Terrence. Back then it hadn't been for Stephen. No, that first time Terrence came to her for a small favor, she'd given into him purely out of sentiment. She had taken Kimmy to visit Stephen and her father in Atlanta. She, her father, and Kimmy had decided to go to the Foxworth plant and take Stephen to lunch. It was there she was reunited with Terrence, and she didn't know what to say to him other than "Hello, how have you been" and "It's good to see you." The conversation hadn't lasted long, but the way he had looked at her, she should've known that encounter wouldn't be their last.

She had to finish this last job to get him out of her life once and for all. But as Jerry chatted about office politics, Havilland wondered if choosing to give into Terrence for the last time was the beginning of her downfall.

CHAPTER SEVENTEEN

*O*ne week later…

"I'm very pleased with these sales figures." Robert's authoritative voice boomed through the speakers of Terrence's laptop.

After his final walk-through with the contractor last week, he was finally able to move into his opulent office, which sat several floors above the plant. He'd happily furnished it with the most expensive décor and sat proudly behind his desk, feeling satisfied that for the first time, he wasn't under someone's watchful eye.

He was now sitting in his leather desk chair, listening in remotely to the weekly sales projection meeting while every now and then, his eyes traveled over to his wall safe, and he thought about the ledger inside. He was more than ready to play that card.

"Claire just informed me her sales team secured a contract with Cherry Hill drugstores. Apparently, their previous supplier wasn't giving them what they needed. Thank you, Claire, and congratulations on the new contract," Robert said, smiling and clapping.

That was a cue for the rest of the executive managers to start clapping and offering congratulations as well. Terrence participated. He was, after all, playing the role of a team player.

"Terrence, how are the plans looking for the opening of the plant in San Francisco?"

He sat up straighter and offered a broad smile for the camera. "Very well, Robert. I did the final walk-through last week, and it's an amazing site. Devon and I are excited to have you and the rest of the board members come up for the unveiling. Even the media is in love with this project."

Robert cleared his throat. "Yes, well, I did see several news articles, and you're right about that. The *San Francisco Chronicle* is very happy about the jobs we're bringing to the city, and the interview you did for them showed good judgment and loyalty on your part."

He paused and to Terrence, it looked like he was trying to swallow dirt.

"Thank you, Robert."

The rest of the executive managers smiled, and it was now Terrence's turn to receive congratulatory remarks. He smiled and nodded his appreciation while keeping his eyes on Robert, enjoying the old man's discomfort. It pained him to give Terrence any smidgen of a compliment, especially in front of others.

"All right, that wraps everything up for the day," Robert said. "Good work, everyone. Terrence, if you don't mind, stay on with me for just a minute."

Terrence waited as everyone logged off the virtual conference and sat back in his chair, waiting for the bullshit that was coming his way. The audience was gone, and Robert no longer had to be the doting father-in-law. The claws were about to come out.

"Now, tell me exactly what the hell is going on up there."

Terrence pretended to look shocked by his tone, but this was nothing new. Their exchanges were always heated, and it was only because they both knew neither of them liked nor respected the other. From the moment Devon introduced him to her father, Robert made it clear he would never accept him as a husband to his daughter. As far as Robert was concerned, his and Devon's marriage was in name only. He gave Terrence a vice-president job, with no real responsibility just to please Devon. He was just bowing to the wishes of his little girl, hoping one day she'd come to her senses and kick Terrence to the curb, but Terrence saw it as his one quest in life to make sure that never happened, simply to spite him.

"I'm not sure what you're talking about, sir," Terrence said. "Like I said, the plant is scheduled to open in the next few months, our hiring managers are overwhelmed with applications, and—"

"Not the plant, dammit! I'm talking about Devon. Why the hell am I getting phone calls from her complaining about you canceling your lunch dates and not coming home on time?"

Of course, it was about Devon. It was always about Devon.

"Since we got here, I've been hitting the ground running, setting up media conferences, meeting with the contractor, finance manager, and inventory sales team. I have a business to run, which will sometimes force me to cancel lunch dates or keep me away from the house."

"I'll worry about the business," Robert shot back. "Your first priority is to Devon."

Terrence's anger swelled. "I'm doing my job. If your little girl is lonely, that's her problem."

"No, it's your problem!" Robert boomed. "Don't force me

to yank you out of California and back here to Georgia. If I get another call from her, that's just what I'll do."

"And who's going to replace me? Everyone else is booked."

Terrence took a moment to calm down because even though he didn't care for the man, the last thing he wanted was to antagonize him even further. At least, not until his plans were complete.

"Listen, you're right that I haven't been spending as much time with Devon, but it's because my focus has been on this facility. This is your business and legacy, and I don't want to screw it up. I'll set things right with Devon, but both of you need to understand that this company is just as important to me."

He could see Robert's features softening just a little, so he began to lay it on thick. "You did me an honor when you entrusted me as vice-president and yes, I know that was mostly for Devon's sake, but nonetheless, you trust me with a lot of responsibility, and I don't want to let you down."

Robert grunted, and Terrence assumed he'd assuaged his temper for now and chose that moment to move on to a more important subject.

"Listen, Robert, this has been the first time in a couple of weeks since I've had the chance to talk to you alone. There's that other matter we need to discuss."

"Later," Robert said brusquely, which only made Terrence's blood pressure rise.

"This can't wait until later. I need to talk to you about—"

"I know what needs to be discussed, and I'm telling you it can wait until later. We can talk in person when I come to San Francisco in a couple of weeks for the opening. Trust me, it will keep until then."

Terrence didn't want to, but he relented. The man always

had to have the final say, and he wasn't about to waste his time arguing with him through a laptop screen.

"Fine."

"One more thing," Robert said and leaned in closer toward the screen. "There are a lot of hungry young graduates out there who would love to take your place. It won't be long before I have better options to oversee the management of the San Francisco facility. Trust me, when I do, you and Devon are coming back here, and you're going to be a husband to my daughter. Even if you are useless at that too!"

CHAPTER EIGHTEEN

*D*evon eyed the plush surroundings of the private investigative firm. It was her second time visiting the office, and it still puzzled her as to why such a high-end firm, whose website advertised corporate espionage cases and high-profile security details, would waste its time with something as old and clichéd as tailing an allegedly cheating husband. But she guessed that her money was just as good as anyone else's, and she was certain she was paying a lot more than she needed to for her cliché case.

"Mrs. Foxworth-Miller, it's good to see you again."

She was sitting in the office of Oliver Meeker, one of the three partners of the firm, when he strode in and offered his hand. She remembered him from the last time she was there when he promised he would have one of his best investigators handle her case. He had also greeted her as Mrs. Miller, to which Devon politely yet firmly corrected. She always included her maiden name in all business dealings. After all, that was the name that held all of the money and respect.

"It's good to see you, too, Mr. Meeker," she said, allowing

him to softly shake her hand. "I assume you have news for me."

"I do," he said, taking a seat in the black executive chair behind his desk. "But, I'm not sure whether you're going to be disappointed or pleased by what my investigator found."

Devon frowned and sat forward in her chair while he removed a manilla folder from his desk drawer and set it between them. He promptly opened the folder and removed several 8×10 color photographs and spread them out. Devon immediately saw that Terrence was in all of the pictures, but it was whom he was photographed with that piqued her interest.

"Now as you can see, in this set"—Oliver pointed to a group of pictures on the left side of the desk"—he's meeting with some men either in restaurants or at the piers."

"Probably something to do with the business," she surmised.

She'd already done a once-over on those pictures and quickly dismissed them. Terrence was handling the opening of the new plant, so it was likely he was meeting with buyers, management, employees, and even the media. Who cared? She had her eye on the second set of pictures to her right. And all of her focus was on the woman.

"We did manage to catch him meeting and speaking to only one woman, but it doesn't look like they're having an affair," Oliver said. "They meet in public and secluded places, but they're just talking. In some of the pictures, you can see them arguing with each other. But there's nothing intimate or overtly sexual."

Devon admitted she wouldn't be too surprised nor would she care if he had a mistress. She was certain of the fact that Terrence would think long and hard before he chose to divorce her, because there was an ironclad prenup in place, and he hardly had any money or investments of his own. So, unless he found himself another heiress, he wasn't going anywhere. She was certain of all of that on her drive over here, but now seeing the familiar face of the woman in the pictures, the tiniest inkling of doubt was creeping its way into her mind.

"Oh, will you please excuse me for just a moment," Oliver said, rising from his seat. "I see one of the other partners just got in from out of town, and I need to speak with him about an urgent matter."

Devon nodded absently, unable to stop looking at the woman. "Havilland. What are you

doing here?" she mumbled to herself.

Out of all the faceless women Terrence could've been meeting, it had to be her, a woman Devon knew personally, and a woman with whom Terrence had an intimate past.

"That won't work. Find another way! This job is way too important."

Devon turned at the sound of raised voices and saw Oliver speaking with another man. He'd closed the door to give them privacy, but she could still hear the muffled and angry exchange. The door was also glass. Oliver's back was to her, but she could clearly see the man he was speaking to, and the sight of him took her breath away. When his eyes slowly slid from Oliver to look over his shoulder directly at her, it all but paralyzed her.

Oliver turned, saw her watching them, and quickly reentered the office full of apology.

"I'm so sorry to keep you waiting, Mrs. Foxworth-Miller."

"It's all right." Devon forced herself to turn away from the man and focus on Oliver.

"I know it's not what you were expecting," he said. "You'd have a hard time proving an affair with these photos, but if you'd like, I can have my team keep at it until we find something."

"No," Devon said, quickly gathering the pictures up and placing them neatly in the folder. She then stood and shook Oliver's hand, who was now frowning at the abrupt end to the meeting.

"I'll take it from here," she said, placing the folder in her oversized Birkin bag and putting on her shades. "Thank you so much for your thorough work, and I'll leave a check for you at the front desk."

She didn't give him a chance to respond but left the office in a hurry. She looked around, glad to see the man was gone and practically threw a check at the receptionist before hurrying to the exit as fast as her six-inch Giuseppes would take her. Once she was tucked away inside her car in a corner of the underground garage, she worked at steadying her breathing, refusing to let the past have its way with her. She shut any impending memories away and pulled out the photos again and stared at the woman Terrence had been meeting. The dates and time stamps correlated with the days when he canceled their lunches or came home late for dinner.

The entire ride back to Pacific Heights, she wondered what could possibly be so important that Terrence and Havilland had reacquainted. If it wasn't an affair, then what was the purpose of these little meetings? What the hell was Havilland doing in California anyway? An icy rage filled Devon as she thought about how eagerly Terrence fought to move out there. Was she the real reason for his eagerness?

She took several more deep breaths. *Keep calm.* The good news is they weren't kissing, embracing, or doing anything remotely sexual in the photos. It seemed to be the opposite. If she looked closely, it became clear that Havilland despised

Terrence. But why? Maybe they did have some sort of relationship and Terrence was ending it.

Devon hadn't really kept track of her after she and
Terrence started dating. She naturally wondered how Havilland had taken the news that Terrence no longer wanted to
be with her, but Terrence said that although she'd been hurt,
she handled the break up with maturity. Devon thought
nothing more of it, especially since she hadn't been the
victim of late-night hang-up calls, her car getting keyed,
windows smashed in, or even secretive text messages to
Terrence about how she missed him. By all appearances,
Havilland had been a part of their past. Yet, now out of the
clear blue sky, she was suddenly very much a part of their
present.

She was surprised to see Terrence's Denali was in the
driveway when she got home. When he left this morning, he
made it seem as if it would be a busy day, and their standing
lunch date would once again be canceled. She wasn't about to
take any more of these damn cancellations, especially now
that she was privy to his secret meetings with his ex-girlfriend. She'd just have to reacquaint herself with Havilland
and then ensure she stayed out of their lives for good. Years
ago, Devon had so easily made Terrence forget his cop girlfriend and set his sights on her. She could definitely do it
again. And whether he liked it or not, Terrence's free time
was about to be cut drastically short, just like it had been in
Atlanta. She didn't need her father—she was more than
capable of keeping her husband's leash tight.

She got out of the car, walked up the entryway to their
mansion while rehearsing what she planned to say to him.
But as soon as she stepped up to the front door, it was
whipped open and Terrence stood there in black, tailored
slacks with a baby-blue, tailored dress shirt that fit his body
to perfection and complemented his dark skin. He had her

mentally swooning. Muscles from his chest and arms slightly bulged, and even the angry scowl on his face couldn't tamp down her sudden arousal. Maybe they could skip lunch, make their way up to the bedroom, and they could work out their frustrations with each other the natural way.

"You called your father again," he accused, opening the door wider to let her inside.

"He wanted to know how things were going," she said, stepping past him and putting her purse and keys on a side table.

Terrence slammed the door and stepped into her personal space. "The next time your father wants to know what's going on, you just tell him everything's fucking peachy."

"Don't curse at me."

"I mean it, Devon. How many times do I have to tell you that what goes on in this house is our business?"

He was shouting now, and she felt a pool of embarrassment well up inside of her at the thought of the house staff listening in once again. They weren't strangers to her and Terrence's shouting matches, but she was really getting tired of being their entertainment. Her father must have reminded him that his only duty was to her. Yeah, he held a vice-president position in the company, but she, her father, and especially Terrence himself knew the role didn't come with any real duties. He was a figurehead, plain and simple, because though Devon wanted her man to work, she didn't want to compete for his time.

She squared her shoulders and raised her head slightly. "You knew when you married me what the deal was. I don't care where you decide to relocate us. Nothing has or will ever change. I come first. I tried to tell you this when we first got here, but you wanted to test me. So, yes, I called my father and told him what was going on, and he obviously felt obligated to call you."

He was staring at her as if this was the first time he'd ever seen her.

"Work, then home and back again. You really do have a nice routine set up for me. Topped with a bit of pocket change to keep me just dependent enough on you."

She didn't say anything to that. What was the point in trying to deny it?

He stepped even closer and Devon was forced to back up slightly. "If you wanted a son, you should've made sure to get pregnant the first night we had sex. That's what you really want, isn't it? Someone to follow you around like a puppy and tied to you. But let me tell you something, even sons grow up and want to get away."

She wanted to spit in his face, but she wanted to jump into his arms even more and have him palm her ass and slam her up against the wall. She was actually turned on by her husband standing up to her. But she knew that if she gave him an inch, he'd want a mile, and she couldn't risk him enjoying just a little taste of freedom. The next thing she knew, he'd want more of it until eventually, he'd want freedom from her completely. Just like her mother had wanted. Just like the man she had seen outside Oliver's office.

"I'm your husband and a fully grown man at that, and I won't be kept prisoner in my own house. I don't care what you or Robert threatens me with."

His phone began to chime, signaling a text message. He pulled it from his pocket, looked at the display and then put it away. "We'll talk about this later," he said, brushing past her.

"Oh, no you don't," she said, moving fast and blocking his exit. "We'll talk about it now."

He narrowed his eyes and then grabbed her by the arms

to pull her away from the door. Devon began to fight him, claw, and smack at him.

"You're not leaving me," she screamed while Terrence blocked her assault.

"Cut it out, Devon!"

But she paid no attention to his commands until she felt herself being lifted into the air over his shoulders and carried into the family room. The next moment, he tossed her onto the sofa, and the air was knocked out of her when her back landed against the cushions. She instantly tried to jump back up, but he was already there to shove her back down with one hand. He put one knee in between her legs and gave her a menacing look as he began to unbutton his shirt.

"Don't move again," he warned.

She lay on her back, staring up at him with shock and anticipation. They'd been at each other's throats for weeks that she hadn't realized how much she wanted him to make love to her. Although he told her not to move, she went immediately for the waistband of her own slacks and shoved them over her thighs and down her legs. As he took off his shirt, she slid off her panties, top, and bra in record time and then reached up for him as he entered her swiftly. She had to get that other man out of her mind, and the intense feelings of her husband stroking in and out of her was just what she needed to shut away the past once and for all.

* * *

Nearly an hour later, Terrence was dressed and Devon was left sated and for the moment, happy. As he closed the front door and headed for his car to meet Rafael Cirillo and his men at Pier 96, he thought of Devon's words to him. She didn't want him to leave her. She wanted him to be completely hers—mind, body, and soul. As he got into his car and looked into the rearview mirror to adjust his tie, he wondered what she'd say if he demanded the same from her. If it ever came down to a choice between her father and him, who would she choose? His gut told him what the answer was, and that only convinced him the path he was on was his only choice. No one was ever going to have his back but him.

CHAPTER NINETEEN

*E*ric sat at his desk, looking at reports but not really seeing them or concentrating at all on any of the work that demanded his attention. He was waiting for word from his surveillance team that they had Terrence Miller in their sights and that the meeting with his buyers was underway. He'd received a tip from Stephen that he and Terrence were meeting with them that afternoon at Pier 96. Eric knew it would only be a matter of time before the man wouldn't be able to resist getting back to business. Now that he was there in San Francisco, far from the watchful eyes of his father-in-law, he probably felt free to continue his illegal operation. Eric wanted so badly to be there to catch the son of a bitch himself, but as much as he hated to admit it, Havilland was right. Because of her, he had a personal connection to Terrence, but his bosses didn't know that. If they had known, he would have never been assigned to lead this case. No one in the office knew about his acquaintance with the man except Havilland obviously, as well as Maya, and she'd promised to not say a word. Still, he needed to find out what Havilland's angle truly was. If she was out to sabotage his investigation, she could've stopped it from the very beginning by telling Carl about everything, including what had happened last fall in Atlanta. But then again, doing so would only implicate her.

A notification came through on his phone, and his team sent him confirmation that Terrence and Stephen had both arrived at the pier along with a man the agency had identified as Rafael Cirillo, a known liaison for the Lupino cartel. Eric pulled up the surveillance images on his computer that were coming through right then. There they all were in clear digital color. He couldn't get audio at that moment, but it would be uploaded later. For now, he was content to see that the evidence against Terrence Miller was piling up.

* * *

Havilland kept one eye on Eric sitting in his office while she frantically sent a text to Terrence on her burner phone. Jerry had excitedly told her that a surveillance detail was being set up for Terrence, and she had only moments to contact him. She knew Stephen would be at that meeting with him, because Terrence never met his buyers without him, and that was only to keep Stephen tied criminally to him.

Havilland: *You're being watched. Stop the meeting.*

She sent the text off and tucked the phone away in her desk drawer and locked it while still keeping an eye on Eric. She resumed her work as though nothing had happened, and waited for her husband's surveillance to come to an end. It didn't take long. When she saw his features turn dark and he erupted with an expletive, she wanted to crawl into a hole. She watched as Eric reached for his desk phone, punched in a number, and began barking orders at what must have been the surveillance detail.

"What the hell happened?" he angrily asked.

He listened to the other caller and pinched the bridge of his nose. "All right. All right! Just send me whatever you got and get back here."

He slammed the receiver down, rested his elbows on his desk and propped his chin in his hands. His eyes stared into space for so long, and then slowly, they scanned the room until finally landing on Havilland. Havilland simply returned his stare, trying her best to keep her face from betraying any type of emotion. But when the look in his eyes turned to accusation, she looked away, not wanting her own eyes to give away her betrayal.

Hours later, Eric walked in the front door and immediately stopped at the sight of his wife and daughter lying on the couch together asleep. The TV was on screensaver mode, which meant they must have fallen asleep watching one of Kimmy's movies. They both looked so peaceful lying there, but he knew Havilland would eventually wake up and want to put their daughter in her own bed. So, he took off his coat, laid it across the chair and went to scoop up the little girl. When she felt herself in his arms, she immediately grabbed for his neck and held on tight but stayed asleep. He smiled and carefully walked her up to her bedroom, laid her down in her twin-sized bed, and pulled the covers up over her. He then kissed her plump cheek and whispered in her ear.

"Good night, honey."

"Night, Daddy," she mumbled but kept her eyes closed.

He switched on her starlit nightlight, closed the door, and then quietly retreated back downstairs to stand over Havilland, who was still asleep on the couch. He wanted to wake her, but knew he wouldn't be as gentle with her as he had been with Kimmy.

Earlier that evening before he left work, he had a meeting with his task force, trying to soothe everyone's wounds about the botched surveillance on Terrence Miller. He wanted to revive their spirits because they hadn't been on this case for more than a couple of weeks and were already logging a lot of hours to bring it all together, and he wasn't going to allow this setback to get the better of him and his team.

"Let's regroup," he'd said. "We have our CI, so if and when Miller makes another move, we'll know about it."

After answering questions and giving directives, he'd dismissed the meeting, but one of his agents, Jerry Hicks, had been slower to get up.

"Jerry, was there something you wanted to add," Eric had asked as he gathered his notes and the photos from the surveillance.

He seemed to shake out of his trance and stood quickly to gather his own things. "No, Eric, I'm good."

Eric had sensed something was wrong but figured Jerry would come to him if it was something important. He went back to his office and began to get ready to leave for home when a knock at the door stopped him.

"Do you have a second?" Maya had asked.

"Sure, come in."

She entered the office, closed the door, and approached his desk with visible apprehension.

"This will sound strange," she said, hesitating, "but do you know where Hav was during the surveillance this afternoon?"

Eric frowned. "She was here at the office."

"Did she get up to leave at any time?"

"No."

"What about phone calls? Did she make any calls during that time?"

"Maya, I was too focused on the images coming through to keep tabs on her. What's this about?"

"It's about Terrence Miller getting a mystery text this afternoon and suddenly, the meeting with his buyers is over."

Eric stayed silent.

"Come on, don't make me say it," she said, leaning forward and pressing her hands atop his desk. "Atlanta."

"All right." Eric raised a hand to stop her. "That's not what's going on here. I kept her off the task force, because I didn't want a repeat of that."

"And you're sure she's not in contact with him again?"

When he didn't respond, she lowered her head and sighed heavily and then looked up at him again. "I know she's your wife. It's why I let it go the last time."

"And I appreciate that."

"But I can't promise I'll be able to do it again. This is such an important case, and it's your career on the line, too, Eric. I respect you too much to see you go down for protecting her."

"Havilland has nothing to do with any of this, and if I find out she does, I'll handle her." He paused and stared at her hard. "*I* will handle her. Is that clear?"

She stared back at him and he noticed subtle defiance in her eyes. When he started to think she was going to be trouble, she nodded and gave a small smile.

"Fair enough."

Now, looking down at a sleeping Havilland, Eric wondered just what he would do if he found out she'd been instrumental in screwing up his surveillance detail and ultimately his case. What would become of them?

* * *

November 2020

"It's just a few days. My dad is more excited to see Kimmy than he is me, and of course there's Uncle Stephen."

"Uncle Stephen!" Kimmy shouted and beamed.

Eric smiled over at her while he leaned against the bedroom door frame, watching Havilland pack.

"It just seems sudden," he said. "What about your caseload at work?"

"I had a few things cleared. There are some pending cases that are in limbo right now and I have a court appearance, but we'll be back before then."

Eric thought back to his conversation with Maya last week.

"What's up, Maya?"

He looked up to find her hovering over his cubicle, holding a file of papers and looking nervous.

"I have something to show you, and just so you know, this is between you and me only. I haven't shown this to Carl."

He frowned, looked at the file, and stretched out his hand to take it. "What is it?"

She still wore the nervous look but handed him the file. "I have contacts in the Atlanta office. A colleague of mine sent me an email asking about an agent who worked here in my division. Apparently, there's an open investigation on a man named Terrence Miller out there."

Eric had barely begun reading the file, but at the mention of Terrence Miller, his head shot up in recognition.

Maya saw it in his face and nodded her head. "I take it you know who I'm talking about. Again, Eric, I want you to know I haven't gone to anyone about this—"

"Sit down," he said, pulling another chair out for her, and lowered his voice to a conversational whisper. "Just tell me what's going on."

"My colleague wanted to know about Hav. He said he was

pulling the file they have on Miller and discovered someone else from a different office had logged in and viewed the file as well. Normally, he wouldn't have paid it any attention, but it seems that their case against Terrence went bust just a few days ago. He and his attorney found out confidential information about the case which allowed him to walk."

Havilland didn't break her rhythm as she continued to pack, but Eric watched her closely when he shrugged and said his next words.

"Well then, maybe I'll tag along. It'll be good for the three of us to get away for a few days."

"Yes, Daddy! Please can you come? Please?" Kimmy asked, excitedly.

But Eric noticed his wife didn't share in the same enthusiasm as their daughter. Her movements slowed, and he watched as her hands shook ever so slightly as she folded several shirts and put them in the suitcase.

Maya paused to let Eric read over the file, but from what he was seeing, he didn't want to read any further. It couldn't be. She wouldn't do this. He closed the folder and went to hand it back.

"You keep it," she said. "I told my colleague I'd look into it but assured him that the agent in question wouldn't compromise a case like that. But if he finds anything else linking her to Miller..."

"I know. I know," Eric said, rubbing a hand over and down his face. "I'll talk to her and find out what's going on. But like you said, Hav wouldn't risk everything to compromise a state investigation."

Maya cocked her head to one side and frowned. "If you don't mind me asking, does she have some sort of connection to Terrence Miller? I believe you, but if there is a connection, and my colleague finds it, I'd like to know ahead of time to not be caught off guard."

Eric looked around once more to make sure there was no one eavesdropping. "They were partners with the Atlanta PD. And they used to date."

Her eyes widened slightly and then she slowly nodded her head. "I see."

A long pause ensued before she asked the next question he'd been trying not to ask himself. "And you're sure there's nothing more between them?"

"Um, yeah, that would be great," Havilland said, finally looking up at him. "But your caseload is more demanding than mine, and what about your interview for the new position?"

"That's not until next week," he said. "It's the same day as your court appearance."

She laughed. "You memorized my schedule?"

But Eric didn't crack a smile and continued to watch her.

She began to stammer. "Well, um, if you can swing it, we'd love it if you came with us. I just don't want anything to jeopardize your interview."

Eric decided to let it go. There were other ways he could find out what was going on, and he hated that he was even thinking about them. He hated that it had come to this in their young marriage. Later on, he lied to her and told her that something came up and he wouldn't be able to go to Atlanta with her, and the relief on her face made his heart sink. He booked a separate flight, and during the entire plane ride, he cursed her, himself, Terrence, and even Maya for bringing this to his attention. But when he drove up to her father's house and saw Terrence Miller kissing his wife, he wished he'd just stayed home, blind and in denial.

CHAPTER TWENTY-ONE

When Devon went to bed the night before, she was confident in her plan. Waking this morning, she was just a little less than sure of herself but continued to get dressed for her drive downtown. By the time she walked into the state government building that housed the California Bureau of Investigation, cleared security, and was directed to the Controlled Chemical Substance division on the eleventh floor, she was questioning the sanity of this plan.

In her research last night, she'd found out through social media that Havilland Currin had changed her name to Havilland Sawyer. She was married to Eric Sawyer, traded in her city cop badge in Atlanta for a state one there in California, and worked with her husband as an agent for the CBI. They also had a daughter named Kimberly. Havilland's social media feed was set to private; however, she knew Havilland had a brother and one search for Stephen Currin, and she had found his social media page. Fortunately, his was set to public view, and Havilland often tagged him in her photos and announcements. Devon saw a picture of Havilland posing with a strikingly handsome white man who must have been her husband and a little girl who must have been their daughter. The three of them were dressed warm in fall clothes and posing in front of a pumpkin patch. The little girl had her small arms barely wrapped around a pumpkin that was bigger than she was, and it was her who Devon couldn't stop looking at. She'd downloaded the picture to her computer, zoomed in, and noticed the girl's eyes and smile were the exact likeness of Havilland. She was her mother's little twin, but there was something else familiar about the child that Devon couldn't place.

As she made her way onto the elevator, she felt her phone vibrate from inside her purse. She pulled it out and twisted her lips in satisfaction when she saw a text from Terrence inviting her to lunch with him later. He'd suddenly been on his best behavior, and she guessed her dad's call had a lot to do with that. But how long would this change last before her father had to make another call? She quickly texted him back, saying she'd love to and would call him later with a time and place.

Although she hated to involve Havilland's husband in this, Devon wanted to see Eric Sawyer and see if he knew that his wife was meeting her husband. She guessed not, but it might do some good to bring him in on this. Maybe he could put a stop to it because it didn't look like Terrence or Havilland was eager to do it.

She admitted there was nothing sexual or romantic about their meetings—she just knew she didn't like it. They were exes, and no doubt Havilland knew Devon was married to Terrence. Who was to say Havilland wasn't after some payback for Devon catching Terrence's eye in the first place? Well, not on her watch. She was putting a stop to it, and if Eric Sawyer didn't pan out, she would handle this herself.

It was a smooth elevator ride up to the eleventh floor, and she immediately saw the office of cubicles with the department name etched on the glass wall. She opened the door and entered the quiet office with only the sound of muffled talking and light pecking on computer keyboards. She panned the space and saw the larger office at the far end that most likely belonged to Eric Sawyer. She found out from the directory downstairs that he was the special agent in charge of the division, and briefly wondered what it was like at home for Havilland, having her husband as her boss, but she dismissed the thought and made her way toward the back office without stopping.

"May I help you?"

Just as she reached the door to the private office, she was stopped by a short and pretty redhead.

"Oh, I'm just here to see Agent Sawyer."

"I'm his assistant," the woman said with a smile. "Do you have an appointment?"

Devon mocked a worried frown. Of course, she didn't have an appointment. What the hell would she say as her reason for seeing him?

"No, I don't have an appointment. This is an urgent yet personal matter."

"Well, I don't know if Agent Sawyer is able to see anyone today," she said and stood from her desk. "If you can wait right here, I'll see if he's able to speak with you. Your name?"

"Devon Foxworth-Miller."

The woman halted and her eyes widened ever so slightly, before she smiled again, stepped past Devon, and knocked on the glass door. So, she was known around there. But why? What business would the CBI have with her or her family?

Devon watched the assistant gesture toward her, then she noticed Eric's eyes also widen and then narrow in suspicion. He also knew her, and something told her she'd stepped into unfamiliar territory. Had she completely misread the situation between Terrence and Havilland? But her time to flee had run out because Eric Sawyer and his assistant were making their way toward her and opening the door.

"Mrs. Foxworth-Miller," he said, offering his hand. "I'm Agent Eric Sawyer. Come in, please."

He was tall, with dark hair and ice-blue eyes that were only magnified against his tanned skin. As she stepped past him into the office, she could tell through his white dress shirt that he was fit with a broad chest, muscular arms, and hard abs. He also smelled good. Maybe Havilland didn't mind so much that her husband was also her boss. Devon thought devilishly to herself that she wouldn't mind if this man bossed her around, either.

"What can I do for you?" he asked, returning to his seat behind the desk and folding his arms across the top, indicating she had his full attention.

Maybe it was the deep-blue eyes, but she suddenly had a hard time looking at him. That strange feeling was creeping up her spine again, telling her this visit was a mistake, only she didn't know why. And since she couldn't come up with a plausible reason why she shouldn't be there, she reached down into her large purse and pulled out a legal-sized envelope.

"I hate to bring this to your attention, but I recently had my husband, Terrence Miller, followed."

God, did she really just admit that? Saying it out loud made her feel foolish and pathetic, and having to say it to a perfect stranger only made it sound worse.

"Why?" Eric asked.

She shrugged. "The short version is he was one man in Atlanta—attentive, communicated with me, kept his lunch and dinner dates, but here in San Francisco, his behavior has changed."

Namely, because her father wasn't around to keep him in line, but that was more than she was willing to say.

A wry smile tickled the corners of Eric's mouth. "I'm not a marriage counselor. What does all of this have to do with me or the CBI?"

He was indeed a handsome man, but she didn't like the way that smile contained a hint of pity. Time to wipe it off his face. She took the envelope, upended it over his desk, and several glossy colored photos scattered between them.

"My Investigator might have found the reason for his sudden change in behavior," she said, locking her eyes on him and searching for a reaction.

His smile slowly became a hard line, and she could tell the exact moment he realized it was his wife in those pictures with her husband.

"I don't know what's going on with these two," she said, after giving him a few moments to digest what he was seeing. "But I thought maybe you could tell me. You may not know this, but your wife, Terrence, and I all met back in Atlanta. Hav and I went to school together, and I met Terrence through her."

He slowly looked up at her and nodded. "I'm aware of all of that."

Devon swallowed. "Then you're also aware that the two of them were with the Atlanta PD as partners. I'm not against old friends meeting for a drink and a chat, but this…" She paused to wave her hand over one picture where both Terrence and Havilland were leaned up against a wooden railing, their elbows nearly touching, and he was staring at her while she looked out at the bay. It was a romantic scene with the sun setting over Angel Island in the distance, and the way Terrence was looking at Havilland made Devon want to scream.

Without thinking, she blurted, "You have to do something."

"Do something?" he echoed.

"Yes! Why are they meeting? What are they talking about? Did he know the two of you lived here in San Francisco?"

He leveled his gaze at her. "I appreciate you bringing these to me, and I don't mean to sound dismissive, but let me suggest that you look for your answers closer to home."

Eric gathered up the pictures, neatly stacked them, and put them back in the envelope. He then went to hand them to her, and she waved them away, gathering her purse and preparing to leave what had obviously been a wasted visit.

"Those are copies. You can keep them. I just thought you should know what was going on. Thank you for your time, Agent Sawyer."

She stood, turned and left the office, closing his door firmly behind her. As she wove her way back through the sea of cubicles, a framed photo caught her attention. The cubicle was empty, so she stepped inside and peered at the photograph beside the computer. It was the same pumpkin patch photo from Havilland's social media account. This had to be Havilland's space, and Devon wondered just how much time she had to rummage through the desk drawers before someone saw her.

"May I help you?"

With disappointment, she turned and met another smiling woman, but this one was tall, brunette, and wore a badge clasped to her trousers.

"I was just looking for Hav. We're old college friends." She reached out her hand to shake the woman's. "I'm Devon Foxworth-Miller."

The same look of recognition passed through the woman's eyes. "Foxworth Pharmaceuticals, of course. Lots of jobs coming to the city."

Devon flashed her media smile, the one she was trained to give to the press whenever her father's business came up in conversation. "Yes, we're very excited about the opening."

"Oh, excuse me, I'm being rude. I'm Agent Maya Landon. Hav should be here any moment. She usually comes in a half hour late because she has to drop Kimmy off at pre-school."

"Kimmy?" Devon asked.

"Their daughter, Kimberly."

"Right." Devon turned and gestured to the photograph on the desk. "Is that her? I haven't seen Hav in so long. I didn't know she had a daughter."

"Yeah, that's her. She's a cutie, isn't she? She just turned four. Hav and Eric had a party for her."

Four? Devon quickly did the math. Through Stephen's social media feed, she saw wedding pictures of Eric and Havilland from two years ago. Did they have Kimberly before they were married? But then a second thought dismissed that entirely. Stephen sent well wishes to his sister on her move to California three years ago. Kimberly had already been born by then. Four years ago, Devon and Terrence were just getting married.

Look for your answers closer to home, Eric had said. An answer was definitely forming, and it was giving her a headache.

"That's nice," Devon said, making a show of pulling out her phone and looking at the time. "I'm going to be late for an appointment. I'll just catch Hav later. It was nice meeting you."

"You too," Maya said, but Devon was already hurrying to the exit and pushing her way out the doors. She needed to get out of there and find some place where she could think.

* * *

As soon as Havilland stepped off the elevator, she nearly collided with a woman who was walking quickly past her to get on. She wouldn't have paid her any mind, only the woman bumped her shoulder just a little in her rush to catch the elevator.

"Excuse me," Havilland said.

The woman turned to face her and instantly, the apology in her eyes was replaced with subtle irritation. She turned away and continued toward the elevator.

"Hold that, please!"

"Devon?" Havilland called, instantly recognizing the familiar face.

Devon rushed through the elevator doors, turned to hit the down button, and looked directly at Havilland. As the doors closed between them, Havilland knew Devon had recognized her, too, and she wasn't pleased at all to see her.

Havilland continued to stare at the closed doors, silently debating whether she should use the stairs to catch up to her. What was she doing there? That question rattled around in her brain as she finally turned and headed into the office. But before she could reach her cubicle, Maya intercepted her.

"You had a visitor. Devon Foxworth-Miller was here looking for you."

"Looking for me?" If that was the truth, why did Devon just ignore her out in the hall?

Maya nodded. "She said you two were old college friends. She was talking to Eric first and then came out looking—"

"Wait? She spoke to Eric?" Havilland asked, bewildered. She quickly excused herself from Maya and hurried to Eric's office without stopping to shed her coat and purse. She knocked on his door, and he motioned with one hand for her to come in. She opened the door, stepped inside and closed it behind her. She then hesitantly came forward, trying to read the look in his eyes.

"What did she want?"

CHAPTER TWENTY-TWO

*E*ric had seen her coming and slid the pictures into his desk drawer before she saw them through the glass door. He wouldn't show them to her, because he wanted her to open up to him herself. He needed that from her.

"Well?" Havilland asked, and he saw the subtle fear in her eyes that she had just been outed. "What did she want?"

He looked away for just a moment, shaking his head in dismay. She wasn't going to tell him.

"Mrs. Foxworth-Miller, got wind of our investigation and came to her husband's rescue by threatening to have her lawyers all over this department if we didn't back off. I told her to do as she pleased."

"That's all?"

"Isn't that enough?"

"It's just that...I thought... How did she know there was an investigation?"

He shrugged. "Who knows? That family has a lot of money and connections, which buys them information."

"What if she tells Terrence?"

"I'm sure he already knows."

She remained silent, and he knew she was too smart to take that bait.

"All right." She turned to the door. "I have some calls to make."

"Anything you want to tell me?"

She turned around. "Like what?"

"Like anything."

"You asked me this before."

"The question still stands." And then he pleaded silently, *Talk to me, Havilland.*

She sighed and a mixture of frustration and sadness came over her beautiful features. "I would tell you I miss you, but that wouldn't be work appropriate, and you wouldn't believe me, anyway."

She then turned, yanked open the door, and left. He watched her go, wishing he could say something, anything to prove her last words wrong. But she was right. He wasn't so sure she missed him, and the reasons were tucked away in his desk drawer.

He pulled out the photos again and spread them across his desk, looking up to make sure no one was hovering nearby his office. In the photos, Havilland and Terrence were talking, arguing, watching the bay together and in one picture, he could see she was crying. He didn't know what infuriated him more—the fact that Terrence had said or done something to hurt her or the fact she felt comfortable enough to show her vulnerable side to him.

Eric remembered the last time he saw her cry. They were taking a walk around the neighborhood, and Kimmy, in one of her wilder, toddler moments was running around them, not paying attention to where she was going and had tripped, fallen, and scraped her knee badly on the asphalt. Blood was everywhere, and both mother and daughter were crying. Eric rushed them all home and then cleaned, disinfected, and bandaged Kimmy's wound while at the same time, handed Havilland tissues to wipe her tears. He told both girls over and over that it wasn't as bad as it looked and that everything would be okay. Finally, they believed him. Eventually, Kimmy went off somewhere to find another adventure, and he sat with his wife at the kitchen table while she alternated between crying and laughing at herself for being hysterical. She told him it had been the first time she'd seen Kimmy bleeding, and he kissed her over and over again until there were no tears left.

They were his family. His girls.

* * *

April 2018

Eric gripped both of Havilland's thighs tightly as she lifted herself up and then slowly back down onto him. She then moved her hips in a slow, rhythmic dance that made him want to come. But he held on, unable to tear his eyes away from her. He was fascinated by the look of pleasure in her closed eyes, opened mouth, and flushed cheeks. It was building within her and intensifying. He wanted to feel her quiver and shake, so he thrust his hips upward and pushed himself deeper into her.

"Eric," she cried out.

Her hips moved in answer to his strokes until finally and deliciously, her orgasm erupted and rolled over her in waves. Eric kept her hips rocking, reveling in the feel of her walls tightening around him. Soon, he felt his own release surge, ultimately overpowering him, and he surrendered to it with a guttural roar.

They lay together for a half an hour longer until she

began to stir, and he felt an alien sense of abandonment that she was once again, leaving.

"Thank you for dinner, handsome," she said, kissing him, and then rose from the bed and began to dress.

He sat up and turned on the bedside lamp. With multiple dates under their belt, he felt things were getting serious between them. But as he watched her put on her bra and panties and then begin to slip back into the dress she'd worn on their date, he realized this is where their evenings always came to an end.

"You know if this is just sex, you can tell me."

Havilland paused in pulling the straps of the dress over her shoulders. "What do you mean?"

He propped himself up on one elbow, letting the bed sheet fall to his waist, and eyed her. "I mean that you don't stay the night and you never invite me to stay at your place."

She pulled the straps over her shoulders, finger combed her curls, and then smiled wickedly as she crawled back onto the bed toward him.

"I have my reasons, and even though I have a lot of fun with your body"—she paused to kiss him fully on the mouth and then slowly pulled away to look him in the eyes with all seriousness—"it's not just sex. I really like you. A lot."

"Then what gives?" he asked, shrugging one shoulder. "You like me. I like you. What's the problem? Let's move forward on whatever this is between us."

She frowned and then smiled. "Isn't that supposed to be my line?"

She was stalling, and it wasn't the first time she'd glossed over this topic. Only this time, he wasn't in the mood for games. Letting his frustration get the better of him, he turned his back to her, angrily flipped the covers off of him and hopped out of bed.

"Eric, wait."

"I'm going to take a shower. Let yourself out," he said, stalking toward the bathroom.

He went inside and shut the door behind him. Fifteen minutes later, he emerged from the bathroom with a towel wrapped around his waist, secretly hoping she'd waited so they could finish their conversation. But she was gone, leaving only the subtle floral scent of her perfume in the air.

* * *

"Sir?"

His assistant, Elena, jarred him from his memories, and he looked over at her standing at his office door.

"Yes?"

"Carl Hewitt is on line three."

"Thank you."

He steeled himself for whatever this conversation was going to be and picked up the receiver.

"Sawyer, here. What can I do for you, Carl?"

"You got your warrant."

Eric slammed his fist atop his desk in excitement. "I'll assemble my team."

"Tell me again why you needed this warrant," Carl demanded. "Robert Foxworth already gave you some pretty damning evidence."

"Not damning enough," Eric said. "The prosecutor will take one look at it and declare it all circumstantial. With an investigation this high-profile, we're going to need conclusive evidence that Terrence is directly involved. Conversations, bank statements, pictures of him exchanging the materials for money, anything along those lines."

"You think he'd keep something like that in his home?"

"We'll see when we get there."

Carl sighed and Eric could sense his misgivings. "I know

you're gung-ho to get Miller and so is Robert Foxworth, but I'm warning you to just tread softly. If there's nothing there, get out."

"I know how to do my job, sir."

Another sigh. "I know that, Eric. But in this instance, maybe you know your job a little too well."

CHAPTER TWENTY-THREE

As Havilland powered down her computer and prepared to leave work for the evening, she sensed something in the atmosphere had changed. Tension filled the department with the anticipation of something about to happen. She got her answer when she noticed Eric exiting his office wearing a bullet-proof vest over his shirt and slacks. She stood and noticed several other agents donning vests, and immediately realized the agents that wore vests were also agents of the task force involved in taking down Terrence. Other agents, like her, who were not a part of the fray, shook hands with the members of the task force and wished them luck.

Jerry passed by her cubicle on his way to speak to Eric, and Havilland quickly grabbed for his shirtsleeve.

"What's going on?" she asked. "New evidence?"

"You can say that," Jerry said, seemingly high off adrenaline. There were agents who loved being at the desk and agents who loved being in the field. Jerry was obviously part of the latter group.

"Eric got a call from Hewitt. Despite the surveillance

debacle, a judge obviously believed he had enough evidence and signed off on a warrant ten minutes ago. We're heading to search Miller's home."

Havilland's heart began to race. *Shit! Shit! Shit!* There was no time to warn Terrence. If they found anything incriminating, he would be arrested, and then everything would be over.

"Congratulations," she said, pasting a smile on her face. "Good luck."

Jerry's smile faltered just a bit, and he paused. "Hav, there's something I want to ask you about. When I told you about the surveillance—"

"Agent Hicks!"

They both turned to see Eric and the rest of the team watching them. "We need you over here."

Jerry turned back to Havilland. "I'll talk to you later."

She nodded and watched with trepidation as he joined the task force for what was likely a discussion on their plan of action. While everyone's attention was diverted elsewhere, she unlocked the top right-side drawer of her desk and reached in the back for the burner phone. But she didn't feel anything. She rummaged frantically around for it and even bent her head to look inside the drawer, and still saw nothing. The burner phone was gone.

"Lose something?"

She sat straight up and whirled around in her chair to find Eric staring at her. She had to admit he looked good as he stood there with his tall stature and biceps filling out the dress shirt and vest. He had always been an imposing figure and sexy as hell to her. But right then, they were on opposite sides of the team, and he was looking at her like she was his enemy.

She stood slowly from her chair and met his stance. He

was a good foot taller than her, but she wouldn't be intimidated, not by a man she'd known intimately for years.

"It's not important. Jerry told me what's going on. Good luck."

He looked at her as if he couldn't decide whether she was being sincere or secretly wishing for his failure.

"I don't know when I'll be home. If it gets too late, I'll try to call and tell Kimmy good night."

She nodded.

"See you later," he said and then turned to his team of agents. "Let's go!"

One by one, they all followed Eric out of the department and huddled toward the elevator with Maya taking up the rear.

"Be careful," Havilland said to her.

Maya gave her a strange look. "You too, Hav," she said cryptically and walked out, leaving Havilland frowning.

When they were gone, the rest of the agents began to pack up and get ready to leave for the night. Havilland dropped down into her chair and wondered frantically how she was going to contact Terrence. If he was caught off guard, he would surely make her pay by hanging Stephen's freedom over her head. There was her personal cell phone, but that was too close to home and could easily be traced. He'd only texted her personal cell one time, and after that, she made sure to put a stop to it. Her work phone was out of the question for obvious reasons. With one last ditch effort, she looked inside the desk drawer one more time and even other drawers, but the burner was nowhere to be found. She knew for certain she'd locked it up after returning from lunch, so someone had to have picked the lock and taken it during any time she'd been temporarily away from her desk.

Eric.

The answer came clear as day. After the surveillance

detail had been compromised, he was onto her. But if he had that burner phone, he knew she was calling Terrence. Was he waiting until he came home to chew her ass about it? Thank God, she'd had the foresight to delete the text messages or she'd really be in deep shit.

Havilland slammed the desk drawer closed in anger, but the anger was all for herself. This was her damn fault. Her marriage and career were a mess, and it was all because of one man. There had to be a way to get Terrence out of her life, but satisfying her promise to him at the same time.

CHAPTER TWENTY-FOUR

When Eric and the rest of his team were let inside by the house staff of the Pacific Heights mansion, they were told that neither Terrence nor his wife were at home. For the moment, they would have the element of surprise, and with the search warrant tucked safely in his back pocket, they had free range access to the entire property. But an hour into the search, he was beginning to think he'd been too hasty in getting this warrant because Miller had obviously not kept anything incriminating in his own home. So far, the only thing they'd managed to confiscate were a few files that appeared to be nothing more than tax documents and a laptop that when powered on, looked to belong to Devon.

He didn't want to give up just yet, though. With Robert's evidence gathered by his own investigators and Stephen feeding them inside information, Terrence was as good as behind bars. He just needed something more concrete to nail the case shut.

But something still nagged at Eric. Terrence had been able to escape prosecution before, and there was no doubt he would be extra careful this time around. If arrested, what could his lawyers use this time to get him off?

Havilland.

The realization came so swift and loud, like a ringing bell, that Eric wanted to bury it back into the deep pile of denial he'd built. Terrence's confidence was because he had Havilland in his back pocket, and Eric was determined to put an end to it. He had to remind himself that everything that went on between them was long before he came into the picture. But he was in the picture now, and no matter what excuse Havilland gave him, her contact with Terrence was going to stop—especially since Terrence was a direct threat to her career and their marriage.

He was upstairs, searching one of the many bedrooms when noise and commotion downstairs put him on full alert. The Millers were finally home. He abandoned his search of a walk-in closet and left another agent to take his place while he went downstairs. This would be the first time in nearly three months he'd seen Terrence, and he was more than ready to look him in the eyes again.

"Agent Sawyer, welcome to my home," Terrence announced as Eric descended the grand staircase. "If you wanted a private tour, you could've just called."

Eric's gaze slid briefly to Devon, who stood by her husband while watching Eric with keen interest. He wondered if she'd told Terrence about their meeting and her suspicions.

He looked to Terrence again and handed him a copy of the search warrant. "Read it over if you like. Just stay out of the way while my team finishes searching the residence."

"Searching for what?" Devon asked and immediately, Terrence took her hand and whispered something in her ear.

Devon frowned at him, but the look he was now giving her demanded she listen to him. She looked Eric's way one last time and then climbed the stairs with a dignified poise. Once she was out of sight, Terrence looked at Eric, and he finally saw the concealed rage in the man's eyes.

"Do what you need to do then get the fuck out of here," he said through clenched teeth.

Another hour passed and Eric was forced to order his team to call it quits, and he had to keep himself from exploding while Terrence looked on with triumph.

"All right, Agent Sawyer, you've had your fun," Terrence's attorney, who'd arrived a half an hour before, said. "I don't know what judge signed this warrant, but obviously you didn't find what you needed. If this happens again, I'm filing for harassment on behalf of my client."

"I haven't even begun to harass your client," Eric said, motioning for his team to clear out. "But you go ahead and file to your heart's content, because believe me, I'm coming back."

He was on his way out with Agents Hicks and Stewart trailing behind him when Terrence called out to him and said a few words. As soon as what he said registered to Eric's ears, something in him snapped and the temper he'd been holding in check could no longer be contained. He turned around in a flash and lunged for the man, who'd been underneath his skin from day one.

* * *

When Havilland got home, she thanked Jeanetta for her help, sent her home, and prepared dinner. As usual, she set aside a plate for Eric in the refrigerator for when he finally came home. Now, she sat at the kitchen table, listening to her little girl go on about her own innocent child-like day with all of its simple adventures while at the same time, trying to disguise how anxious she felt for the moment when Eric would walk through the front door.

When she finally heard the key turn in the lock, she unconsciously sat up straighter in her chair, listened to the front door open and shut, his keys dropping to the console table and then the sound of heavy footsteps echoing on the hardwood floor. When he finally appeared in the kitchen doorway, his cerulean eyes went directly to her sitting at the table in the alcove, only she couldn't read him at all.

"Hi, Daddy!"

Seconds later, his eyes trailed to Kimmy, and a smile reluctantly creased the corner of his lips as he watched her push around the broccoli on her plate. He went over to her, bent down, and kissed the top of her mass of curls and whispered into her ear.

"I have ice cream, so eat every last bite of that yucky stuff."

Kimmy giggled and at the promise of ice cream began to shovel the vegetables into her mouth.

"Slow down, please," Havilland admonished and then turned to watch as Eric removed a carton of ice cream from a plastic bag and place it into the freezer. He then opened the refrigerator, grabbed a bottle of water, uncapped it and took a swig.

"You're home earlier than I thought you'd be," she said.

He didn't say anything and tossed the empty plastic bottle in the trash can.

After several minutes of nothing but the sound of her daughter's fork hitting the plate, Havilland's patience had run out. She had to know everything.

"How did the search go?"

"Can we talk about it later?" He turned around and leaned against the counter, looking at her with a stern expression.

She clamped her mouth shut but narrowed her eyes in

aggravation. Eric ignored her stare and turned to leave the kitchen.

"I'm going to take a shower," he announced.

"Daddy, when you come back, we can have ice cream!" Kimmy said, excitedly.

"Absolutely, honey," he said and then left without another word.

CHAPTER TWENTY-FIVE

Havilland kissed Kimmy good night and left the room as Eric tucked her in. She wondered if Kimmy noticed they no longer stayed in the room together to wish her good night. Of course, she did, but she never asked what prompted the change in the nightly tradition, and Havilland was grateful for that. So, as Eric laughed with her, Havilland waited in the bedroom, changed into her pajamas, and paced the floor. Then she realized that even if she did get Eric to talk to her, he wasn't about to tell her everything.

She stopped pacing, grabbed her phone from the nightstand, and texted Jerry.

Havilland: *What happened?*

The reply came back in a few minutes.

Jerry: *We raided Miller's home, looking for more evidence but couldn't find anything solid.*

Havilland sighed with relief. She wanted to know who this CI was, but knew Jerry would never reveal that to her. A moment later, another text from him came through.

Jerry: *Did Eric tell you what happened?*

Havilland: *No. What happened?*

Jerry: *He nearly fought Terrence. Stewart and I had to get him out of there fast.*

Havilland frowned. They were fighting? Why?

Before she could ask for details, she heard Eric's footfalls passing by the bedroom. She knew he was heading to the spare room, but that wasn't happening tonight. He was going to talk to her first, and then he could go hide out in his new bedroom. She rushed to the double doors and flung them open just in time to see his back as he headed down the hall.

"You're not going to bed without talking to me," she hissed, careful not to raise her voice too loud and disturb Kimmy.

He paused in his steps, put one hand on the railing that overlooked the downstairs living room, and slowly turned to look at her, but he didn't say a word.

She stepped out of the room and into the hall. "What happened tonight? I'm still an agent. Can't you share anything with me?"

"He wasn't arrested if that's what you're worried about."

She recoiled. That assumption coupled with the derision in his voice was worse than a slap.

"That's not what I'm worried about. I just want to know what's going on. We used to share things like this."

"*Used* to," he emphasized.

"Fine. But we could go back to that and back to the way things were if you'd just—"

"Just what?" he asked, stepping close to her. "What do you want me to do? Let it go? Forget what you nearly cost us and yourself? Forget what I saw?"

He was so angry. She could hear it in his voice, even though he kept his tone low. But there was something more, something deep in his eyes. He was hurt, but he also seemed genuinely worried for her.

In a moment of desperation, she asked, "Do you want to leave me?"

That question must have shocked him because he went very still.

"Well, do you? Or is your plan to just stay with me and continue to punish me for what I've done? Are we only staying together to just make each other miserable because I don't want to live like that. I'd rather you just leave me!"

They must have realized at the same time that she was beginning to shout because he immediately backed her into the master bedroom. He turned to close the doors softly behind them and then advanced on her.

"Yeah, I'm still pissed, and maybe one day I'll get over it. But until then, I'm not going anywhere and neither are you. You're my wife, so ride it out."

He grabbed both of her forearms, swung her around, and pushed her up against the closed bedroom door. In an instant, he had his body molded against hers and Havilland let out an involuntary cry of surprise at the feeling.

"You're *my* wife," he said again, and to her shock and delight, he kissed her.

The moment, she felt his lips on hers, she didn't waste time. She was so afraid that he would realize what he was doing, that he still hadn't forgiven her, that he was still clinging to his anger and then release her and walk out. She had to take advantage of this moment.

She freed herself from his grasp and pulled his shirt over his head. He grabbed it from her, threw it behind him, and ran his fingers through her curls as she kissed and swept her tongue along the apex of his chest. She then wrapped her arms tightly around his neck and returned her mouth to his. Eric slid his fingers inside the waistband of her panties and roughly shoved them off. She stepped out of them and broke the kiss once again to pull her own T-shirt over her head and fling it in the same direction as his. A rush of excitement began to overtake her. He was obviously not wasting time, either, because the moment she was completely naked, he hoisted her in the air by her ass and carried her to the bed. He then laid her down, spread her legs, and his intense eyes looked directly at her as he shed his pajama pants and entered her with abandon.

That first contact was too much and yet not enough. The feeling of him deep inside of her made her crazy with wanting. It had been too long. She tried to take hold of his broad, strong shoulders, but he snatched her wrists before she could touch him and slammed them down onto the bed above her head. She lay trapped and completely at his mercy as he bent low and kissed her lips, her neck, and then lower still to lick and take feather light bites of her erect nipples. All the while, he moved in and out of her, claiming her as his.

"Christ, Hav," he groaned.

She locked her legs around his waist and cried out as she felt him going deeper and deeper. She greedily took each powerful thrust of his hips, looking into his eyes and silently telling him just how much she missed him.

But there was something off. They were joined together in the most intimate way possible, but this wasn't lovemaking. There was something different about the rhythm of his movements as well as the way he was staring down at her. He wanted to possess her. He wanted it known that she was his. He needed to prove it to himself and to someone who was not in the bed with them. So, she gave herself to her husband and let him take his fill until soon they were coming together, filling the bedroom with the sounds of their sensual cries and moans.

Ten minutes later, when Havilland came out of the shower, she poked her head out of the bathroom and wasn't surprised at all to find the bed empty.

* * *

Eric sat in the armchair of the spare bedroom, thinking about the woman on the other side of the wall. He hadn't meant to touch her, but after the disappointing raid at Terrence's mansion and those last taunting words he'd said to him, Eric was ready to burst. He'd thought eating ice cream with Kimmy and tucking her in for the night would be just the salve he needed for his wounds. But the moment Havilland threw open those double doors with fire in her eyes and breasts heaving under a T-shirt that barely skimmed her upper thighs, he knew he wasn't about to go to bed without fucking her. *Damn.* Walking out of that bedroom and once again, leaving her to sleep alone was the hardest thing he ever had to do.

He leaned forward to rest his elbows on his knees and gripped strands of his hair. What the hell was he doing? How long was he going to keep punishing her and torturing himself?

Before those thoughts could run amuck, his phone rang by the bedside table. He got up, checked the caller id display, and swiped the screen to answer it.

"Sawyer."

"I heard you raided my daughter's house," Robert said.

"We were looking for evidence."

"What I gave you should be plenty to put him behind bars."

"Except, it's not," Eric responded bluntly. "Any good DA wouldn't dare touch it and risk getting embarrassed by your son-in-law's high-priced lawyers. It's all circumstantial. We need more."

Silence fell on the other end, until Robert spoke again.

"Maybe I can help with that. You have plans Friday night?"

"Isn't that the night of your big party?"

"I'm personally inviting you. Just make sure you and your team are there. I'll get you your hard evidence."

CHAPTER TWENTY-SIX

Havilland picked up her desk phone on the second ring. "Agent Sawyer."

"Can you come in here for a minute? I need to talk to you."

It was Eric. His authoritative tone rang crisp and clear from the other end.

"I'll be right there."

She hung up the phone and closed her eyes, praying this wasn't going to be about what happened last night. Although Eric didn't like to discuss personal business at work, he might just make an exception if it was weighing heavily on his mind. But she wanted none of it. They were married, and the last thing she wanted to hear was her own husband apologizing for making love to her. That would launch a rocket blasting her self-esteem away.

She stood, smoothed out her skirt, and walked the short distance to his office. He was leaning against the front of his desk with his arms and ankles crossed, already anticipating her arrival. Before she raised a hand to knock, he beckoned her inside.

"Sit down," he said, softly. The cuffs of his dress shirt were undone, with the sleeves rolled to his elbows and his tie somewhat askew. It wasn't even noon yet, and she could see it was already turning out to be a stressful day for him.

She hesitated before taking a seat, wanting instead to straighten his tie for him. But that would mean standing inside his personal space, and being close to him would only reawaken memories of last night and how much she wished he'd stayed with her. Even if he was still angry with her, just the simple act of him lying next to her would have been more than enough to give her a peaceful sleep.

She took a seat in one of his guest chairs and looked up at him. "What's going on?"

He returned her stare, and the way he was looking at her made her second-guess the reason for this meeting. There was something else he wanted to talk to her about, and it looked as though he was struggling to find the words.

"Eric, what is it?"

He let out a heavy sigh. "You heard about the party celebrating the opening of the new Foxworth plant, right?"

"Sure, it's been all over the news."

How could she not? Robert Foxworth obviously had a hefty advertising budget because every news channel, radio commercial, Billboard, magazine, and social media ad in the Bay area was announcing the opening and praising the Foxworths for bringing more jobs to the city. As a celebration, Robert was coming to town to join his daughter and son-in-law to throw a huge black-tie event with the major stockholders and board of directors.

"I want you to go with me."

She frowned. "What for? It can't be for cover because Terrence knows we're both agents."

"No, not for cover. I need you to wear a wire."

She gaped at him. "He's not going to confess anything to me."

"I know it's a long shot, but the fact of the matter is he trusts you. He may just slip up, and when he does, I want to hear it."

"Did Hewitt approve this?"

Eric looked insulted, and she wished she could take it back, considering the hostility between the two men.

"This is my operation, and you've been pressuring me to get you involved, so here's your chance. Just get him to open up. That's always been your gift."

Although she wasn't entirely sure about this and truthfully thought it was a waste of time, he couldn't have handed her a better way to stay involved. She needed to be at that event because she had an agenda of her own that he knew nothing about, and his invite would ensure it stayed protected.

"I'm in."

He nodded. "Good, it's short notice, so you may want to call your mom or Jeanetta now to see if either are available to watch Kimmy that night."

"I'll do that."

She stood to leave, but he grabbed for her arm lightly to stop her. "Hav, listen about last night—"

"Don't," she said, raising a palm to stop him. "I know it doesn't change things between us, so can we just chalk it up to the tension of the evening?"

He looked regretful, and she wondered if maybe she'd assumed the wrong thing.

But he then simply nodded. "Yeah, we can do that."

CHAPTER TWENTY-SEVEN

When he came home that evening, Eric found Maya just where she said she'd be in her text message. He pulled into his driveway, but instead of going into the house, he walked a few feet up the sidewalk to her car, opened the passenger side door, and got in.

"I'm sorry to show up like this," she said.

"What's going on?" he asked. "Why didn't you just come inside?"

She had a worried look on her face that only seemed to intensify with each second that passed.

"Just so you know, I'm only looking out for you. I don't want your career to end because of—"

"Maya, what's going on?"

"I'm sorry, but I was so angry about the stakeout and then the fact that we found nothing at Miller's house. We've been logging hundreds of man hours in this case, and even with a CI, we're still no closer to catching this asshole."

"I know," he said, placing a comforting hand on her shoulder. "We're going to get him."

"We'll get him when he no longer has help."

He frowned. "What do you mean?"

She let go a sigh. "I've had my suspicions for a long time, and don't you dare tell me you didn't either, especially after Atlanta."

Havilland. Of course, this was about Havilland.

A feeling of dread came over him as she pulled a plastic evidence bag from her purse and handed it to him. Inside was a cell phone. He looked up at her curiously.

"It's a burner phone I found in Havilland's desk."

"What the hell!" he erupted. "You're illegally searching through her things, now?"

"I had a hunch, and that hunch was right. I pulled the records." She paused to hand him three stapled sheets of paper. "Terrence Miller's number shows up over twenty times. She deleted the text messages, but it's obvious they're in contact, Eric."

He couldn't keep denying it to himself anymore, not with proof staring him in the face. His mind went to the photos Devon brought to him that showed in clear color Havilland meeting with Terrence. It was either an affair or she was protecting him from prosecution, or even worse, it was both. Havilland had something going on with Terrence Miller, and more than likely, she was the reason his investigation was going nowhere. But he had to remind himself he had an ace up his sleeve, someone more powerful than both Terrence and Havilland—Robert Foxworth. That eased his temper a bit, but he hated that this was happening all over again.

He looked into the passenger side mirror at the reflection of his house, where Havilland was inside with Kimmy. As much as he wanted to, now was not the time to go in there, slinging accusations. There were other ways to get the answers he needed. History was repeating itself, and just like last time, he was going to have to set up his own wife in order to get at the truth. With that thought, a new wave of fury and regret tore at his heart. She was putting her career and marriage on the line for a man she was once in love with, and what kept him up at night, what kept him giving her the cold shoulder for three months, what kept his anger and jealousy fed...was the thought that she might still be.

* * *

April 2018

Eric sat at his cubicle while filling out the report to a case he just closed and tried not to obsessively look at the time. Ever since their last encounter at his apartment nearly a week ago, he and Havilland had been avoiding each other at work. If she caught him staring at her, he'd look away and vice versa. They were back to the little game they'd played when they first became acquainted, only this time, Eric wasn't amused by it. He liked her very much, but he wasn't just going to be her fuck buddy. He wanted more than that with her. He wanted her to be exclusively his, but it was obvious she didn't share those same feelings. He needed to just end things with her, but he also didn't want it to be awkward around the office with her.

That afternoon, when he came back from lunch, he'd found her waiting for him at his cubicle.

"Hi," she'd said.

"Hey," he'd replied, holding his breath and wondering if this was the moment the awkwardness would begin.

"Listen, would it be all right if we had dinner tonight? There's something I need to tell you."

He shrugged. "I'll be working late finishing up a report, but you can meet me here."

"Okay," she said, looking relieved. "I'll be here around seven."

At seven-fifteen that evening, Eric had powered down his

computer and pulled out his cell phone to call Havilland. Maybe this dinner was for her to break up with him or maybe even confess that she was married and that this whole time, he'd been a complete sucker. But somewhere deep inside, a part of him would readily accept whatever terms she wanted. If all she wanted to give him was a slither of her time, he knew he'd take it in a heartbeat just to be with her, and that pissed him off because he'd never wanted any woman that much, not even Christina.

Just as he was about to call and see if she was on her way, he heard the elevator ding and stood up in time to see Havilland walking slowly into the office. He put his phone away, grabbed for his coat, and shrugged it on.

"I was just about to call you," he said dryly, already chalking up this evening to be a complete fail.

She was looking at him with a nervous smile and still walking slowly toward him, so he figured this really was the moment they were about to break up.

"Listen, we can do this here," he said, grabbing his briefcase, then heading toward her. "We don't need to go out if—"

His words and steps came to an abrupt halt when he was finally in front of her and realized why she'd been walking slowly. Clutched in her hand was a much smaller hand of a little girl, more like a toddler, trailing beside her and dressed in a pink overcoat that seemed to swallow up her tiny form.

"Sorry, I'm late," she said. "It's the first time I had to get the both of us ready for a date."

He still didn't move or speak but continued to dart his eyes between her and the child. They had the same brown eyes, same nose and mouth, and same chestnut complexion. She was a miniature version of Havilland.

"This is Kimberly," she said. "But I call her Kimmy."

He realized now why she looked so nervous. She did have a confession to make, but with all the possibilities swarming through his head, this one had not once occurred to him. Yet, looking back now and thinking about her actions, it all made sense.

"This is my daughter." She knelt down and smiled at the girl, who was shyly looking up at Eric, studying him as much as he was studying her.

"Kimmy, this is Mommy's very good friend, Eric. Can you say hi?"

He was holding his breath, suddenly feeling nervous himself, but when her small, soft voice spoke that one simple word, he exhaled and felt a warmth flood over him.

"Hi."

He slowly knelt down to be eye level with her and smiled.

"Hi, Kimmy. It's very nice to meet you."

He moved his gaze over to Havilland, who was staring back at him with such naked hope, and he suddenly felt like a jerk for doubting her. She was a mother, and she had been waiting to be sure about him before she introduced him to the most special part of her.

"So where would you ladies like to go to dinner?"

CHAPTER TWENTY-EIGHT

*F*riday night…

Downstairs in the living room, Eric was pacing back and forth in his tuxedo, talking on the phone and giving a member of his team last-minute instructions when he heard both Jeanetta's and Kimmy's voices squeal with awe and excitement.

"Mommy, you look beautiful!"

"Mrs. Sawyer, my goodness! That dress was made just for you!"

Eric had slightly turned his head and in the moment he saw her, everything stopped.

Jesus Christ.

She hadn't worn that dress in so long. It had been an impulse buy before they were married when he'd asked her to be his date at some fancy dinner function. He didn't remember much about that night except for after the dinner was over when they couldn't get back to his place fast enough.

It was a red, floor-length evening gown with that soft,

airy-looking fabric she called tulle, and he had to admit that the color red against her brown skin was the greatest pleasure to his eyes. The part that made him salivate, though, was the deep V neckline, which accentuated her generous breasts. And it was backless, which meant she wasn't wearing a bra. But the detail that made his dick hard were the two discreet front slits trailing up each of her legs and ending at thighs that knew how to straddle him perfectly.

"Thank you," Havilland said, beaming from the compliments. "I'm glad it still fits."

Oh, it fits all right, Eric thought to himself. She had gained more curves when they got married, but she looked so good, and damn, every time she moved, those curves swayed underneath the material, tempting him to no end.

She'd pulled her hair into an updo, creating a mass of curls that sat up on her head like a crown, with only a few ringlets let loose to frame her face. The style left her delicate neck exposed to him and called for his mouth.

"I hope you have your gun, Mr. Sawyer," Jeanetta said, laughing. "You may have to remind some men tonight that she's yours!"

Havilland was still smiling, but when she turned her direction to Eric, her smile dipped slightly, and he realized he was gaping at her.

"Hello? Eric are you still there?"

His caller. He'd forgotten all about them.

"Yeah, I'm here. We'll touch base when I get there."

He hung up without waiting for a reply and returned his attention back to his wife.

Now she was looking unsure of herself. "Maybe I should go change."

"No," he said, quickly. "You look..."

Suddenly words failed him.

"Sexy, stunning, gorgeous," Jeanetta replied, still having fun at Eric's expense. "Any of those words will do."

"I think she looks really pretty," Kimmy said, softly.

"We'd better get going," Eric said, stepping up to offer his hand to help her down the rest of the stairs.

After a flurry of good nights and good-night kisses for Kimmy, Eric helped Havilland into her coat and escorted her out the door. They walked the short distance to the driveway in silence. When they got to the car, he opened the door for her, and as she passed him to get inside, he inhaled the scent of her sweet fragrance and recognized it as a perfume he had given her for her birthday. When he got into the driver's seat, he put the key into the ignition and hesitated before turning the engine over. He slowly turned to look at her. She was facing forward, but when she felt him watching her, she looked over at him, her big brown eyes so clear even in the shadow of the car's interior.

"You look amazing."

The most ravishing and yet shy smile he'd ever seen spread across her lips, and it both unnerved and warmed him.

"Thank you."

A few months ago, it wouldn't have taken him so long to compliment her. Hell, a few months ago, he would've called this entire thing off, sent Kimmy to Jeanetta's for the night, and spent the entire evening showing Havilland just how amazing she looked. It only illustrated just how far they'd moved away from each other.

He suddenly realized they were staring at each other, and before he acted on impulse and kissed his wife, he abruptly looked away from her, turned the ignition, and began the trip across the bay to the Bayview district and home of the newly built Foxworth plant.

He needed to confront her about the phone records Maya

had found, but he didn't know how to bring it up without revealing another agent had illegally searched her property. It would only lead to a huge fight between them and tension between her and Maya. Besides, if everything panned out tonight, Terrence Miller was going to need more than his own personal CBI agent to keep his ass out of prison.

CHAPTER TWENTY-NINE

"Double the amount for the next order," Terrence said.

Stephen frowned. "Cirillo wants more?"

"Yeah. Can you get it done? You know it will mean more money for us."

They were having a last-minute business conversation in Terrence's office upstairs as guests began to file in for tonight's celebration.

Stephen nodded but Terrence noticed the slight hesitation. "What is it?"

"Nothing. I'm still thinking about that last meetup with him. You never told me why we had to end things so quickly."

"I got tipped that we were being watched."

Stephen widened his eyes in surprise. "Being watched? Who's watching us?"

Terrence shrugged. "DEA, FBI, CBI. Who cares? I got it handled."

"Well, I care," Stephen said, indignantly. "Doesn't it worry you that we're being watched in the first place? Listen, Terrence, I got in this to make money, not to go to prison."

"We share the same goal."

"But something tells me we're veering off course here. We've made plenty of money, and maybe it's time to stop, close down shop, and walk away."

Terrence looked at him hard and then without warning, he grabbed him by the collar of his tux and brought him close to his face.

"Have you been talking to the cops?"

"Hell no!" Stephen said immediately.

"Then why the sudden cold feet?"

"I told you, it's a feeling I have."

"Well, fuck your feelings! There's shit going on that you don't know about nor would you understand, and until I've accomplished everything I set out to do, we're not shutting anything down. So, get your shit together, package the product, and collect your money. That's all you need to worry about!"

"All right!" Stephen shouted.

Terrence shoved him away and pointed a finger in his face. "Don't forget I saved your ass many times, including from those boys who wanted to break your limbs for not paying them. I paid that debt."

"And I've repaid you for it in favors many times over," Stephen said and then added under his breath, "So has my sister."

"What did you say?"

Before Terrence could advance on him again, the door to his office opened, and Robert Foxworth poked his head in.

"Pardon me, I didn't mean to interrupt. Terrence, my daughter is looking for you, and the media and other guests are beginning to arrive. You may want to come down and be a host."

"I'll be right there," Terrence said, stepping back from Stephen and now glaring at Robert. He was the one he wished he could send a fist right into his jaw.

Robert hesitated at the door, dividing a look between the two men, and then he settled his eyes on Stephen.

"Everything all right, son?" he asked him.

"I'm good, Mr. Foxworth," Stephen said. "Thank you again for inviting me."

"Of course! You're one of our best chemists. There was no way I was excluding you. If you need anything, let me know."

"Appreciate it, sir."

Robert's cell began to chime. He pulled it out from the inside of his tuxedo jacket, read the text, and then something dark passed over his eyes.

"I need to take this," he said and looked at Terrence. "Get downstairs now, please. This is your event."

Terrence gave him a mock salute as Robert closed the door behind him. He then counted to ten, headed toward the door, and opened it slowly. He looked down the corridor to see that Robert was heading into another private office and ushering in a woman with long, brunette hair, wearing a floor-length rose-gold-colored gown. Any other time, Terrence would've applauded the old man for living a little and doing something to get that stick out of his ass. But, he didn't look too happy to be entertaining this particular woman. Just before they went inside and closed the office door, Terrence was able to catch a brief stint of their conversation.

"I'm not going to say this again. I told you on the phone that my attorney will contact you," Robert said in a hushed tone.

"I'm tired of passing messages back and forth," she replied. "I need to look you in the eye when we make our deals."

CHAPTER THIRTY

Instead of parking by the valet just outside the doors of the new facility, Eric parked the car two blocks away, behind a waiting surveillance van. Both he and Havilland got out of the car, knocked on the van's doors, and were promptly let inside. The agents then got busy carefully wiring Havilland while Eric coached her on her role.

"Try to stay by his side as much as you can and get him comfortable enough to start talking."

"I'll do my best, but this is his party. I'll have to compete with his father-in-law, wife, board members, and even the media for his attention. This isn't going to be easy." She paused to frown at Eric. "What are you hoping to get him to say?"

"We got a tip about another meeting with his buyers to finish the deal that was aborted last time," Eric said. "With any luck, he'll let slip when and where it is."

"To me?" she asked incredulously. "You expect too much."

"And you're doubting yourself, when I know for a fact he trusts you more than anyone else in that room."

She looked up at him as a wave of guilt swarmed her. How much did it pain him to just admit that?

He looked at his watch. "We need to get going. Remember, I'll be listening the whole time. If I get any sense that you're in danger, I'll be right there."

She nodded. "I know. You always are."

At that last word, she felt something pass between them that temporarily made her forget they were surrounded by a team of agents. They continued to stare at each other until Jerry broke the silence.

"You two need a moment alone?" he joked.

Eric ignored him and addressed the other agent who'd been wiring Havilland. "Are we ready?"

"She's good to go."

Eric shoved open the van door, jumped out, and then turned to offer a hand to Havilland who hopped out after him. He tucked an earpiece into his ear and motioned for her to test her mic.

"Testing. Testing," she said.

"We hear you loud and clear, Hav," one of the agents responded. *"Good luck in there."*

Eric escorted her back to the car, opened the driver's side door for her, and handed her the keys. She took them from him, but he didn't let go of her hand until she gave him her full attention. Havilland looked at their clasped hands and then up at him.

Without speaking, he bent down and brushed his lips so close to her neck that she could feel the sensations against her skin, and it made her shiver with desire for him. He barely touched her, but moved his lips along the curve of her neck and then up to her ear where he whispered just loud enough for only her to hear.

"I miss us."

* * *

Havilland walked into the grand hall and allowed one of the attendants to take her coat. She could sense several eyes on her and immediately felt exposed, not because of the dress but because she was there to once again thwart her husband's plans. She gripped the matching clutch in her hands and made her way through the throng of guests in search of her target—or in actuality, Eric's target.

However, even in this large space, it didn't take long before she felt his presence behind her, as though he'd been awaiting her arrival. She slowly turned and he was there, looking handsome and stylish as only Terrence could look in a white, tailored tuxedo jacket. Seeing him staring at her made her heart sink because she wished to God it was Eric standing in his place and that this was just a normal night where the two of them got dressed up, went out for dinner and dancing, laughed and enjoyed themselves, and came back home to kiss Kimmy good night and make love like they were dating again.

I miss us.

"Hav," Terrence said, coming forward. "I'm glad you could make it. There's something I need to talk to you—"

"It's good to see you, too, Terrence," she said and turned her head slightly to the right. She held it there for a moment, hoping he got the hint.

When she turned back to face him, his eyes had gone hard, but instead of saying what was racing through his mind, he continued to walk forward, took her elbow gently in his hand and leaned forward to kiss her cheek. He stayed there a moment longer and whispered into her ear.

"You look stunning."

She knew he saw the wire, but just as she'd hoped, he

didn't mention it. Instead, he kept talking as though everything were innocent.

"Have you seen your brother?" he asked. "He's around here somewhere."

Havilland looked around the hall that was growing with guests by the minute. "No, I didn't know he'd be here."

"Of course, he'd be here. He's our star chemist."

Havilland frowned at the bitterness she heard in his tone, then she looked behind his shoulder and smiled and waved.

"He's over there, talking to your father-in-law."

Stephen waved back, but when Terrence turned and looked at the two men speaking, Havilland saw Stephen's demeanor change instantly. She then looked at Terrence and that silent, slow-burn temper of his had returned.

"Something wrong?" she asked.

He turned to her and smiled. "No. Nothing. You know, this soiree reminds me of the last time you and I got fancy together. You remember?"

She rolled her eyes. "Don't be a bastard, Terrence. Of course, I remember. In fact, it should be a very memorable occasion for you because that's where you met your wife."

He nodded, took two glasses of champagne from a passing waiter, handed one to her, and took a sip of his. He watched her over the rim of the glass with amusement dancing in his eyes at the memory.

* * *

October 2015

"I did tell you that you look great tonight, didn't I?" Terrence asked, taking Havilland's hand as they both took the short walk from the parking lot to the auditorium of Spelman College.

"Three times already," she said, clutching his hand tighter

and leaning forward to steal a last-minute kiss before they entered a roomful of people.

"Well, I'll probably tell you again some time tonight," he said, his eyes roaming up and down her body.

She felt sexy whenever he looked at her like that. Tonight, she went for the classic little black dress but made sure it clung to every curve of her hips, butt, and thighs, and accentuated her narrow waist. Her breasts were pushed together in the sweetheart neckline, and she smiled whenever she caught him staring.

"I appreciate you being my date," she said. "I promise we won't stay too long since we have a shift tomorrow."

"It's all right," he said, opening the door to the auditorium. There was music playing loudly on the speakers, so he had to raise his voice. "Just know that I'll be expecting payment later."

He winked at her, and she gave him another shy smile and then looked around the hall. Round tables adorned with white tablecloths were placed strategically around the open space. Balloons showcasing the school colors of Columbia blue and white were hung throughout the room, petunias of the same colors were placed in small vases as center pieces, and a large blue banner hung center stage that read: *Welcome 2002 Alumni.*

Normally, Havilland would've blown off the night, but she and Terrence had been dating for nearly five months now, after she finally broke down and violated her "do not date your partner" rule. He'd flirted and made advances for months, and she couldn't deny how helplessly handsome he was with his handsome milky brown skin and deep, dark eyes that mesmerized her. He had a soulful, smooth tone that was like molasses dripping from his mouth every time he spoke. It was no secret around the department that several of the female cops, and some of the men, had propositioned him at least once, but he seemed to only be interested in her —the one who didn't want to date him.

They found a table that had not been filled yet, and Terrence sat down while looking around at the throng of women brimming with incessant and lively chatter.

Havilland noticed his uneasiness and chuckled. "Relax, I'll get you a drink."

"Don't be long," he warned.

She leaned over and whispered playfully, "Just tase anyone who gets too close."

She turned and headed for the open bar and had to stand in line as many others had the same idea. By the time she ordered a martini for herself and a whiskey and soda for Terrence, twenty minutes had passed. As she made her way back to the table, she saw that not only had Terrence relaxed but he had found company.

"Hi, Hav," the woman said, turning to look up at her. "You look great! I was just talking to your handsome friend here."

Havilland smiled indulgently and handed Terrence his drink. "Well, I'm sure you introduced yourselves, but just in case, Devon Foxworth, this is Terrence Miller. Terrence and I work together at the Atlanta PD." She turned to Terrence. "Devon and I were in school together."

"Hav, I remember you were interested in law enforcement in college. It's great to see you went after what you loved," Devon said. "Me, on the other hand, I just took a job as my father's assistant in his office. It's the only way I'm going to learn the drug business."

"That's why your name is so familiar," Terrence said, snapping his fingers. "Foxworth. As in Foxworth Pharmaceuticals?"

"Guilty," Devon said, flashing a brilliant smile.

Havilland felt Terrence's interest suddenly heighten, and Devon eyed him just a little longer, seemingly sensing his growing interest as well before she turned back to Havilland.

"Hav, I read the alumni roster, and I saw you got both a Bachelor's and a Master's degree in Criminal Justice. Congratulations, but I thought for sure you'd do something else with that instead of becoming a cop."

Havilland felt her back stiffen because that sounded like a backhanded compliment. But what was more surprising is when Terrence had the nerve to agree with her.

"Thank you," he said, clinking his glass against Devon's. "I keep telling her that she has the education to be more than a cop. Go to law school or something."

They smiled at each other in agreement and Havilland spoke up. "I always enjoyed the investigative work. I'm hoping to move up to detective one day. I'd rather catch the criminals than prosecute them."

Devon and Terrence shared another look and then shrugged and shared a smile. Finally, someone else caught Devon's attention, and she politely excused herself.

Havilland turned to Terrence and frowned. "What was that about?"

"What?" he asked.

"I like being a cop."

"I know you do," he said. "I just think you're selling yourself short. You have a lot of talent and could be doing more. Is it wrong for a man to want more for his girlfriend?"

"I thought we were done with this topic. Just because you regret your career path, doesn't mean I do. I like my work, and I have plans to move up the ranks."

"That badge isn't paying you shit. It's not paying me shit!"

There it was again. His constant reminder that their chosen profession wasn't providing him with the comfortable lifestyle he craved.

"Terrence, don't start. You're not making much money

yet, but it doesn't mean you won't ever get to that point," she said. "Put your time in, move up the ranks, and eventually, you'll be living more comfortably. Maybe you should go back to school and study something to help with your career."

"Forget it," he said, annoyance filling his voice.

The problem was that he wasn't patient. Terrence wanted that comfortable life now, and his frustration came from the fact that he didn't know exactly how to go about getting it.

She tried consoling him some more. "We're both investing in our pensions. And if things get more serious, we can start saving for a nice house to pay with cash. We're doing a lot better than most people our age."

"Yeah, I guess."

She frowned. "You guess?"

"Obviously, some people our age are doing much better," he said.

She saw as he slid a look over to Devon, who was now engaged in conversation with some other girls Havilland recognized from school. Terrence must have sensed her watching him and the fact that he was being a jerk because he suddenly turned toward her, leaned over, and kissed her.

"You're right. I'm sorry. Let's enjoy ourselves and our night off together."

That melted a little of the ice off her shoulders, and she gave him a small smile. The rest of the night continued on pretty uneventfully, but every now and then, Havilland would catch Devon staring over at them, particularly at Terrence. And what concerned her even more was that Terrence would inconspicuously stare back.

CHAPTER THIRTY-ONE

"Terrence?"

Havilland and Terrence turned to see Devon looking spectacular in a cream-colored, form-fitting, strapless gown. Havilland recognized the designer because ever since college, Devon wore nothing but the best.

"Dad wants to do a toast with the board members. We need you over there."

"I'll be right there, honey," he said with an outstretched hand. "You remember Havilland, right? It's Havilland Sawyer these days, excuse me, Agent Havilland Sawyer."

Devon took his hand and came forward, smiling. "Of course, I remember. How are you doing, Hav?"

Havilland smiled back and could already see Devon wasn't about to mention the fact that they'd already crossed paths at her job.

"It's good to see you again, Devon."

"So, the name change must mean you got married," Devon said, maintaining her mock enthusiasm. "Why didn't you invite your husband to the party?"

"Work ran late. Maybe he'll be here later."

"As long as he's not busy raiding our house again," Devon said snidely, and Havilland noticed Terrence's fists tighten. That was obviously what he wanted to talk to her about, but now was not the time.

"So, you've met him," Havilland said and mentally cheered at the look of derision that fell across Devon's flawless face.

"Oh, Dad's gesturing for us," Devon said, encircling her arm with Terrence's. "Excuse us, Hav."

Havilland nodded with a feigned smile and watched as the couple walked away.

"I told you this wouldn't be easy," she said, murmuring to Eric and the rest of the team into her wire.

"You okay?"

She turned with a start to find her brother standing by her side and this time emitted a smile that was genuine.

"Yeah, I'm good. Just battling old memories. I saw you speaking with the big boss earlier," she joked. "Robert Foxworth must be impressed with you."

"Something like that," he said, shrugging and taking an hors d'oeuvre from a passing server. "I just came over here because it looked like you needed some rescuing."

"Thanks, but I can handle the Millers and the Foxworths."

"I'm not so sure in that dress," he said, looking her up and down. "Who told you to come outside dressed like that?"

"Shut up," she said, laughing.

"I'm serious! I need to go get Eric and have him come stand guard over you. This is his job."

"He may or may not be here tonight."

"What are you talking about? I just saw him a few minutes ago. He and what looked like some other agents just went upstairs to the corporate offices."

"What?" Havilland whirled around in the direction of the elevators. "Are you sure?"

"They may have been dressed in tuxedos, but they were

obviously law enforcement. I saw Mr. Foxworth use his pass and key in a code to let them upstairs."

"I'll be right back," Havilland said, handing Stephen her glass and hurrying to the women's restroom.

When she got inside, she checked under the stalls to ensure she was alone and then spoke into her mic.

"Commander, this is Sawyer, come in. Commander? Eric, are you there?"

"He cut comms temporarily, Hav. Is something wrong?"

She recognized Agent Stewart's voice over the radio.

"What's going on? Why is he in the corporate offices?"

"Your target is Terrence Miller. We need you to maintain visual contact."

Havilland remained silent as she tried to think. Then it hit her. This was all a ruse. Eric was going after something else, and she was put in place to distract Terrence while he retrieved it.

"Dammit!"

"Hav?" Agent Stewart called, but she didn't respond. Instead, she hurried toward the bathroom exit and started to reach for her mic to turn it off. But Maya was already entering the bathroom, holding a glass of water.

Havilland dropped her hands. It was too late to turn off the mic, and it didn't matter anyway, because Maya was still wearing one and it didn't look as though she was going to let Havilland out of her sight any time soon.

"Hav? Hav, are you there?"

"She's fine, Stewart," Maya said, locking the bathroom door. "I've got eyes on her here in the bathroom. She just wasn't feeling well."

She paused to hand Havilland the glass of water. "Here, drink this down. You look flushed, and it will help you feel better."

Havilland's eyes went from the glass to the woman in the rose-gold evening gown currently blocking her exit.

"Go on, take it."

She finally outstretched one hand, took the glass from Maya, and simply held it without taking a sip.

"Feel better?" Maya asked, knowing the other agents could only hear them.

"I'm fine. Thank you, Maya."

"I hate these large crowds too," she said. "Eric and the others are almost done. We'll just wait here until he's finished, and then you can go see him."

Her eyes spoke volumes, namely, that what she was saying wasn't up for discussion, so either they were going to fight each other for all the men listening in, or Havilland would just have to stay put.

She finally sighed, put the glass on the sink and braced her hands on the porcelain edge. They waited, both regarding each other with combative silence and both obviously wishing they could freely say what they wanted to each other. Finally, the taut silence came to an end when they heard Eric's voice through the mic.

"We've got it," he said. "I repeat, we have the ledger."

Maya smiled. "Nice job, Commander."

Soon, more congratulations followed, but only Havilland scowled and touched her earpiece.

"Commander, what's your twenty?"

"Upstairs in the corporate offices," Eric said.

"Stay where you are. I'm coming to you."

"Copy that."

Havilland stalked her way to the bathroom door, only to be blocked once again by Maya. They stared each other down, and just when Havilland thought the men were about to hear the girl fight of their fantasies, Maya slowly reached her hand up, turned the lock, and stepped aside. Havilland threw open the door and brushed by her without a word.

As she headed to the elevators, she caught Terrence's eye. He looked at her curiously with the silent question as to what was going on, but she subtly shook her head, stepped onto the elevator, and proceeded up to the offices. When she got upstairs to the plush, quiet surroundings, one of the agents let her inside what must've been Terrence's office. She immediately saw a wall safe with its door wide open, and then her eyes trailed to Eric. He was holding an evidence bag with what looked to be a leather-bound book inside and currently engrossed in conversation with Robert Foxworth.

"We appreciate your help and cooperation in getting us access," Eric said. "We have the warrant here for you and your attorney."

Robert waved a hand. "I know you went by the book on this one. It's too risky not to. Hopefully, everything you need should be in there to secure an arrest."

"We'll have it analyzed as soon as possible," Eric said and then noticed Havilland. "Will you give me a moment please, sir? I'll be in touch."

Robert nodded, took another long look at the ledger, and then turned to head toward the office door, barely sparing Havilland a glance. But before he could leave, a ruckus was heard just outside the door and in seconds, Terrence stormed in, breathing fire.

"What the hell is going on in here? Why are these people in my office, Robert?"

"Obviously looking for something of yours," Robert said, matching his furious tone.

"And you just let them in?"

"They have a warrant, Terrence! What did you expect me to do? They were looking for one particular item."

Eric held up the evidence bag. "And we found it."

The color seemed to drain from Terrence's face as he saw what Eric held in his hands.

Robert stepped forward. "I have board members downstairs, stockholders, and the goddamned media. How do you think it would look if I had the CBI traipsing all over the place conducting a search and seizure operation? I gave them access to your office to keep things quiet. So, maybe you need to be telling *me* what the hell is going on!"

"You son of a bitch." Terrence stepped just as close to Robert until the tips of their shoes met. "I know what you're doing, and I promise I'll see you in hell first before you take me down."

Eric, obviously having heard enough, spoke up. "We have what we need, Mr. Miller. We'll leave. You throw a great party, by the way."

Terrence looked at the ledger again and then stared long and hard at Havilland.

Eric moved in front of her, blocking his view. "Anything else you want to say?"

Terrence's eyes met his. "I'm glad you and Mrs. Sawyer enjoyed yourselves." He sent one more hostile look to his father-in-law and then left the office.

Robert shook his head in disgust and then turned to Eric. "Let me know what you find out. I want this thug out of my life and my daughter's life once and for all."

Then he was gone, and one by one the team of agents filed out of the room with murmurs of congratulations for Eric.

"Congratulations, sir." Maya walked up to them and patted him on the back with an engaging smile. She then turned to Havilland. "You too, Hav. We appreciate you stepping up and agreeing to the wire."

Havilland simply nodded.

"See you back at the office," Maya said to Eric.

Eric nodded. "I'm right behind you."

With that, she left and finally, Havilland was left with her husband, feeling like an outsider. He placed the bagged ledger onto the desk and turned to her, patiently waiting for her objections.

"You used me as bait. You never expected for him to say anything incriminating."

"No," Eric admitted. "He's too smart for that. I'm sure he guessed from the moment he walked up to you that you were wearing a wire."

"So, this was all just a ploy to get in that safe?"

"I needed him distracted."

"You had a warrant. Why didn't you just demand him to open it for you?"

A devilish smile painted his lips. "This was more fun."

"You could've told me what you were planning," she said.

"I could've, but there was too much risk involved."

"What risk? Apparently, the rest of the agents knew about it."

"They're on the task force. You're not."

Her temper finally erupted. "Fuck you!"

She turned and started to walk out, but he snatched her arm from behind and turned her back around to look at him. "Don't talk to me like that."

She shook her arm free. "You still don't trust me."

His steely blue eyes, which were cold at the beginning of their conversation, now went soft and warm. "I want to trust you. I really do."

"So, what's stopping you?"

"Can't this wait until we get home?"

"Answer me, dammit!"

He looked toward the closed office door, probably to

ensure there weren't any shadows lurking on the other side. He put one finger to his lips and slowly lifted her right leg. Havilland put one hand on his shoulder to keep her balance and watched his hands disappear underneath one of the slits of her dress. She felt his hand trail up her inner thigh to where the mic was strapped. He turned it off, unclasped and removed it, and tossed the gear onto the desk behind him.

"I'd prefer the rest of the team didn't hear us arguing."

"You're going too far with this," she said.

"I'm doing my job," he countered.

"Is that right?" she asked. "Well, let me ask you something: do you want him in jail for his crimes or for the fact that he and I had a relationship?"

His jaw hardened to granite as his eyes danced around the office and then settled back to her. They dipped lower to watch her cleavage rise and fall with each breath and once again slowly trailed up to her face.

"You really do look great in that dress."

She sighed. "Eric, what are you doing?"

In a flash, he grabbed her waist and brought her up hard against his body. While she melded to every inch of his frame, he pulled up the folds of her gown and moved his hands up the backs of her legs to palm her ass.

"It's my favorite."

She didn't know how he accomplished it, but suddenly the tone in his voice had her softening toward him. "I know. I wore it for you."

"Did you?"

"Yes."

He stared directly into her eyes as he slipped his fingers in between her thong panties and traveled down to that hot and moist center. Havilland whimpered and fell against him, but Eric kept her flushed tightly against his chest, making his fingers dance.

"I've been wanting to do this all night." He leaned forward to whisper in her ear. "Who are you wet for?"

Havilland bent her head toward his ear, bit his lobe, and sucked it gently between her lips. "I stay wet for you," she said, panting.

He growled like a predator, lifted her by the waist, turned and planted her ass onto the desk. He spread her thighs apart, quickly unbuttoned his slacks, and grasped the back of her neck with one hand while trying to free himself with the other. Havilland gripped both of his shoulders, and the two of them clutched at each other, anticipating that blessed moment when he would push himself inside of her.

But as soon as she heard the loud rapping at the closed office door, Havilland knew the moment was lost.

"Goddammit!" he hissed and then shouted toward the door. "What is it?"

"Agent Sawyer, Agent Hewitt is requesting to see you at headquarters," someone called from the other side.

He exhaled a deep breath. "All right. I'll be right there."

Havilland was already adjusting her panties when Eric turned back around, grabbed her by the waist, and helped her off the desk. When he tucked his dress shirt back into his trousers and zipped them up, he stared at her, and the two of them shared a fleeting look of regret.

"You say you don't trust me, but then you can't keep your hands off me," she said. "What is this, Eric? Either we're moving forward or we're standing still."

He grasped her face between his hands. "You make me crazy every time I look at you. I wanted to tell you everything, but I know you want this case to go away. Even if it means my career."

She tried to shake her head within his grasp. "That's not true. I would never jeopardize your career."

"But you'd jeopardize your own—for him. That's why I can't move forward, Hav, and I don't know if I ever will."

"Don't say that."

"I have to go."

He released her and walked out of the office, leaving her feeling deflated and defeated.

CHAPTER THIRTY-TWO

The next morning, by the time Eric woke, Havilland was gone, leaving him a note about running errands. He poured Kimmy a bowl of sugary cereal and sat her in front of the TV to watch cartoons in her pajamas. After making himself some coffee, he went into the home office and retrieved the ledger from his safe. He hadn't wanted to leave it in the evidence locker over the weekend, and instead brought it home with him last night. Sitting at his desk, he flipped through the pages and aside from a few names and dates, it was all basically numbers that began to blur together. But he knew that hidden underneath all of those numbers was the key to Terrence's arrest. However, he couldn't concentrate on any of it for thinking of last night's events. His team had scored a major victory in retrieving the ledger, but his mind was on someone else.

Once he left her last night, he returned to headquarters, debriefed his team, and filed the necessary reports. He took an Uber home and by the time he arrived, the house was dark and quiet, to which he felt both relief and disappointment. On one hand, he didn't know what to say to her, but on the other, he'd been tempted to once again put aside his anger for the moment and finish what they had started in the executive office that evening.

He flipped the ledger closed, locked it in the safe and left the room. He wasn't getting any work done, and it was a sunny and pleasant Saturday morning. He grabbed his jacket and the small pink jacket Kimmy wore. Sometime in that half hour he'd tucked himself away in the office, she had dressed herself but had resumed her seat in front of the television. Time to give them both a break.

"You want to go to the playground?"

"Yeah!" she cried out happily, jumped up, raced up the stairs to put her sneakers on, and was back in less than a minute.

He laughed as he slipped her jacket on for her and ushered her out the front door.

"Is Mommy coming?" she asked.

"No," he said, turning to lock the door behind him. "She left earlier to go run an errand. It's just you and me, honey. Is that cool?"

"Cool."

As he strapped her into her car seat, Eric thought about Havilland's absence, and then he thought about what Devon said when she came to see him.

You have to do something.

* * *

He sat on a park bench, responding to messages and emails on his phone while at the same time, keeping an eye on Kimmy running around the park and playing with kids she'd met only five minutes ago. It was odd to him how children could so easily open up to each other.

"Eric?"

He looked up from his phone and was struck by the sight of familiar light-brown eyes, sun-golden hair and a smile greeting him.

"Christina," he said, returning her smile and rising to meet her for a hug.

"Wow, it's so good to see you," she said. "How long has it been?"

He shrugged. Five, almost six years. It's good to see you too. What've you been doing with yourself?"

He left the rest unsaid, but they both knew he was really asking what she'd been up to since she quit the CBI after their breakup.

"I went back to school and finished my accounting degree."

He raised his eyes, impressed. "That's great. You always wanted to go into that field."

She shrugged. "That's what I tried to tell my dad, but he insisted my finance skills would be better used as an agent."

He invited her to sit down on the bench beside him. He then looked away for a moment and found Kimmy happily playing on the slide and smiled.

"He thought he was doing what was best for you."

"Absolutely. By interfering," she said on a laugh and then followed his gaze. "Is the little girl yours?"

He nodded.

She's pretty. How old?"

"Four."

"I also heard you got married."

"That's right. A little over two years now."

She smiled. "So, you're still a newlywed."

Eric thought about it. Havilland and he were newlyweds, but they weren't acting like it. They should be living in wedded bliss with their daughter right now, but sadly, they were at war with each other.

He spied another glance toward Kimmy and saw that one of her shoes had come untied. He called her over and in seconds, she was at his side. He gestured for her to put her little sneaker on his knees and while he tied it, he resumed his conversation with Christina.

"Your father told me you were married now, but I didn't know you had kids."

"Stepkids," she said, nodding to twin boys playing on the jungle gym. "I'm getting some bonding time in with them. They're about the same age as your little one here."

"This is Kimberly, but her mother and I call her Kimmy. Kimmy, this is Christina, an old friend of mine."

"Hi," Kimmy said with that familiar shy tone she always reserved for strangers.

"Hi, Kimmy," Christina said with a beaming smile.

"All right, you're all set," he said. "Thirty more minutes, and then we need to get going."

"Okay," she called and ran off to resume her play.

Eric hesitated before turning back to Christina. "Your father never wastes a moment to keep me updated about your life—"

"Don't pay him any mind," she said. "He doesn't know the whole story and refuses to believe I had anything to do with our breakup."

"It's all right, but that's not what I was going to say. He told me you have your own practice now. I hate to ask, but there's this case I'm overseeing, and I'd like to have someone outside the agency take a look at some numbers."

She nodded and smiled. "I'd love to help you, but my specialty is forensic accounting. So, unless you need to find some money, I'm probably not your girl."

"Actually," he said. "That's exactly what I need."

CHAPTER THIRTY-THREE

Havilland walked up to the black Denali parked on a secluded corner in Hunter's Point near Pier 96. She looked around and saw there were only a few other cars on the street before opening the passenger door and climbing inside. She shut the door and for just a moment, the two of them shared the silence. After a full minute, she looked over at him and saw he was watching her expectantly.

She sighed. "I'm not wearing a wire."

"Can't be too sure with you," Terrence said, his voice low and teeming with animosity. "Tell me you didn't know what was going on."

"I didn't," she said, matching his tone. "At least, not until it was already underway. I couldn't have stopped it."

"I didn't ask you to stop it. I asked for a heads up," he said through clenched teeth. "Just like I wanted a heads up before he decided to raid my goddamn house."

"Someone took my phone," she began and stopped when he abruptly slammed an open palm against the dashboard.

"I thought we had an understanding. You keep me

informed of everything, and I stay out of prison. And if I stay out of prison, your brother stays out of prison too."

She glared at him, hoping he could see in her eyes just how much she despised him and the hold he continuously had over her.

His face a morphed into a crooked smile. "I see you do remember. You know you were always irresistible to me when you're furious."

"Is there a reason you called me here?"

"I'm calling this whole thing off. I've got a passport and papers, so after I tie up a few loose ends, I'm out of here. But your husband has the accountant's ledger, and I need it back before I can leave."

"Where the hell do you think you're going?" she asked, gaping at him.

"This is over."

"Oh, no you don't! You don't bring me into your shit and then just call it off when you feel like it. You came to me, Terrence. I've come too far, risking everything for you and Stephen—my career and my marriage. It's over when I say it's over."

"This whole thing is screwed up," he shouted. "I need to start looking out for myself."

"When have you not looked out for yourself?"

He looked away from her and stared out the window. He didn't seem to be looking at anything in particular, so she assumed he was attempting to calm himself.

"I'll give you until the end of the week to get that ledger back. As long as the CBI has it, I'm not safe."

Her eyes widened. "You're crazy. You're actually asking me to steal evidence?"

He swung his gaze back to her, his midnight-colored eyes now fierce. "You have a better idea? Besides, it's about par for what you did for me in Atlanta."

"That was just passing along information. This is something entirely different. I could go to jail."

He went silent, and his face was completely blank as if he were mentally communicating to her that he didn't give a damn about her or the risk she was taking.

"There's got to be another way."

"Either I get the ledger or your brother goes to prison."

"You know what? Do what you have to do," she said. "I'm sick and tired of your threats against my family. I'll get him a good lawyer. You manipulated him just like you did me, and I'll be damned if he goes down for your greed."

"If you feel confident that the one lawyer you can afford on your salary will be enough against my slew of lawyers, then get out," he said.

"You mean the slew of lawyers your father-in-law will get for you?" she asked, sneering and got so much delight when his jaw hardened into stone.

She'd definitely struck a nerve.

"I'd love to be in on that conversation when you demand that Robert Foxworth and his debutante daughter hire you the best defense team to keep you out of prison."

He still didn't say anything, and she gave a slight chuckle and grasped the car door handle.

"Good luck with that."

Just as she cracked the door open, Terrence finally spoke. "These are dangerous people, Hav."

"So what?"

"If I don't get that ledger back, there's no telling what they'd do or who they'd go after."

Something about his words had her pausing. She closed the door again and stared. "If you're talking about Devon, you and Robert can hire protection for her."

He shook his head. "Going after Devon isn't enough to hurt me. There's someone else. Someone more innocent."

She felt her heart begin to speed up as her mind deciphered what he was trying to tell her.

She shook her head slowly from side to side. "No, that would never happen. How could it? You've never spent time with her." Furious tears filled her eyes. "You haven't seen her since she was a baby."

He shrugged. "It's not hard for these people to find out she's my daughter. I need the ledger. I need the ledger or Kimberly—"

He didn't finish that sentence, because the next thing she knew, she was attacking him. She smacked him and used his momentary shock to climb over the console to scratch and claw at every piece of flesh she could get her nails into. She screamed, cried, wailed but kept hitting him, her only goal to kill him. Just kill him and this would all be over.

"I hate you!" she screamed over and over. "I'll kill you! Do you understand me? I'll kill you if something happens to her!"

He managed to wrestle her hands away from him, tighten his arms around her, and put her back to his chest. He immobilized her, but she only leaned against him and kicked in the air, determined to break free.

"Havilland, stop!" he yelled. "Stop it!"

"Let go of me!"

"I'm sorry, okay? I'm sorry for all of it!" he shouted above her screams and cries. "I never wanted it to come to this, but I have no other choice. I'm a dead man if this doesn't work out."

"I'll bury you myself," she promised.

"Listen to me. Just get the ledger. Get the ledger, and I'll leave town. Forget everything else. Forget about our arrangement. I promise, you'll never see me again."

He still had his arms wrapped around her, but she'd

stopped kicking and fighting him, and now the two of them were filling the silence with their heavy breaths.

"I know I don't have a relationship with Kimberly. She doesn't know me, but she's still a part of me, and these men know what it would do to me if something happened to her. We've been at this for too damn long, and I'm tired. I just want it to end."

The tears that had welled in her eyes finally escaped and streamed down her cheeks as she thought about the complete mess her life had become. He was right. They had been going at this for nearly a year, and he wasn't the only one who wanted it to end. He was promising to leave town, but as far as she could see, there was only one way to make it all stop. There was only one way to keep Stephen out of prison and Kimmy safe from his enemies. She was going to have to kill Terrence.

As if in a trance, she felt herself nodding her head. She would get the ledger for him, but he wasn't going to leave with it. He wasn't going anywhere.

"I'll do it."

* * *

Devon stared through binoculars in shock and horror at the two people parked several yards away from her. She'd rented a small sedan to tail Terrence around town because he would've definitely recognized her Range Rover. She followed him all around the city, eagerly waiting to catch him involved in something. And boy, did she catch him.

What had possessed Havilland to viciously attack him like that? What had he said to her? Devon thought she was about to witness the murder of her own husband and had pulled her cell from her purse to dial 911. Then Terrence had somehow restrained Havilland. He kept his arms around her until she calmed down, and even then, he didn't let her go.

Havilland wasn't a mistress. This—what she was witnessing—was something deeper. Something hostile. There was no love between these two. She zoomed in on Havilland and saw the tears flowing, but she wasn't sad, she was furious. It was the look of a woman who'd reached her breaking point and was ready to do something dangerous.

Devon slowly put down the binoculars and a cold shiver coursed through her body and she instantly recognized the fear. She was afraid. Not afraid of Havilland, but afraid *for* Havilland.

CHAPTER THIRTY-FOUR

Two days later…

Havilland showed her badge to the clerk sitting behind the plexiglass window.

"I need to review the evidence for the Dawson case. I have a court date coming up and need to refresh."

"Fill the form out," the clerk replied in a bored tone and handed her a clip board with a pen.

She quickly scribbled the necessary information and handed the form back. The clerk glanced at the information, tapped a few keys on his computer, and spoke once again in the same monotone voice.

"Box 71389. Do you know where you're going?"

"Yeah, I'm good. Thanks."

She was buzzed in to the evidence storage, took the appropriate route all the way to the back, but instead of taking a left where the Dawson evidence box was stored, she took a right in search of the Miller evidence box.

She grabbed a step ladder and placed it directly below the high shelf, climbed up, and grabbed for the box labeled *Miller*. She pulled it out, quickly lifted the lid, and dug around inside until she came to the medium-sized leather-bound journal she'd recognized from the evening of the party. She quickly flipped through it, viewing names aligned with numbers and figures that were completely foreign to her, but readable to the trained eye.

She gripped the ledger in her hands, wishing to God there was some other way. Stealing this would slam the lid closed on Eric's case for good, but only Havilland knew there had been no case to begin with. It was all a smoke screen—a case perfectly crafted to hide what was really going on. She wished she could just tell him everything, but revealing to him what she knew would bring it all crumbling down, and she was so close to the end. But could her marriage hold on that long?

She tucked that thought away to be pondered at a later time and also tucked the ledger into her purse and hurried toward the exit. She signed out of the evidence room and turned in the direction of the elevators. She needed to get to the employee parking garage fast to store the ledger in her trunk. But just as she made one step toward the elevators, she halted and found that Maya was once again, blocking her escape.

"Everything all right, Hav?"

Havilland could feel her heart beating out of her chest. "I'm good. I spent too much time in there catching up on a case and realized I have an appointment I need to get to." She pulled her cell phone out to look at the time. "I'm going to be late. I'll see you later."

"Sure thing," Maya said, stepping to the side, and as Havilland walked past her, she didn't miss Maya's subtle gaze downward at her purse.

* * *

Maya trailed Havilland down the hall and peeked around the corner to make sure she got on the elevator. When the elevator doors closed, she rushed back to the evidence locker, showed her badge to the clerk, and recited the evidence box number she now knew by heart.

The clerk narrowed his gaze through the glass partition at her. "Weren't you here for the same box this morning?"

Maya sighed with impatience. "Yes, I was. Do you need me to fill out your forms again?"

The clerk eyed her for a moment longer and then buzzed her inside. "No. I'll just notate that this is your second entry today."

Maya rolled her eyes and pushed through the door into the evidence locker room. "You do that."

When she got inside, she hurried to the box that contained the case evidence against Terrence Miller. She rummaged through it, and smiled widely when she didn't find what she'd been looking for.

"I've got you now," she muttered to herself and pulled her cell from her hip holster and dialed the last number she'd called.

"Sawyer." Eric's voice sounded on the other end of the line.

"She has the ledger," Maya said, looking around to make sure she was still alone.

A long hesitation came from his end of the line. "You're sure?"

"That ledger was in here before she went in. After you checked it into evidence this morning, I made sure to watch the locker all day. It's gone now."

"All right. I can see her coming back to her desk now. She wouldn't be carrying it on her, so she must have stashed it in her car. I'll take it from here."

"Are you going to arrest her now?" Maya asked, mentally

calculating in her head how fast she could get back to the department to witness the scene.

"No. She stole it for Miller. She's going to take me right to him, and I'll get them both."

"Will you?"

"Will I what?"

It was Maya's turn to hesitate.

"Spit it out, Maya."

She sighed. "Terrence Miller is one thing. I know you want to see him go down, but when the time comes, are you absolutely sure you'll be able to arrest your own wife? Or are you going to, once again, let her skate by?"

"I told you before, I'll handle her."

"How much more evidence do you need to see to realize her loyalty isn't to you?"

There was a long pause before Eric spoke. "Agent Landon, I thank you for all you've done, but you're crossing a line. I'm still your superior, and I'll handle it from here. Is that understood?"

Her mouth tapered into a thin line, but she didn't press the issue any further. "Yes, sir."

CHAPTER THIRTY-FIVE

Havilland's mind was in a whirlwind. Maya had seen her coming out of the evidence room, and if she was curious enough to review that surveillance footage, anyone would see her taking that ledger. She had to talk to Carl Hewitt. He was the only one who could fix this for her —that is if she could get him to have a meeting with her, or at the very least, return her calls and texts. She was beginning to feel cornered, and that all the plotting and scheming she'd done was for nothing. She wanted so much to talk to Eric about all of this—he had always been her trusted go-to source to air out her problems. But how could she even begin to tell him that this whole time, she'd been trying to sabotage his case? He was going to want to know why, and that wasn't something she could reveal.

She finished making the peanut butter and jelly sandwich, cut it into two triangles, and put it on a plate. But before she carried the plate along with a glass of milk to Kimmy, something told her to first make the call she'd been avoiding.

She put the plate back on the counter and grabbed her

cell from her purse and stepped into the den to make a phone call.

"Deputy Director Holladay's office. How may I help you?"

"This is Agent Havilland Sawyer. Is he in?"

"One moment, Agent Sawyer. I'll see if he's available."

A few minutes later, she heard his familiar voice, which was a comfort to her with everything that was going on.

"You nearly missed me," he said. "I was just on my way out."

"I need to see you."

Pause.

"I'm on my way to the airport right now. I'll be out of town for a couple of days. Can it wait until I get back?"

Hell, no! Everything was fucked up, and she was desperate.

She looked up to the ceiling and silently cursed, then she let go a breath and tried not to sound as scared as she was.

"Yeah. Sure."

Another pause.

"Agent Sawyer, I may be completely wrong, but you sound stressed. Are you sure everything is okay? I know it's been a long time, and it's all right if you're feeling like the walls are caving in."

Havilland forced herself to get it together. "There are a few things going on that I didn't anticipate, but I'm sure it can keep until you get back."

David paused as if he could still hear in her voice that everything was not all right. "Fine," he continued, "but I should tell you that Terrence called me about four weeks ago. He was concerned about whether or not you could follow through with this."

That was rich. He was the one threatening to leave town, but she couldn't follow through with this?

"I'm sorry," Havilland said. "He shouldn't have done that, but I have everything covered."

"What does Carl say?"

She wanted to tell him he wasn't answering her phone calls, and she was afraid maybe he was putting distance between them in case he needed to serve her up as a scapegoat later. But revealing that would only force David to pull her out, when this had been her idea from the beginning.

"As a matter of fact, I have a meeting with him tomorrow," she lied. "I'm sure I can talk to him about my concerns then." She added a small laugh for effect. "I guess I'm just a little impatient."

The doorbell sounded and Havilland left the den to answer it. She opened the door without first looking to see who it was and froze with surprise.

"Agent Sawyer? Havilland, are you there?" David called through the line. "Is everything all right?"

"Yes, I'm fine. We'll talk when you get back into town."

Without waiting for his reply, she disconnected the call and confronted her past.

* * *

"It's good to see you again, Hav."

"You, too," she said, stepping to the side. "Come in."

"Thank you." Devon stepped over the threshold and swept past her, leaving a waft of expensive perfume in her wake. She pulled her shades up onto her head and took a moment to observe her surroundings.

Havilland closed the front door and followed Devon's gaze as it moved about the living room. She tried to see it through her eyes and immediately knew the curtains, furnishings, and general decor couldn't compare to what Devon was used to. But Havilland loved her home. She and Eric had picked the house out together, although he always insisted he simply let her have her way and agreed to whatever she wanted as long as it didn't mean a long commute to work for him.

"This is nice," Devon said and then finally turned around to Havilland.

Her brown-eyed gaze was now assessing her as though she were looking for an answer to something.

"Let's go in the kitchen," Havilland said, ushering her through the living room and into the space that shared the kitchen and family room.

The television was still on along with the happy sounds of cartoons, but Kimmy was nowhere in sight. Havilland guessed she must have gone to the potty and was glad her daughter wasn't around just now to see the distressed look on her face.

"I want to thank you for not letting the cat out of the bag at the opening," Devon said, placing her purse on the kitchen counter and taking a seat at one of the barstools. "Terrence doesn't know I visited your workplace, and I'll let him know about it in my own time. I also want to apologize for brushing past you on my way to the elevator without speaking to you. I guess I wasn't yet ready to talk."

"But you are now?" Havilland asked.

"Yes, I am. So, to get straight to the point: what exactly is going on between you and my husband?"

Havilland stared at the woman dressed head to toe in designer clothes. Her makeup, hair, and skin were flawless, and she still had that way of walking into a room and immediately commanding attention. Still, underneath all of that, Havilland sensed dwindling self-confidence and wondered how she could have ever been envious of her. Yes, she had turned Terrence's head and made him forget Havilland ever existed, but all those days and nights of despising her had been a waste of time. She had Eric's love even though these days it didn't feel like it, and she especially had Kimmy. She was a fortunate woman on the verge of losing it all.

"If you think we're having an affair—"

"No, I don't. I mean, I did at first, but then I saw you two together."

"You saw us together. When?"

Devon sighed. "I'm not a stupid woman, Hav. I followed the two of you because my gut was telling me something was happening."

"I promise you, there's nothing illicit or sexual going on between us. His contact with me is for official purposes only. If you want more than that, then talk to him."

Devon's eyes flashed with amusement. "Speaking of husbands, you sound just like yours.

He fed me the same line when I went to see him."

Havilland went cold. "You talked to Eric about this?"

"I showed him some pictures of you and Terrence meeting. I'm sure he still has them." She paused and shrugged. "In hindsight, I know it was petty of me, but I was hoping he'd have some answers for me."

Havilland wanted to throw something. Pictures? At this very moment, Eric had proof that she was meeting with Terrence. What more did he need to see her as his enemy?

"Okay, that's enough. This may sound rude, but I need you to leave. Now."

Devon raised her hands in acquiescence. "Wait a minute. Just wait. I'm not doing a good job of this, because I'm not used to doing it."

"Doing what?"

"Apologizing."

Havilland stilled and Devon took that as her cue to continue.

"I don't know what's going on with you and Terrence, and yes, my first thought was that the two of you were rekindling your relationship. Then, I saw you with him at one of the piers along the Embarcadero. You attacked him."

Havilland shook her head in regret. "I wish you hadn't seen that."

"It's all right. I know he must've said something to provoke you because he's done it to me many times. But it showed me what I needed. What I saw in your eyes wasn't love for him. You and I may not have been very close, but I've only seen you look that way once, and it was in college when you got news of your father's heart attack. It was like someone mixed rage and fear together in a bottle, shook it, and then released it. You had that same reaction with Terrence."

Havilland didn't know what to say. She remembered the day she got the call from her mother that her father was in ICU from a massive heart attack, and the doctors weren't sure he was going to make it. She was in between classes and once she'd registered what her mother was saying, she heard herself screaming and could feel people surrounding her and holding her up to keep her from collapsing. She hadn't known Devon was there.

Devon continued. "Since my mother left years ago, my father has sort of adopted this habit of protecting me by keeping secrets from me. Terrence is doing the same thing. He's involved with something, and he won't tell me what it is, but it's causing problems in our relationship. Maybe it's that karma I don't really believe in, but I've always wanted you to know that I'm sorry for whatever part I played in hurting you. I've just been too cowardly to say it or even admit to myself that I did something wrong."

The kitchen filled with silence as they regarded each other with uncertainty. They weren't friends, but they weren't enemies, either.

"Mommy?"

Both Havilland and Devon turned to the small voice. Kimmy stood on the border between the kitchen and family room. Her feet seemed to be poised at the edge as though she were afraid to step one foot into the kitchen without knowing what to make of the two women.

"Go finish watching cartoons, honey. I'll be right there."

"I never got my sandwich," she said, quietly.

"Oh, I'm sorry. Mommy had a phone call and then a visitor. It's there on the counter with a cup of milk. Can you take it back into the family room with you without spilling it?"

Kimmy nodded but was now looking at Devon.

"Go ahead," Havilland prodded her.

She slowly headed toward the kitchen counter and stood on her tip toes to reach for the small plate and sippy cup of milk. She held the cup in the crook of her arm and carefully balanced the plate with both hands.

"Good girl. I'll be right there."

Kimmy nodded but again looked to Devon, and the two seemed to engage in a staring contest.

"Kimberly!" Havilland's tone snapped her out of her daze, and she quickly turned and headed back into the family room. Havilland then looked to Devon, who was still staring after her child.

"Devon?"

Devon slowly turned back to face Havilland and smiled. "You have a very beautiful family." She pulled down her shades, grabbed for her purse, and left the house without another word.

CHAPTER THIRTY-SIX

Terrence paced back and forth in his office like a caged lion. He could feel the walls closing in on him.

What the hell was taking Havilland so damn long to get that ledger? He'd spoken to her two days ago. How hard was it to snag a book from the evidence locker? It drove him insane thinking about that ledger in the hands of the CBI because the information in there was his insurance, his bargaining chip, his lifeline.

"Mr. Miller. You have a call on line one."

His assistant's voice sounded through the intercom on his phone. Any other day, her soothing syrupy tone would be calming to him, but today, it irritated the hell out of him.

"I said no calls! Take a message."

"Yes, sir," came her clipped reply.

Screw this. He wasn't about to stand around like a fool waiting to be arrested. To hell with Robert Foxworth, Cirillo, the CBI, and the DEA. He had a forged passport with a new name and identity along with an emergency stash kept in a safe at home. No more thinking. He was gone. But what would he tell Devon? He had a passport for her, too, but would she agree to leave the country with him?

His phone vibrated on the desk, nearly causing him to jump out of his skin. He was on edge and needed to calm down. He snatched up his phone and swiped through it to find an incoming text from Havilland. A wave of relief swarmed him when he read her message.

I have it.

"It's about damn time," he muttered and rapidly texted her back to bring it to his home later that night. That would be perfect. He would go home now, pack, and hopefully Devon would be there, and he could somehow convince her to go with him. He was going to take the ledger, leave the country, and finish his deal with Havilland later. She would just have to understand.

He looked at his watch. It was nearly four-thirty, and if he left now, he could just make it to the bank and clear out his safety deposit box of cash. That, combined with the money in the safe at the house, would be more than enough to sustain him while he stayed hidden for a while.

After closing up his office and telling his assistant good night, Terrence pushed the speed limit as best he could in San Francisco traffic and made it from the industrial sights and sounds of Bayview to the Financial district in record time. He cleaned out his safety deposit box, and before he knew it, he'd returned to the more elite and exclusive views of Pacific Heights. But when he saw the town car and driver parked outside his home, he immediately got a feeling of foreboding. When he unlocked the front door, stepped over the threshold and heard his name, the feeling intensified. He turned to his right, where the sitting area was, and found not only Devon waiting but his father-in-law, as always, by her side and as always, looking disappointed.

"What's going on?" Terrence asked. He placed his briefcase full of cash on the floor, shrugged off his coat, and flung it onto the side of a corner armchair.

"Come sit down," Devon said sweetly and gestured with a hand to the sofa opposite her and her father. "Can I fix you a drink?"

"No," he said, taking a seat and then nodding toward his father-in-law. "Good to see you again so soon, Robert."

"To be honest, I never left. After that fiasco at the opening, I took a suite at the St. Regis to make sure things stayed running smoothly."

Terrence spread his arms. "Well as you can see, the CBI didn't have anything on me to convict me. I'm here and I'm running this side of the business just fine."

"Yes, but you see, my concern is the fact that you're being investigated in the first place," Robert said.

He was sitting on the arm of the sofa beside Devon and leaned forward.

"Do you really think having my vice-president led away in handcuffs is something my board of directors want to see?"

"I wasn't led away in handcuffs. Like I said, they have nothing."

"They must have something, or you wouldn't be under investigation! Before the week is out, I wouldn't be surprised if they found something to charge you with."

"And I bet you're just praying for that."

"Okay, enough!" Devon sliced a hand through the air and then turned to look up at Robert and put a hand on his knee. "Dad, Terrence is right. They haven't arrested him for whatever happened at the party and whatever the legal issues are, I'm sure our lawyers will take care of it. Besides all that, there was something else you wanted to talk to Terrence about, right?"

Robert looked at her for a long time, and Terrence could

see he didn't like the fact that she interrupted his rant. But after a moment, he visibly exhaled and patted her hand.

"I'm going to let the legal issues work themselves out. If you say I have nothing to worry about, I'll just have to trust your word on that. However, my job is to protect my business at all costs and keep the board and major stockholders satisfied. So, I'm going to have to force you to take a leave of absence until this investigation is settled."

Terrence couldn't stand the man, but at that moment, he could've kissed him. He just gave Terrence the excuse he needed to get out. Oh, he would do more than take a leave of absence. He was going to disappear.

"I hope you understand that I am well within my rights to fire you, but—"

"But then how would you and Devon control my every move if I went to work for someone else?"

Robert shot up. "You ungrateful little shit! I brought you into this family, into my business, and into my money only because my daughter wanted you. I've given you everything, and you turn around and embarrass us by getting yourself mixed up in some investigation."

Terrence rose as well and stepped toe to toe with him. "I wouldn't be mixed up in an investigation if someone didn't offer me up to the CBI in the first place."

Devon frowned. "What are you talking about?"

Terrence kept his eyes on Robert. "Do you want to tell her, or should I?"

Robert's face turned deadly.

"Dad?"

After a tense and awkward silence, he slowly turned to look at his daughter and when he did, his facial features magically transformed into something more congenial.

"I have no idea what he's talking about."

"That's what I thought," Terrence muttered.

Devon divided another confused look between them and then turned to her father. "Dad, can you give us a moment alone to talk?"

Robert nodded. "Fine. I'll be at my hotel. Call me when you're ready to go, and I'll have my driver pick you up on the way to the airport."

She nodded and accepted a kiss from him on the cheek. He walked past Terrence on his way out and didn't look at him at all.

As soon as the front door closed soundly, both Terrence and Devon spoke at the same time.

"Tell me what's going on, Terrence."

"Why are you going to the airport?"

She cocked her head to one side and looked impatient. "Answer my question first."

Instead of answering her, he went to the side bar, realizing he wanted that drink after all.

"Do you remember when we first got together?" Devon asked. "I told you that you would love this life. You would never want to go back to being a cop."

"I remember," he said, placing ice and pouring whiskey into a glass. "I remember because it was true. I knew from the moment I met you that you would be my ticket to a life of privilege. It's what I always wanted for myself. I'd been looking for a way out of law enforcement and living paycheck to paycheck, and there you were."

"But what about Havilland?"

He paused only slightly at the mention of her name and then turned with his drink in hand to look at her. Devon watched him hard, but his face remained stoic.

"What about her?"

"She wasn't as concerned with wealth and privilege like you were. She liked being a cop. Is that why you left her?"

"Among other things. We were growing apart."

"Are you sure about that?"

"What's this all about? You got something you want to ask me?"

"I know she's in San Francisco, and I know you've been seeing her."

He shrugged. "It's nothing important, and it's definitely nothing for you to be concerned about."

"If it's nothing, why didn't you just tell me about it?"

"All right, fine. Let's get it all out. I'll start. I'm not having an affair with her." He took a sip of his drink and nearly choked when she asked her next question.

"What about your daughter?"

"My daughter?"

"I know Havilland had a baby, and I did the math. She got pregnant when we were together, didn't she?"

"No," he said quickly and then sighed heavily, wishing this conversation could have come up at a more convenient time. "She was pregnant when she and I broke up, only I didn't know about it until she came to me a couple months after you and I started dating."

"And what did she say?"

"She told me she was going to have it, and that if I wanted to be in the baby's life, it was up to me. I didn't want a child. I told her how I felt, and never heard from her again. The next thing I heard, she'd moved out here to California to be near her mom."

Devon scoffed and began pacing the room.

"What's your problem?" he asked.

"My problem is my husband can't tell me what is going on and as his wife, I get every excuse in the book about why it's the worst time for us to have a baby—"

"Are you serious?"

"And yet, he has no problem making a baby with his ex-girlfriend! I've seen that little girl.

. . .

Take away all of Havilland's features, and I can see you in her."

"I never meant to have a baby with her."

"But you were never going to tell me, either."

"If you had come to me, I never would've denied it. I may not have wanted to be a father, but I wouldn't deny having a child."

"Is that why you're really here? Did you jump at the opportunity to move us out here because you knew Havilland and your daughter were out here?"

"No, that's not it at all, and I didn't tell you about Kimberly because for one, I don't have a relationship with her, and I knew it would hurt you because you wanted a baby."

They were quiet for a while until Terrence realized what she'd said. "When did you see her?"

Devon looked uncomfortable for a minute and then seemed to shore up her confidence. "I went to see Havilland."

"What? Why the hell would you do that?"

"To find out what was going on with you two!"

"Nothing!" he shouted. "There's nothing there!"

"No, there absolutely is something there. I have pictures, and I saw the way you look at her! I just wanted answers."

He stared at her, dumbfounded. "You had me followed? You thought we were...You know what? Forget it. I don't have time for this. I came home to ask you to go away with me, but I see you have other plans with your father."

She nodded. "I'm going back to Atlanta while you're on your leave of absence, and I want you to come with me."

"No. I have a better idea. Leave the country with me. We'll travel for a few months around the world."

Devon stared at him in disbelief and then let out a laugh. "Travel the world a few months? We can't do that. What about your work?"

"Screw that job. I'm on a leave of absence anyway."

"Screw that job? You mean my business that I will one day inherit? You want to walk away from a mid-six-figure position to go play for a few months?"

He didn't have the heart to tell her it would be more than a few months. With the way she was reacting, he was glad he didn't tell her it just might be forever.

She shook her head and left the room to head for the stairs. "Stop talking crazy. I need to finish packing. The flight leaves at nine-thirty, so you should get upstairs and pack too. I expect to see you on that plane with me tonight."

"Were you ever in love with me?"

He'd followed her out of the living room, and she paused just as one heel touched the first step of the staircase.

She turned around slowly. "Why would you ask me that?"

He shrugged one shoulder. "Sometimes I wonder if I'm just a do over for you. Maybe even a consolation prize." He came toward her. "Was there someone else? Someone you really wanted? Someone who maybe wasn't as easily tempted by you, your father, and the promises of"—he paused and waved his glass of whiskey around their opulent surroundings—"all of this."

The slightest flicker in her eyes told him he'd struck a chord somewhere close to the truth, but she was an expert at masking her feelings, because in the next instant, it was gone and he questioned if he'd even seen it in the first place.

"We all have a past, don't we?" she asked and then tossed his words back at him. "Did you ever love *me*?"

Terrence sighed, realizing they'd once again hopped on

that old merry-go-round, but this time, he wasn't going to play with her. "Truthfully, Devon, I love the life you gave me."

A shimmer of tears came to her eyes, but rather than let them fall, she remained composed and dignified. "That's what I thought. Well, if you want to keep it, be on that plane at nine-thirty."

With that, she turned and he listened to the sound of her heels stomping up the stairs. He swirled the ice in his glass and thought about how he'd arrived at this very moment, beginning with the day he and Havilland were reunited.

* * *

October 2019

"When you asked me to lunch, I figured it would be at some cozy bar and grill," Havilland said, looking around the spacious dining area.

Servers strolled by dressed in uniforms that reminded her of tuxedos, the table linens and napkins were cloth, the champagne was served in crystal stemware, and she was pretty sure there was a sound requirement because she could barely hear the conversation of the couple beside them.

Terrence looked around sheepishly. "Yeah, it's pretty fancy, but I take a lot of clients to lunch and dinner here that I hardly notice it anymore. Plus, they know me very well, so I always get a good table."

She smiled, unwrapped the cloth napkin, and placed it on her lap. "This never used to be your style, but I see a lot can change in five years."

He nodded and leaned forward, placing his forearms on the table. "Speaking of changes, imagine my surprise when I see you came to visit Stephen with not only your father, but your daughter."

She didn't respond but looked at him across the table as the server poured them both glasses of Pellegrino.

"Are you ready to order lunch, Mr. Miller?" he asked.

"Give us just a minute," Terrence said.

"Of course."

He waited until their server was gone before continuing. "Were you never going to tell me you had her?"

"You didn't want children, Terrence. But I did," she said. "Why did I need to tell you?"

"You're right, I didn't want a baby, but she is my daughter."

Havilland shook her head slowly. "She already has a father."

"Fine," he said, sitting back. "I deserve that, but I would at least like to meet her."

"I'll think about it, but how about you tell me why you asked me out to lunch. From the tone of your voice, it didn't sound like a friendly catch-up."

He reached for his own cloth napkin, unraveled it, but proceeded to clench it between his hands. "Your brother tells me you work for the California Bureau of Investigation."

"That's right."

He looked around, ensuring there was no one close enough to overhear their conversation and report back to Robert or Devon.

"Do you ever have contact with other agencies like the GBI?"

Havilland shrugged. "Sometimes, there are interagency communications if the case warrants it. Why?"

He paused.

"Terrence, what is it?"

"I'm going to ask you for a huge favor, Hav. You have no reason to help me given the way things ended between us, but I'm hoping you'll at least think about it." He hesitated, looked around the exquisite restaurant once more and then stared at her, certain that he looked as desperate as he felt.

"I'm in trouble."

* * *

The cell phone buzzing in his trousers brought Terrence out of his memories and back to the present. He put down the glass of whiskey on a nearby table and fished the phone out of his pocket, checked the display, and frowned before answering.

"What is it?" he asked.

"Rafael wants to see you," Stephen responded immediately. "He's been trying to reach you all afternoon, but you haven't been answering your phone. That made him nervous."

Terrence pinched the bridge of his nose. He had been purposely ignoring Cirillo's calls because he was too busy making plans to leave the country.

"All right, where are you?"

"I'm on my way to the pier now."

"Give me twenty minutes."

He hung up the phone and fought the urge to holler out a string of curses. Instead, he grabbed his keys and called up the stairs to Devon.

"Devon! I'll be back in an hour."

He didn't receive a response from her and wasn't even sure if she'd heard him or not, but it was all fine to him. He preferred to leave without a bunch of questions being tossed at him, especially when he had no answers to give her.

CHAPTER THIRTY-SEVEN

Three hours later...

Maya was livid. She'd been waiting in this big empty mansion for the past half hour, and he still hadn't shown up. She knew how to cut the feed to the video cameras outside and did so before picking the lock to the French patio doors and letting herself inside. He said he would be there, but she wanted to catch him off guard in case he tried to pull a fast one on her. She'd come to distrust him these past few weeks. She'd seen one too many signs that he was just dicking her around until he could find a way to cut ties with her. Just like now. He promised he'd be there, so where was he, and more importantly, where was her damn money?

Sitting there in the quiet den, she thoroughly regretted ever getting involved in this plan. She should've just stayed on the side of the law. The side where Eric was. But after working with him for years and seeing him choose one woman after another over her, she was done. First Christina, which wasn't a big deal because everyone knew Christina had no business being an agent. When she finally realized it herself and resigned as well as ended her relationship with Eric, Maya was ecstatic that she'd get another chance with him. But nearly a year went by and he just wasn't interested. She started to think that maybe Christina really did a number on him, but then Havilland joined the CBI and Eric only had eyes for her.

But Maya considered herself anything but a quitter. She backed off and allowed Eric to enjoy wedded bliss, but she still kept an eye on Havilland because something told her the woman was hiding something.

And she was. Yet with every fragment of proof Maya gave to Eric showing him that his wife was corrupt, he continued to sweep it under the rug. The man was blinded by loyalty— or was it love? Either way, she was done protecting him. And now with this latest event, she wondered just what Eric planned to do. Havilland was caught stealing evidence. That was grounds for termination as well as criminal charges, and if he let it go, Maya would be forced to report him to Hewitt and Hewitt's boss. That saddened her because not only did she care for him deeply but she knew that going to Carl Hewitt about this would bring Eric up for disciplinary action too. Carl still believed Eric broke Christina's heart, forcing her to resign from the agency, and he would give anything to exact his revenge on Eric.

But as much as she'd fantasized about being with Eric, she'd fantasized about his position more. She would love to be Special Agent in Charge.

She spun slightly in the leather desk chair and then sighed aloud. She reached into her pocket for her cell and then pulled it out to dial a number she knew by heart. There was no way she was saving his name in her contacts.

The phone rang and rang, and she felt her blood pressure rise when she got voicemail. She was done playing his game, and it was about time she taught him a lesson.

"I know what you're up to," she started as soon as the recording beep sounded. "You're trying to fuck me over, but it's not happening. I'm going to arrest that bitch Havilland, and then you're next."

She pressed *end*, deleted the number from her call log, and stood to leave.

"Bastard," she muttered, but just before she exited through the French doors, she heard a faint sound from somewhere in the house.

She turned around and perked her ears up to listen. Someone was heading toward the den where she was.

That asshole. Had he been there the entire time?

"Is that you? I'm in here!" she called. "I've been waiting long enough, and you'd better have the money I earned by keeping you out of prison!"

CHAPTER THIRTY-EIGHT

Havilland bypassed the front door of the mansion and crept around to the rear of the home just as Terrence had instructed her. She came to the back patio, and there, just like he'd said were a pair of French doors, which would be left unlocked for her. What he hadn't told her was that the doors would be wide open with one of the glass panels shattered.

Instinct and training instantly brought Havilland's gun from her holster to her hands along with her flashlight. She turned in a full circle, searching her surroundings and straining her eyes and ears for any sign of movement, but she only saw the trees in the backyard and beyond those were the darkened waters of the bay and the now shadowed structure of Alcatraz.

She braced herself against the outside wall of the home and used only her head to quickly peek around the corner and then shined her flashlight into the room that led directly from the patio.

"This is Special Agent Sawyer with the CBI," she called. "Is there anyone inside?"

Silence.

She stepped one sneakered foot inside the room, wincing at the sound of crushed and broken glass beneath her shoe. She stepped another foot inside and swung the flashlight from corner to corner. Judging from the desk placed in the center of the room and the bookshelves that lined the walls, she could see she was in the den. She reached for a desk lamp and yanked the chain over and over, but only the insistent clicking sound returned with no light to fill the room.

Where was Terrence?

Havilland moved through the room with her gun and flashlight leading the way, all the while keeping her back close to the wall for cover. She didn't get too far because as soon as she rounded the other side of the desk, her foot kicked something heavy and immovable. She shined her flashlight down and trailed it along a body lying motionless and then immediately backed away in shock as familiar and now dead, sightless eyes stared up at her.

No. It can't be.

Maya's head was turned in an awkward position, indicating her neck had been broken. Havilland took several deep breaths to compose herself and then knelt down and checked for a pulse. When she didn't find one, panic seized her, and somewhere in her head a voice was screaming at her to get out of there. Fast. No one could know she had been there. She could hurry back to her car, drive a few blocks down the street, and make an anonymous 911 call. But that plan was swept away the moment she heard something that told her she was not alone in this big house.

Havilland looked up from the body on full alert, absolutely certain her ears weren't deceiving her and that what she'd heard was the slightest creak of a heavy footstep on a wooden floorboard. She stood to her feet, and her arm came up again as she aimed for the darkness from where the noise had come.

"Come out now, and show me your hands."

Her heart was beating fast as adrenaline coursed through her. Add to that, she was fearful, not because of the danger she may be in but the possibility that she was going to have to subdue and arrest whoever this was and then later explain how she happened to be in Terrence and Devon Miller's home.

The sound of movement grew louder and more distinct. Whoever was there was slowly following her instructions, and she held her breath, keeping her gun aimed in the direction of their footsteps. When they finally came into view, their body was cast in shadow, but she could see the outline of a tall man with his arms extended and aiming something right back at her.

"Drop it!" she commanded as her finger slightly brushed the trigger. "I said drop it now!"

Just as she was about to shoot, the man spoke and the instant familiarity of his voice sent a renewed dose of fear straight up her spine.

"No, Hav. You drop it."

She stared wide-eyed and mouth agape as the man stepped forward, shedding the darkness around him.

"Eric?"

"Yeah," he said, his voice level and cold. He stepped closer with his gun still trained on her. "Now slowly put down your weapon and face the wall. You're under arrest."

"Eric—"

"Save it."

"Don't do this, let me explain."

"You've had weeks to explain to me what the hell you've been up to, now time's up. I don't want to hear anything you have to say."

He took one dangerous step toward her, aiming his gun at the center of her chest. "I said drop your fucking weapon and face the wall. Now!"

She kept her gun raised for one tension-filled moment and then slowly lowered her arms and dropped the gun. It landed with a thud on the carpeted floor between them.

"The bag too," he commanded.

She did so and then turned with her hands raised and faced the wall. In the next instant, she heard Eric's footsteps come up behind her. He pushed her against the wall, grabbed one arm, and then the other to pull behind her back and handcuff her wrists together.

"Havilland Sawyer. You're under arrest for evidence tampering and theft."

She leaned her forehead against the wall and closed her eyes, listening to him read her Miranda rights. But after several agonizing moments, he stopped speaking, and she thought maybe she zoned out from shock. But then he turned her around to face him, looked her in the eyes, and slowly pressed his forehead against hers.

"Why, Hav?" he asked and then slammed a hand against the wall behind her. "Why?"

"I didn't do it," she said. "I didn't kill her."

He stepped back, bent to the ground where her messenger bag lay, and slid his hand inside to pull out the ledger.

"You're going to tell me you didn't take this, either?" he asked, shoving the book in her face.

Without waiting for an answer, he turned and threw the ledger against the opposite wall. The sound of the book smacking against the wall coupled with a rage she had never seen in him made her jump.

"Maya knew what you were doing," he said. "She was planning to report you. She got tired of me protecting you and was going to Hewitt about you. Your career was over, and now here she is dead at our feet."

"I didn't do it. Yes, I know she found out what I'd done, but I would never have killed her. Please believe me. There's so much I want to tell you, but I can't!"

"You know, honey, I don't really give a rat's ass about any of that right now," he said, his voice dripping with sarcasm and fury. "All I want to know is where's Terrence?"

"I don't know."

"Don't give me that! You were here to meet him to give him that ledger. Where. Is. He?"

"I said I don't know!"

He stepped back and shook his head in aggravation. "It's Atlanta all over again, only this time, an agent is dead, and if you didn't do it, then he did. Did you tip him off? Is that why he's not here?"

She leaned against the wall and eyed him with malice. "What's the matter with you?"

"Are you seriously asking me that? My wife is protecting a goddamn criminal! She's stealing evidence, and I need to decide if I'm going to put her, Kimmy's mom, behind bars or as always, let her get away with it!"

"Oh, please! Come down off that cross, Eric. You never saved my ass for me. You did it for yourself," she said, an accusatory bite in her voice. "God forbid your name loses any of its shine!"

That seemed to stun him, and she didn't know what made her speak so freely, but she did know that it was the most honest she'd been with him in months.

"Never mind," she mumbled.

He folded his arms across his chest. "No, go on. You got something on your mind? Say it!"

She narrowed her eyes and accepted his dare. "You're so concerned with keeping your name and career free of blemishes, and that includes me. I may not have been an agent as long as you, but I've been in law enforcement for just as many years, and sometimes this job gets dirty. Sometimes, I get dirty, but I do my job!"

"You really feel that way? You really think I'm just protecting my name?"

"I'm the one in handcuffs, aren't I?" she asked, twisting around slightly to show him the cuffs on her wrists. "Not you, Mr. Perfect who arrived here before me. What were *you* doing here? How do I know you didn't—"

She shut her mouth before she nearly said it—something she could never take back. But his look told her he already knew what she was going to say.

"Eric, I—"

"Forget it."

He closed the space between them and without explanation, turned her around and grabbed her wrists. In the next instant, she felt the handcuffs fall off, and he was ushering her out of the house.

"Go home," he said, once they were outside.

"What are you going to do?" she asked, rubbing the feeling back into her wrists.

"I have to call this in."

"Then what?"

"Then, I'm going to handle things. Don't worry. It's not the first time I've covered for you."

She narrowed her eyes at him, but he ignored her and pulled out his cell phone to make a call.

"This is Special Agent in Charge Eric Sawyer. We have an agent down. I repeat, agent down. I need backup at…"

Eric began to relay the address to dispatch, and Havilland looked around, wondering what would happen next. She still didn't know where Terrence was and if it was really him who killed Maya. What had she been doing there in the first place?

She was pondering that question when something Eric said snapped her attention right back to him.

"Put an APB out for Terrence Miller and take Stephen Currin into protective custody."

She stepped up to him. "Eric, what are you doing?"

"Not now," he said, ending his call and slipping his phone into his back pocket.

"I want to know what's going on."

"And I want you to get in your car and get out of here. This place will be swarming with agents very soon. How are you going to explain why you're here?"

"How are *you*?" she asked.

He shook his head. "Havilland, go."

"Not until you tell me what my brother has to do with this."

"He turned state's evidence against Terrence Miller weeks ago. He's a Confidential Informant. All right?"

"Did he come to you?"

"No, I offered it to him after Robert Foxworth gave us his name as someone involved in Terrence's drug trafficking scheme."

She shook her head. "Robert Foxworth? Eric, listen to me, you can't have Stephen as a CI."

"He's already a CI. He's already given statements and evidence. Your brother is deeply involved."

"You're using him."

She could see he was losing patience with her. "I didn't hold a gun to his head, and I'll see to it he gets immunity. It's not my fault he got involved with Miller. Seems like the two of you can't resist that guy."

"I want him released, Eric. If it ever gets out that he's working with the CBI—"

"Why should it get out? Who's going to tell? You?"

"Really? You'd think I'd rat on my own brother?"

"You've been interfering with this case from the very beginning!" he shouted. "What else am I supposed to think?"

She stepped up to him, pleading with her eyes. "Maybe I can't stop you from walking away from this investigation, but I don't want my brother involved anymore. Promise me you'll let him go."

His eyes remained cold. "I can't promise that, because I'm not going to do it."

"This case is really that important to you?"

"No, an arrest is what's really important to me."

"What about you and me? Is our marriage important?"

"One has nothing to do with the other."

"Yes, it does! The deeper you get into this case and the harder you go for Terrence's arrest, the further we grow apart. You have this obsession, and it's affecting your judgment."

Without warning, he grasped her forearm and drew her into him, hissing angrily in her face. "You're damn right I have an obsession, and whose fault is that? If you don't like what's going on, then maybe you shouldn't have had your fucking lips on him."

Tears came to her eyes, but before she allowed them to fall, she shoved him away from her hard and he backed up, letting her storm past him down the stone walkway. She got into her car and tires squealed as she pulled from the curb and sped away.

CHAPTER THIRTY-NINE

"I'm sorry I'm late," he said, sliding into the booth. "It's been a long night, and I got away as soon as I could."

"Eric, it's okay." Christina leaned forward in the booth and clutched his hand. "Dad called and told me about Agent Landon's death. I'm so sorry."

"Thank you. With me calling her parents, questioning Robert Foxworth, and speaking to my team, I should've just done this another day."

"No, because it would've been on your mind, and you probably wouldn't have gotten any sleep tonight," she said, smiling sympathetically. "I'm here. Let me just tell you what I've found, and you can take it with you and read over my notes later."

He nodded and for the first time that evening, he felt his shoulders slump from the weight he'd been carrying from the moment he confronted Havilland at the Miller's mansion.

Things had been in a whirlwind ever since Maya's body was taken to the morgue. Eric and a team of agents took several state-issued vehicles and raced to San Francisco airport to detain Terrence Miller for questioning. But the only one they found was Robert Foxworth, waiting impatiently for his daughter. They escorted him and his attorney off his private plane to Atlanta and explained that Terrence was at large and wanted for questioning in the death of a CBI agent. When Eric asked the whereabouts of Devon, Robert Foxworth flew into a rage, admitting she never made it to the airport.

"This is ridiculous! Instead of wasting your time questioning me, you need to find that thieving bastard. He's run off, and he's taken Devon with him, and most likely by force."

"What makes you think it was by force?" Eric asked.

"She was ready to leave here and return to Atlanta. I was going to have my driver bring her to the airport, but she never called. I've tried calling her several times, but she doesn't answer. She may not always answer my calls, but she damn sure returns them. Now, her phone is going straight to voicemail. God knows what he's done with her. I'm telling you, something is wrong."

"When was the last time you saw or spoke to your son-in-law?"

"He came home around five-thirty this afternoon. Devon and I were there waiting for him, and I told him I was putting him on a leave of absence because of this whole investigation. We had a few words, and then Devon asked me to leave to give them some privacy. That was the last time I saw either him or my daughter."

"I appreciate you doing this so quickly for me," Eric said as Christina laid the photocopied pages of the ledger in front of him beside their cups of coffee. "I know you have other clients and work to do."

"It's fine," she said laughing. "I owed you for being so patient with me. You knew from the start that the CBI wasn't for me. I belonged in the private sector, and only you had the guts to tell me to my face something I've known all along. And you got my father's wrath for it."

"I can handle it." He shrugged. "So, what did you find?"

"Something very important. You can see he's definitely hiding money. Any competent accountant can decipher these figures. He's not making it a secret that he's embezzling from the company. He has the account numbers and the names of the shell corporations that are hiding the money. He also has the list of the buyers, the materials they purchase, and the weight."

"What are you saying?" Eric asked. "That he was trying to get caught?"

Christina paused and looked up at Eric with a frown. "Maybe not trying to get caught, but he must've known that if this ledger ever fell into the hands of the authorities, it would be more than enough to prove his illegal dealings."

He looked at the photocopies she pushed across the table toward him, and wondered why Terrence would have his accountant create such an easy trail to decipher that led straight to Terrence's own guilt. As Christina explained the figures he was looking at in layman's terms, something didn't sit well with him. He understood everything she was saying, but something was off about the figures she was showing him.

"Hold on a minute," he said, going into his briefcase and pulling out the ledger he'd taken from the scene of Maya's murder. He'd taken it from Havilland and then threw it across the room in a blind rage at her blatant deceit. After she left the Miller's home, he went back inside, grabbed the ledger, and put it inside his car before the other agents and EMTs arrived at the scene.

He opened it and flipped to the pages Christina was referencing, and immediately saw what had him confused. His eyes glanced back and forth from the ledger to the photocopies several times to be sure he wasn't hallucinating.

"These aren't the same numbers."

"What?" she asked. "What do you mean?"

He flipped the ledger around so that she could see for herself.

"Compare the numbers in the ledger to the photocopied pages. They're all off."

She did so, and after several minutes, she looked up at him, wearing the same confused expression as him.

"What's going on?" she asked. "Which one is right?"

Eric frowned as he attempted to review the timeline of events in his head. That Saturday morning, after Christina agreed to help him, she and her boys followed him and Kimmy home where he retrieved the journal and then went to the office store to photocopy the pages for her to examine. The journal then remained in his safe the rest of the weekend until Monday morning when he checked it into evidence.

"You have the photocopied pages of the ledger I got from Terrence's safe the night of the party. I kept it with me all night, locked in my own safe at home. There's no chance anyone could've gotten to it and tampered with it. Havilland doesn't even have the combination."

"So, these pages are from the original ledger. But that means…"

He looked at the leather-bound journal between them. "This one is a forgery."

He assimilated the rest to himself. Havilland, never would've attempted to steal a forged ledger from the evidence room. Someone else on his team must have switched the ledgers early Monday morning after he checked it into evidence. But who, and just as important, why?

"You said this guy wasn't stupid, but maybe he should consider firing his accountant," Christina said.

Eric focused his attention on her again. "What do you mean?"

"The photocopies don't have this information, but this

ledger, the forgery, is showing actual bank account numbers. It would literally take two seconds to find out who those account numbers belong to."

He stared at her in disbelief. "So, someone replaced the original ledger with this fake one, and not only do we have proof that my suspect is receiving money from illegal goods, but I also have proof that he's depositing it all into his personal accounts."

She nodded. "If you go by the forged ledger, you have this guy dead to rights. Your case came gift-wrapped with a pretty bow." She paused to frown. "I may not be an agent anymore, but I still have instincts, and Eric, that smells like a setup."

* * *

When he pulled into the driveway, he didn't see her car. It wasn't parked in the garage either, and neither was Jeanetta's car. He pulled out his cell to first dial Jeanetta, but after a brief conversation, he discovered Kimmy wasn't with her.

"Is everything all right, Mr. Sawyer?" Jeanetta asked.

"Oh yeah, sure. Everything's fine. Hav probably had to make a late run to the store or something and took Kimmy with her."

"Okay, well call me if you need anything."

"Thanks," he said and quickly disconnected the call.

That excuse he gave her sounded like bullshit to his own ears. He dialed Havilland's phone and cursed when it went straight to voicemail. He quickly got out of the car, leaving his files and briefcase inside. He raced up the porch steps, unlocked the door, and let himself inside.

"Hav," he immediately called out on the off chance she was home, but the house was still and empty.

He went up the stairs two at a time and with one glance at

Kimmy's room door ajar, he knew she wouldn't be in there. She liked her door closed when she slept because the starlit night light they gave her would swirl around her entire room. Her bed was empty, and as much as he hated the thought, something told him to check her bureau drawer and closet. The bureau drawer had some clothes in it, but it was sparse. A look in the closet told him her Doc McStuffins suitcase was gone, and Eric felt the first sense of fear shoot up his spine.

He left Kimmy's room and went across the hall to the master bedroom. He crossed to the closet and threw it open only to find it just as sparse as Kimmy's closet, and Havilland's luggage was gone too. With one last semblance of hope, he went to the dresser they shared, but before he could pull open a drawer, he saw the note with his name taped to the mirror. With hands slightly trembling, he removed the note, unfolded it and read Havilland's cursive.

Eric,

Kimmy and I are fine. We'll be staying with my mom for the time being. I won't be at work for the rest of this week. I know what you did for me was at great risk to your career, but I need you to believe that everything I've done was for good reason, and I will explain everything in time. I love you, and I hope when this is all over, we can...I don't know. I just wish things didn't get so fucked up.

Hav

He sat down on the edge of the bed and read it again, then slowly lay down on the bed, clutching the note in his hands and thinking about all the nights he left her alone in this room.

CHAPTER FORTY

November 2020

"I'm sorry for popping up like this. I know you're here to spend time with your family."

"It's okay," Havilland said, stepping out onto the porch into the sunlight. "What's going on?"

Terrence stood there with his hands braced on the porch railing. He was dressed casually in designer jeans, white sneakers, and a pressed white polo shirt that looked great with his complexion.

"I may be moving to San Francisco," he said.

Havilland's eyes widened in disbelief. "What?"

"Yeah. My father-in-law is expanding the business and wants to begin operations in California."

"Does Holladay know?"

Terrence shook his head. "No, because it's not confirmed. But I'm telling you as a heads up. So, hopefully if all goes well, you won't have to hop on an airplane to do me favors anymore. Thanks to you, the GBI dropped their case."

Havilland felt her stomach growing queasy. This wasn't good news for her at all. Terrence being twenty-five hundred miles away in Georgia was one thing, but Terrence in her backyard was something else entirely. How was she supposed to keep this kind of thing from Eric?

"You're worried," he correctly guessed.

"Yeah, I am."

He pulled away from the porch railing and stepped toward her. "Hav, nothing has to change. In fact, everything will be a lot simpler with me close by." He paused and shrugged. "Maybe I can even see Kimberly once in a while."

The look she gave him made him put his hands up in surrender. "Or not."

"You haven't been in her life since birth. She doesn't know you, and you didn't want her to begin with."

"So, I guess people can't grow and change."

"Not you," she said.

"Touché. All right. It was wrong of me to behave that way. I know you have a family and she has a father she knows and loves. I'm not trying to interfere with that."

She wanted to keep her guard up around him, but maybe the issues he'd been facing had humbled him in some way.

"I was wrong about a lot of things, Hav."

The tenor in his voice suddenly changed. It was still the same deep baritone, but what was once firm, clipped, and no-nonsense was now soft, comforting, and melodic. She hadn't heard that tone in years, but she knew what it meant and now looked at him warily.

"Is this confession time?"

He stepped closer. "I just wanted you to know that I'm sorry for the way I treated you. Hell, I'm sorry for everything. You shouldn't have had to pick up and move across the country because I was being a jackass."

She held up her index finger. "My move wasn't because of you. I'd always had plans to move out to California to be near my mom. When I found out I was pregnant and we seemed to be at the end of our relationship, it made the decision easier."

"Still, maybe if I hadn't been so stupid, then..."

He trailed off and Havilland shrugged her shoulders. "Then what? We'd be together?" She sighed. "Terrence, trust me. We would've eventually made each other miserable. It's much better this way."

"Is it?" he asked, and before she could form a response he took her by the waist, pulled her toward him, and kissed her.

She was completely immobilized with shock. This wasn't Eric kissing her; this was Terrence. *No!*

She started to raise her hands to shove him away, when all of a sudden, she didn't feel his arm around her waist anymore. His lips weren't pressed against hers anymore, and she was no longer suffocating from shock, confusion, and outrage. The relief she felt nearly brought her to tears. But then she saw what, or actually who, had pulled him away from her.

Eric caught Terrence off guard and managed to send several punches to his face, before Terrence recovered and began fighting back, landing several blows of his own.

"Both of you, stop!" Havilland screamed as they tumbled off the porch and were now on the lawn. She followed after them, but getting in between two adult men fighting was dangerous. She shouted for help and in seconds, Stephen and her father, Anthony, came out of the house and finally succeeded in breaking them apart.

"What the hell's going on here?" Anthony shouted. "Why are you two out here fighting?"

Eric and Terrence stood there breathing heavily and exchanging murderous glances. Both had obviously gotten the better of each other as Terrence held his side and was sporting a rapidly swelling eye while Eric was trying to nurse a bloody nose with a busted bottom lip.

"My apologies, Mr. Currin. There seems to have been a misunderstanding," Terrence said on shallow breaths.

"You're fucking right about that," Eric spat.

Havilland pulled a tissue from her pocket and was trying to help him stop the bleeding, but he only snatched the tissue from her and attempted to nurse himself.

"I'm sorry to cause a disturbance. I'll leave." Terrence paused to take one last look at Eric. "I'll see you around, Agent Sawyer."

"Yeah, look me up the next time you're in San Francisco. I'm not hard to find."

Terrence smiled through his swelling eye and sent him a mock salute. He then spared a momentary glance for Havilland and then turned to walk down the street to his car.

"I'll get you a towel and some ice for that lip," Stephen said and hurried back into the house.

"Mommy?"

They all turned and saw Kimmy standing behind the screen door.

Eric hissed an expletive and immediately turned away to shield his injuries from Kimmy's eyes. "I don't want her to see me like this."

"Stay there, honey," Havilland said.

"Is that Daddy?"

"I've got her," Anthony said. "You two stay here. I won't let her come out."

He walked back up to the porch steps, opened the door, and picked Kimmy up, carrying her farther back into the house and tickling her.

As her giggles faded away, Stephen reemerged and handed Eric a clean towel and ice pack.

"Thanks," Eric said.

"Don't mention it." Stephen looked between the two of

them, but Havilland gave him a glare, silently telling him to go away.

He nodded and walked back into the house. When they were finally alone, she put her hand on his arm and tried to assess the damage, but Eric instantly pulled out of her grasp and gave her a look that told her to back away. She did so but still had questions she wanted answers to.

"When I texted you an hour ago, you said you were about to go in a meeting. Obviously, that wasn't true. Were you trying to surprise us?"

"No, I was coming to see if it was all true."

"If what was true?"

"You're feeding him confidential information." The bleeding seemed to have stopped, so Eric took the towel from his nose and grabbed for the bag he'd dropped in his attempt to get at Terrence. He pulled a file from it and handed it to her. "Your movements haven't gone unnoticed. The GBI has contacts in California, but thank God, someone alerted me about this before it got to our bosses."

She read through the file and suddenly felt faint. In the back of her mind, she knew this could happen yet believed she was being careful at covering her tracks. But staring up at her were reports linking her Agency ID to the GBI's case against Terrence Miller.

"They were investigating him," he said, "and by giving him access to information, you just succeeded in getting the GBI's case to blow up in their faces. Or was that your plan the whole time?"

She looked up at Eric and saw a fury in his eyes she'd never seen before. This was more than just about her feeding Terrence information. He'd seen him kissing her.

"I was about to push him away. I never expected him to kiss me."

He said nothing, but the fury didn't lessen.

"I don't love him, Eric. I love you."

"Then why are you doing this?" he asked, gesturing to the file in her hands.

She opened her mouth and closed it several times, unsure of what to tell

him.

"Are you going to answer me?"

"It's not what you think."

"Then what is it?"

"I can't talk about it now, but if you just give me some time. Wait—listen to me!"

He was grabbing his bag off the curb and walking away. "I'm catching the next flight

back home."

"Eric, wait," she said, trying to grab ahold of him again. "Let me get our things packed.

Kimmy and I are coming with you."

"No. I don't want to have to explain bruises and a bloody nose to her, and"—he paused

and she saw despair and regret fill his eyes—"Christ, Hav, I can't be around you right now."

* * *

"Mommy?"

Havilland came away from the events of that day and found Kimmy looking up at her.

"Yes?"

"When are we going back home?"

"Are you tired of me already?" Lola was cleaning up the breakfast dishes and turned to look at Kimmy with mock sadness.

"No!" Kimmy said with childlike shock. "I just miss Daddy."

Havilland smiled through the ache in her heart. "I know you do, and it won't be much longer. Can you just be a little more patient?"

Kimmy nodded, but there was still sadness in her eyes. Havilland leaned over and kissed her soft cheek and whispered into her ear. "Thank you."

When she ran off, Havilland turned to find her mother staring at her.

"Have you talked to Stephen?" Havilland asked.

"Never mind Stephen. He can take care of himself. What about you and Eric? He's called here every day this week and spoke to Kimmy. It's been five days. When are you going to speak to him?"

"I can't talk to him until I can tell him everything. I've kept a lot of secrets from him these past few months, and we're at our breaking point. I don't want to lie to him anymore, Mom. He still won't listen to me about Atlanta and now with this investigation involving Terrence—"

Lola sighed heavily. "Why did you ever—"

"He needed my help. That's all I can say. Trust me, no one wants this whole thing over with more than me."

Lola nodded and her eyes turned sympathetic. "I know you do, Hav."

CHAPTER FORTY-ONE

Nearly a week had passed since Maya's brutal murder, and the department was still in a flood of confusion. Eric was balancing calls from his superiors as well as holding meetings with his agents and requesting hourly updates on the whereabouts of Terrence Miller. Now, he was on his way to a meeting with Carl Hewitt and Hewitt's boss with nothing to tell them.

"Sir, the deputy director of the DEA is here to see you."

Eric was gathering file folders for his meeting and looked up at Elena with a frown. "The DEA? Did we have a meeting scheduled?"

She shook her head. "He doesn't have an appointment. I told him you were busy, but—"

"It's okay. I have a few minutes." He glanced down at his watch and then up at the door to his office as Elena escorted in a man with his similar height and build wearing a dark-gray suit.

"I'm Agent David Holladay, Deputy Director of the San Francisco DEA."

Eric grasped the man's hand for a firm shake and

gestured for him to sit down. "What can I do for you, Agent Holladay?"

"Well, I told your assistant I needed to speak with Agent Sawyer, but I guess I should've been more clear. I'm actually looking for Havilland Sawyer."

A pain he hadn't expected welled up in Eric's chest at the very mention of her name. She wasn't home. Kimmy wasn't home. His family wasn't home.

"I'm her husband. She'll be out for the rest of the week, but if it's important I can pass the message along to her."

If she'll take my calls.

"You're Eric Sawyer?" David asked and then nodded slowly. "That explains a few things."

Eric frowned at the cryptic response and realized he didn't have time for this.

"I don't mean to be rude, but if this isn't urgent, you'll have to excuse me. We're dealing with a lot around here today. One of our agents was murdered almost a week ago, and we have a missing suspect."

"Yes, I saw the picture and announcement in the lobby downstairs. Agent Maya Landon. Please accept my condolences."

"Thank you."

"But before you have your assistant walk me out, maybe you can tell me how I can reach Agent Sawyer. She's not answering her cell phone, and I've lost contact with my witness who is also her CI."

Eric's brow furrowed again. "CI? Hav—I mean, Agent Sawyer doesn't have a CI. She has a case that's pending, but she hasn't even interviewed witnesses for it, yet."

"No, the case I'm referring to has been underway for almost a year. It has to do with Foxworth Pharmaceuticals."

Eric could feel his fists begin to tighten. What the hell had she done now? Did she really tell a DEA deputy director that she was part of this case to get information?

"Agent Holladay, we have a task force already established for Foxworth Pharmaceuticals. We're even close to an arrest, but since Agent Landon's death, he's been missing, and we've been chasing our tails ever since, trying to locate him."

David narrowed his eyes. "Who's the suspect?"

"Terrence Miller."

He stared at Eric in what looked like disbelief. "You're not serious."

"Yeah, I'm serious. He's been under investigation for stealing, trafficking, and selling narcotics ingredients from his father-in-law's company."

David lowered his head, and a string of expletives raced from his lips in undertone. "That's what had her so upset."

"Say that again?" Eric asked.

David raised his head to look up at Eric. "That's what had Agent Sawyer so upset. The last time I spoke to her, she sounded as if she was coming undone, but she wouldn't tell me what the problem was. Now it all makes sense."

Eric had had enough. "What makes sense? What are you talking about?"

David expelled a long sigh. "Your investigation…it's all involving her CI."

"What?"

"Terrence Miller is Agent Sawyer's CI. He turned state's evidence almost a year ago and she's been his contact."

Eric felt the room beginning to spin, but he had to keep it together. "State's evidence for what?"

"Against Foxworth Pharmaceuticals," David said. "Miller isn't the man you want. Robert Foxworth is the one trafficking and selling narcotics ingredients. He's stealing from his own company."

CHAPTER FORTY-TWO

*E*ric knew he'd heard the words. He just wasn't sure if he'd heard them correctly or if his ears had suddenly begun to fail him.

"We've been investigating Robert Foxworth for years," David said. "He's slick, clever, and always able to cover his tracks. From what we discovered, he and his buyers set up a network of pill mills to eventually sell the narcotics to once the materials were used to create the drugs. But it looks like he got greedy and cut ties with the organization who was buying the pills from him and went directly to the mills himself. That was a mistake. Now, he's in deep with them, so it was time to burn it all to the ground. When Devon married Terrence Miller and Robert brought him into the company, we never thought he'd bring him into the illegal side of the business too. But it seems Terrence was his way out."

Eric had been leaning forward in his chair, hanging on every word. Now he sat back and pondered what he was hearing. "He needed a scapegoat. He came to us, offered up Terrence on a platter, and gave us evidence to bring down Cirillo too."

"Exactly," David said, nodding. "If you've listened to Robert Foxworth speak for any length of time, you'll know there isn't any love lost between him and his son-in-law. He'd have no qualms about sending him up the river for his crimes."

"Where does Havilland come in?"

"Well, it seems Terrence grew wise to what Robert was doing. He was the one who always met the buyers. He was the one who always arranged shipment and delivery of the product, while Robert wouldn't come within ten feet of the dealings. Terrence must have realized he was being set up to take the fall in case shit went left, and he was right. We began to tail him, and we saw the moment he sought out Agent Sawyer for help. That's when my office got involved. She agreed to be his contact, and she would relay everything to me directly."

"But she hid and destroyed evidence to keep Terrence from being convicted."

"Only because that was the agreement. He promised to testify against Robert Foxworth in exchange for immunity. No charges could come to him."

David paused as he must have seen the cloud of anger cross Eric's face. "Agent Sawyer, your wife was conducting her own investigation, and your investigation into Terrence was interfering with that. Yes, he was involved in stealing and selling the ingredients, but only because he had to be in order to keep Foxworth from suspecting anything."

She could have come to me. She could have talked to me. I'm her husband.

David leaned forward. "I know this is all a lot to take in, but you can rest assured she was always acting under orders from the DEA and the CBI."

Eric narrowed his eyes. "I'm in charge of this department. I'm her boss. She wasn't acting under my orders."

David paused. "No, Agent Sawyer, I was referring to your boss, Carl Hewitt. She was acting under his orders."

CHAPTER FORTY-THREE

Havilland, her mom, and Kimmy were all gathered together on the floor playing Candyland. Havilland and Lola were just going through the motions and letting Kimmy win—something Havilland and Eric always did when they played this game with her. Kimmy, who wasn't quite old enough to know the rules of the game, played just for the colors, the characters, and the candy places while the adults simply indulged her. They were laughing at her when the doorbell rang.

"I'll get it," Havilland said. "Are you expecting someone?"

Lola shook her head. "No, but it could be Janice from next door. She said she'd return the casserole dish I lent her last week."

When Havilland opened the door and got a look at the man on the threshold, relief flooded through her and she smiled.

"Stephen!"

"Hey, big sis." He smiled and came forward, enveloping her in his tall and broad frame.

"Oh, thank God!" Havilland heard her mother say behind

them, along with Kimmy shouting for her Uncle Stephen to give her a hug too.

He did so, lifting Kimmy up to embrace and kiss her and then lowering her to step past them and greet their mom.

"Hi, Mom."

"Hi, Mom." She echoed and then drew him into her arms. "That's it? Where have you been? No call, no text, not even a damn smoke signal! We've been worried about you!"

He pulled away from her, looked at Havilland, and then back to Lola. "I've been in protective custody."

"What? Protective custody? What's going on?" Without waiting for an answer, Lola turned to Havilland. "Did you know about this?"

Havilland nodded. "I knew where he was, but all I could tell you was that he was safe. I thought Stephen would want to explain everything to you himself."

"She's right, Mom. I was safe, but I made a terrible, greedy decision, and now I'm facing the consequences."

Lola put her fists to her hips. "Well, I'm waiting. Tell me what's going on."

Havilland went to close the front door, but a hand slapped against it, stopping her movement. She turned around and her heart leaped in her chest for the second time. Her eyes slowly trailed him from his worn sneakers to the faded jeans and up the length of his body to his torso. She took in the dark hoodie sweatshirt and the matching baseball cap worn low, shielding his eyes. He was in shadow, but she knew it was him.

No matter how long they stayed away from each other, she'd recognize her husband anywhere. He stepped forward with his hands tucked in the pockets of his hoodie and slowly lifted his head, reacquainting her with those fathomless blue eyes.

Without a word, she opened the door wider and heard a joyful squeal behind her.

"Daddy!"

Eric smiled and went to his knees with open arms as Kimmy barreled toward him. She fell into his arms and squeezed so tight that Havilland immediately felt guilty for keeping them away from each other for even one week.

"Yeah. I forgot to mention who drove me here," Stephen said.

Eric picked up Kimmy, hugged and kissed her some more, and patiently answered the questions she threw at him.

"Are you coming to stay with us? Can we come home?"

"Soon, honey," he said, laughing. "I'll come for you, soon."

"Me and Mommy," she clarified.

He put her down gently and finally, finally his eyes found hers, and when they looked at each other fully, she suddenly didn't want him to say a word. She wanted to fall into his arms just like her daughter had and have him never let her go.

"Yeah. You and Mommy."

Lola stepped forward and took Kimmy by the hand. "Why don't we give you two a moment alone. Kimmy, come with me, and we'll see about your dinner."

"Good idea, Mom, because I'm starving," Stephen said.

"Of course, you are," Lola said, narrowing her eyes. "And don't you think I've forgotten that you owe me an explanation. Once Kimmy goes to bed, you're going to tell me everything."

"Yes, ma'am," he said, following her into the kitchen.

When they were left alone, Havilland cleared her throat and said the first thing that came to her mind. Well, in truth, the second thing because the first thing she wanted to say was that she'd missed him, terribly, but she wasn't sure he was ready to hear that.

"I owe you an apology. I know you're not using my family and that as deep as Stephen got involved with Terrence, becoming an informant was the only way he wouldn't face prison time. You saved his life."

"Don't thank me for that. He's your brother, and I know you worry about him. Besides, the case is on hold right now."

"What do you mean?"

"I'll explain later, but right now, my visit is two-fold," he said, taking a small step toward her. "I know you wanted some space between us, but that's going to have to wait. You're needed back at the office."

CHAPTER FORTY-FOUR

"I appreciate the two of you coming down here after hours. Have a seat."

When Havilland entered the conference room and surveyed the scene, she immediately wanted to turn around and run away. Carl Hewitt, an agent she recognized from Internal Affairs, and a union representative were present. From the looks of this scene, these men were there to get answers, and if the correct answers weren't given, both her and Eric's jobs would be in jeopardy.

Standing behind her, Eric must have sensed her apprehension because he put his palm to the small of her back and kept it there as a silent comfort. He then pulled one of the chairs out for her to sit and took the seat next her. They sat elbow to elbow together across from Hewitt and the IA agent and even with their own representation beside them, it felt good to have Eric next to her. She hoped her presence and the feel of his forearm slightly touching hers was as much a comfort to him as it was to her.

"As you both know, when an agent is killed in the line of duty, there's a lot of paperwork to be filed and a lot of questions to be answered," Carl began. "This is Agent Bergman with Internal Affairs. His department has nearly concluded their investigation into Agent Maya Landon's death, but there are still some details that need to be clarified, details that involve the two of you."

Carl then nodded to Agent Bergman, who officially began the meeting.

"The time is six thirty-seven pm," Bergman said for the recording device. "Present is Special Agent in Charge Eric Sawyer and Special Agent Havilland Sawyer, with their union representative, Agent Jameson. Both Agents have agreed to attend this interview at the request of the Internal Affairs Division to answer questions regarding the death of Agent Maya Landon. More specifically, we are seeking clarification of their whereabouts on the night in question."

Agent Bergman paused and then continued. "First, I need to mention for the purposes of full disclosure, that the exterior cameras to the Miller's home were shut off at seven twenty-two that evening, so we don't have footage of Agent Landon actually entering the house. Before that, we have footage of Terrence Miller leaving the residence at precisely six fifty-eight pm. Between that time and the time the cameras were shut off, no one was seen entering or leaving the residence."

"So, you have no proof as to whether she was in that house with someone or alone?" Jameson asked for clarification.

Havilland turned to Agent Bergman, who nodded in confirmation. Why would Maya visit Terrence and Devon's home? Did she have a connection with them that no one knew about? She slid her glance sideways toward Eric, but he appeared just as confused as she was.

"We'll have to accept the fact that there are some questions that only Agent Landon could've answered. However, the cameras seemed to have been turned back on remotely at eight seventeen pm, and we have footage of SAC Eric Sawyer knocking on the front door at eight thirty pm and then letting himself in the back door. Can you explain your reason for being there, Agent Sawyer, and what led you to let yourself in through the back?"

Havilland could already anticipate Eric's answer. It was too easy for him to explain that he was following up on a lead that had to do with his investigation. But what could she say?

Eric cleared his throat. "I had a question about the investigation for Mrs. Miller, and she agreed to meet me at that time. When I arrived at the residence, I knocked on the front door but didn't see any cars in the driveway or detect any movement from inside the house. I went around to the back, called for Mrs. Miller or any household staff, but I didn't receive an answer."

"Then what?" Bergman prodded.

"In the rear of the house, I found the patio French doors open and glass broken. I pulled out my weapon, announced myself again and stepped inside. Maya was lying there on the floor, and from what I could see, her neck had been broken. I immediately called for an ambulance and went searching the rest of the house for any signs of the perpetrator."

Havilland tried her best to keep as still as possible. Eric hadn't called an ambulance until after they were outside, just before he let her go. Why didn't he tell Bergman the truth?

"As her superior, can you provide any insight as to why Agent Landon would be visiting the Miller's residence?"

"No, I can't," Eric said. "Agent Landon went to the Miller's home without my authorization. Whatever business she had with them, she was conducting alone and not under my orders."

Just as Havilland assumed, he had the investigation as his

justifiable cause for being at the Miller's home. He was in the clear, but how in the hell was she going to explain herself?

She dreaded the moment the IAB agent's gaze would swing her way and pose the same question to her. Could she simply end the meeting by walking out of there, or would they just bring her back and force her to answer the question?

She looked in Carl's direction, hoping to communicate with her eyes that she needed help. He knew exactly what she was involved in. He could step in right now and tell the IAB agent that she was involved in an investigation of her own. But would he do that with Eric sitting there? He'd insisted on absolute secrecy from the start. Only a particular few were to ever know about the task force she was involved in with the DEA in order to prevent leaks. But when Carl's eyes met hers and then instantly fleeted away, Havilland realized she was on her own.

"Agent Sawyer." Bergman finally turned to her. "The camera feed recorded you arriving on scene about five minutes later. What was your reason for being at the Miller's residence?"

She opened her mouth to speak, still not knowing what she was about to say.

"I asked her to meet me there."

Havilland heard his voice, but couldn't really believe he'd spoken. She slowly turned her head to look at her husband and saw that his lips were indeed moving. He was giving her an alibi.

It's not the first time I've covered for you.

Bergman's gaze returned to Eric. "I'd appreciate it if you'd let Agent Sawyer answer my questions, directly. But since you did speak, it was my understanding that you established a task force for the Miller investigation and that Agent

Sawyer here wasn't part of that task force. Why would she be accompanying you in an official capacity?"

Eric leaned forward, jabbing his index finger onto the table to illustrate his point. "Agent Sawyer may not have been on the task force, but she did assist my team in the confiscation of evidence against Mr. Miller on the night of the Foxworth Pharmaceuticals party. She showed great poise and efficiency that night and I asked her to assist me again this time. Also, I was hoping a female presence would make Mrs. Miller more comfortable."

"Agent Landon is a female, and unlike Agent Sawyer, she was on your task force. Why not ask her?"

Havilland spoke up. "Because I know Devon."

Bergman turned to her and motioned for her to continue, and she did, praying that no one could hear the slight quiver in her voice.

"Devon Miller and I went to college together. We weren't very close, but we knew each other well enough to recognize one another after so many years. That's why Eric asked me to go. However, because I'm acquainted with Devon, Eric had to make the decision not to include me in the task force against Terrence Miller."

"I see," Bergman said, filling his legal pad with notes. "Agent Sawyer, would you please describe the scene as you encountered it?"

Havilland took in a breath and began reciting what happened in her own words. This part of the story was easy because it was mostly the truth. The only detail she left out was Eric pulling a gun on her and arresting her. The remaining questions went equally as smooth as she continued to recite what she saw in the den of the Miller's home. Then Agent Bergman asked one last question.

"I hate to get personal, but it looked as if the two of you had a disagreement outside the house, and then there's a view of Agent Havilland Sawyer leaving the scene before EMTs and backup arrived. Why did you leave so early?"

This time, Havilland had been anticipating it and already had an answer crafted for herself.

"I secured the scene with Eric—I mean, SAC Sawyer, first. After that, I left in order to begin tracking down both Terrence and Devon Miller and their housing staff."

"I authorized her to leave," Eric chimed in again. "Time was of the essence."

"And the disagreement?"

"I regret my actions," Eric said, and Havilland guessed he was envisioning pulling her up against him and hissing in her face. She was thinking about it, too, and wondered what it must've looked like from the IAB agent's point of view.

Then maybe you shouldn't have had your lips on him.

"We did have a disagreement, but I can assure you, it was a personal matter that has no bearing on the case or Agent Maya's murder."

Bergman looked ready to insist on more details, but Jameson sat up, giving him a stern look. "They answered your questions about the timing, and the video feed shows they followed protocol. Unfortunately, we may never know what Agent Landon was doing there in the first place, but I think you have more than enough to close this investigation. A look into the agents' marital disagreements is crossing the line."

Bergman nodded regretfully, looked down at his notes, and then closed the notebook with a thud of finality. "I don't have any more questions at this time," he said, rising from his seat. "Thank you both for your cooperation."

The movement seemed to trigger everyone else to stand, including Havilland, who was ready to run out of there, but she was forestalled by Eric's hand on hers. She looked down and realized he had remained seated and was glaring across the table at Carl. Both men regarded each other with hostility as the room cleared and then finally, it was just the three of them.

Havilland sat back down, realizing she was to be a part of a second meeting.

Carl was the first to break his stare and looked at his wristwatch impatiently. "I have somewhere to be, so let's keep this brief."

"Sure thing," Eric said. "I just want to make something clear. The next time you have any of my agents, especially my wife, working on a case that directly opposes mine, give me a fucking heads up."

* * *

Eric could feel Havilland's shocked eyes on him. No doubt she was wondering how and when he found out, but he would deal with her later. The entire ride down to the office, they hadn't said much to each other, except he'd explained to her that after another long day, he'd come home, showered and changed and went to pick up Stephen to take him to see her and her mom. On his way to the safe house, Carl called him, saying IAB had questions for both him and Havilland and that they both needed to return to the office. She'd only uttered a few words in response, still determined to keep her secrets, and that was fine with him. For now. Besides, Deputy Director Holladay had given him more information than he'd been prepared for, and what he couldn't get out of his mind was that Havilland and he had been on opposite sides this entire time. That was unacceptable, and he laid part of the blame at the feet of the man sitting in front of them.

Carl's eyes narrowed. "Let's try that again, Agent Sawyer, with more respect."

"Well, you see, Carl, the funny thing about respect is that

it's a two-way street. You didn't give me the respect to inform me that one of my agents was conducting an investigation that involved my suspect."

Carl shook his head. "I had reason to believe Robert had someone in the department on his payroll, and I couldn't risk him finding out we were onto him. The less people involved, the less likely there would be leaks."

"There are no leaks in my department."

"Are you so sure about that? Agent Landon was killed in the home of the man you were investigating and you, yourself, admit to having no idea why she was there. And whether Terrence Miller was Havilland's CI or not, I warned you from the beginning to proceed cautiously with the investigation."

"Warning me to proceed cautiously and outright telling me that I'm going after the wrong man are two different things. You could've brought me in. You just chose not to because of this crap with Christina."

Carl seethed. "You leave my daughter out of this."

"How can I when you constantly use my past relationship with her against me? What happened between the two of us is our business, and it has nothing to do with any of this. The fact remains that you sat there and listened to Robert Foxworth go on about his son-in-law, knowing the whole time he was lying, and yet you still said nothing to me."

"Agent Sawyer, I'm your superior, and even though I have no obligation to explain anything to you, I understand your frustration. But you must understand that Terrence Miller's safety was important. We needed his testimony, and if it got out that he was working with the CBI and DEA, Robert Foxworth would have used every connection he had to get rid of him, not to mention what Cirillo and his bosses would do to him. This was a joint task force with the DEA, and I wasn't about to let it go bust."

"Yeah, and I'm sure a joint task force with the DEA did wonders for your career. Did you ever think about what would happen if Robert Foxworth found out Havilland was onto him?"

Carl nodded to Havilland. "With all due respect to Agent Sawyer, she knows the risks of this job."

Havilland turned to Eric and put a hand to his arm. "He's right. I knew what I was signing up for when I took on Terrence as a CI."

"There, you have it," Carl said, glancing at his watch again. "Anymore grievances you feel like airing? I told you I have another appointment."

Eric scoffed and shook his head in disgust. He stood from his seat, signaled for Havilland to get up, and started to follow her out the door when he stopped and turned around.

"You know I met with Christina the other day."

His announcement bought a scowl to Carl's face, but Eric pressed on.

"I needed her expertise on this case. From one father to another, how about you be proud of what she has accomplished instead of disappointed in not following the life you laid out for her."

"Get out," Carl said.

"Absolutely. Sir."

Eric left the conference room and firmly closed the door behind him.

CHAPTER FORTY-FIVE

"Robert, I know you're worried about Devon, but this is a situation we need to get out in front of now," Keith urged.

For the past week and a half, Robert had been holed up in his hotel suite, waiting for something to happen, like news of Devon's whereabouts or Terrence's arrest. He was also waiting for the all clear from the CBI to leave California and return to Georgia, but Robert cared the least about that, because as far as he was concerned, he wasn't going anywhere without Devon.

He'd been pacing the suite back and forth and instantly stopped and whirled around to face his attorney. He stomped over to where he sat in an oversized armchair in the sitting area of the suite.

"Listen to me," he said, "my daughter is my number one priority right now. Everything else—the business, the Colombians, can go to hell for all I care. Until I hear she's safe, nothing happens. Nothing else matters! You got that?"

"All right," Keith said, throwing up his hands in surrender. "I get it."

At that moment, Robert's cell phone rang on the small table beside the chair. He picked it up, saw it was a blocked number, and answered immediately, silently praying it was his daughter on the other end of the line.

"Devon? Devon is that you?"

"Sorry to disappoint you, Robert, but it's Terrence."

Robert angrily pulled the phone from his ear, put it on speaker, and placed it back on the table, so that his lawyer could hear the conversation.

"What have you done with my daughter? I swear to God, if you harm one hair on her head—"

Terrence's deep voice echoed in the suite. "Devon isn't with me. I assumed she was with you."

"Well, she isn't! So why the hell are you calling me?"

"I'm calling you, because Cirillo wants to pull out of the arrangement."

Robert went silent and narrowed his eyes in suspicion. "What do you mean he wants to pull out? What the hell have you done?"

"The CBI's sudden interest in me has spooked him."

"If he pulls out, we'll be left with raw materials we can't use and in the hole for two million dollars," Robert barked.

"I know, but there was no swaying him, at least from me." Terrence paused on the other end. "I convinced him to hold off until he met with you, personally."

"I don't have time for this right now, Devon is missing, and I have the CBI breathing down my neck about you because one of their agents was killed. Why can't you do Devon and me a favor and turn yourself in?"

Terrence chuckled. "You'd like that, wouldn't you? Well, let me tell you something, old man. If I go down, Foxworth Pharmaceuticals goes down with me, and I think you know what I'm talking about. Devon missing won't be the only thing you have to worry about if I turn myself in and start talking. You want to take that chance? It would be a shame that after years of building up this business, you'd have to see it all come crashing down."

He was taunting him, and Robert knew it. He leaned over the table, gripped the edge, and gritted into the phone.

"What do you want?"

"Meet with Rafael, ease his fears, finish this deal, give me all the money, and I'll disappear."

Robert laughed, ignoring Keith's hand gestures for him to hang up. "That's ludicrous! This is supposed to be a five-million-dollar deal, and you expect me to let you walk away with all of it?"

"Yeah, I do, because there's something else I know. That CBI agent who was killed..." He paused, and Robert could hear him snapping his fingers on the other end of the line. "Landon. Maya Landon, that's it. I saw your little pow wow with her at the party. You didn't look too happy, Robert. Was she trying to shake you down? Well, it doesn't matter, but it sounds to me like you have a pretty good motive for wanting her dead and gone. Is the CBI aware of your relationship with the victim?"

Silence.

"Nothing? All right, well, if you'll excuse me, I have some CBI agents to meet," Terrence said. "Have a good night."

"Wait." Robert looked over at Keith, who wore an unreadable expression. "I'll give you your money. Let's just end this."

And by ending it, he was going to put an end to Terrence once and for all. The only one walking off that pier with the money would be him, while his son-in-law's body would be later found floating somewhere in the bay.

CHAPTER FORTY-SIX

*E*ric opened the front door and allowed Havilland to go in ahead of him. She stepped inside, walked to the middle of the living room, and stood still. It was deathly quiet, and she was all too aware of him coming up to stand behind her. It was just the two of them there with nothing else between them. No secrets left. Everything she'd tried to keep hidden from him for so long was now fully exposed.

She turned around to face him. "Are you hungry?"

He tossed his coat across an armchair and stepped up to her, shaking his head.

"Are you sure? I don't mind making something quick."

He moved in closer. "Don't you think it's time you and I talked?"

She sighed heavily and nodded.

"Good, because right now, I don't want anything from you but answers."

"But we're not going to talk; we're going to argue," she said.

"I'm not afraid of arguing with you. But first, why don't you go ahead and ask me what you want to know."

She swallowed. "How long have you known?"

"I found out a couple of days ago. Your contact at the DEA came to see me. He's been looking for you."

"Eric, you have to understand that if Carl hadn't sworn me to secrecy, I would've come to you."

He cocked his head to the side. "You sure about that?"

"Yes! I never wanted this between us. I wanted so many times to tell you." She paused. "But then I thought..."

"You thought what?"

"I thought you would take it the wrong way. I thought you would read the entire situation wrong and assume I was helping him because...because I'm in love with him, and I'm not!"

"Then what is it? Why did you agree to be his contact?"

Her face and voice turned apologetic. "He helped Stephen out of a jam, and then he needed my help, and...dammit Eric, he's Kimmy's father."

He closed the distance between them. He was so close to her face she felt the warmth of his breath against her skin and saw the anger flash through his eyes as he bore them into her.

"*I'm* her father," he said, pointing to his chest. "*I* adopted her because I love her and want to bring her up with you. I don't give a damn where she came from. She's mine. You got that?"

"Okay," she said. "You're right. You're the only father she knows, and I never should've said that."

She instantly felt ashamed. She could see the comment hurt him, and he was having a hard time composing himself.

After a long, taut silence, he spoke again.

"The night Maya died, you left with Kimmy. Why?"

"I was scared. You had already put me in handcuffs. Maybe you believed I really killed Maya. It wouldn't matter if

Terrence was my CI and Carl knew about it. He couldn't protect me from a murder rap. I had motive."

"I took the handcuffs off," he said.

"Only because I nearly accused you of the same thing."

"No, that's not why I did it," he said. "I took them off because I couldn't stand to see you in them, and I don't want anyone to take you away from your daughter. Haven't I proved that to you over and over again? Didn't I prove that tonight?"

"I don't want you to have to come to my rescue," she said. "You put too much on the line for me already."

"So, you run off," he asked, his voice rising. "Don't you trust me enough to talk to me?"

"I've always trusted you," she said, matching his tone. "That was never our problem."

"Then what was it? Why did you leave?"

"I had no other choice. I'm not perfect, Eric."

"I never wanted a wife who was perfect. I want a wife who's honest with me."

"That's it, right there," she said, pointing a finger at him. "I've lied so much, that you stopped trusting me!"

"But I never stopped loving you!"

Their words echoed among the four walls, and they stood there together in the middle of the room, their ears ringing with the truth in his words.

"I'm sorry," she said, softly. "I'm sorry I left, I'm sorry he kissed me, and I'm sorry I broke your trust enough to force you to follow me all the way to Atlanta just to see that."

"You really think it was just about that damn kiss? No, Hav, what pisses me off is that you lied to me for months. Me! Tell me one occasion when I've never had your back? I don't give a damn what's going on in the office or where the leak is coming from, I would've been there for you."

CHAPTER FORTY-SEVEN

Havilland turned on the shower and watched in a daze as the water streamed from the nozzle. As wisps of steam rose, she slowly and methodically removed every item of her clothing and then stepped in. She positioned her body directly beneath the shower head, closed her eyes and allowed the hot water to drench her hair and run over and down her body.

As soon as Eric uttered those words, it was as if they were both rendered speechless. Neither one of them had anything left to say to the other, so she used what energy she had left to trudge past him up the stairs. After her shower, she would dress in an old T-shirt for pajamas, climb under the comforter of the bed, and go to sleep. Eric would just have to take her back to her mom's house tomorrow.

That thought brought tears to her eyes. There, in the seclusion of the shower, she allowed them to flow freely down her cheeks, mixing with the water and eventually disappearing down the drain as though she hadn't been crying at all.

She and Kimmy should be there in their home. But Eric

hadn't denied her last words. He didn't trust her, and what was a marriage without trust? Then again, how could they ever hope to begin restoring that trust if she was living elsewhere?

The bathroom door swung open, and his sudden presence startled her. He hadn't used their master bath in nearly three months, but now he stood before her, bracing his hands over one of the dual vanity sinks and staring at her through the mirror. Havilland slowed down her lathering and stared back at his reflection. For a moment, neither of them moved or spoke, and then he finally turned from the sink to face her, grabbed hold of the shower door, and opened it. Steam fell out and drifted around them as he continued to watch her. She stopped lathering herself altogether, put down the bodywash and stood completely still.

"Would you have really left me?" he asked.

Her breathing became shallow as she stared at the desperation and fear in his eyes at the possibility he could've lost his family. What a mess she'd made of things.

"No," she said on a weary sigh. "If you hadn't come for us, I would've found a reason to come home."

He tugged off his sneakers, stepped into the shower, fully clothed, and closed the door, trapping her inside with him.

"Eric, your clothes are getting wet."

"I know."

"Let me get out, and we can talk."

"I don't want to talk anymore," he said, pulling his T-shirt off and dropping it to the shower floor. "Nothing's getting solved."

"It definitely won't get solved like this," she said, but couldn't resist running her hands across his chest.

"Maybe, but I don't care. I want you, Hav. I've never stopped wanting you. We can figure the rest out later. Just let me have you tonight."

He gently pushed her naked body against the wall, brushed the damp strands of her hair away, and framed her face in his hands for a deep and longing kiss. Havilland accepted it with greed and ran her hands up and down his back with the warm water flowing between her fingers. He kept his hands to the sides of her face and alternated between kisses that were hungry and rushed and kisses that were slow and sensuous.

* * *

Eric was serious. There was still so much that needed to be said, but the last thing he wanted to do was talk. Releasing her face, he turned her around and pressed the front of her body against the glass shower door. He undid the button of his now drenched jeans, slid the zipper down, and reached inside to pull that throbbing part of him free. He slowly guided himself into her, and instantly felt her walls tightening around him. It nearly undid him.

"Goddamn!" he groaned out loud and forced himself to slow down.

"No, Eric!" she cried out, turning her head to the side and pressing her face against the shower door. "Give it to me rough!"

She splayed her hands over the door, and he intertwined his hands with hers while taking her relentlessly from behind. He was mesmerized by her ass bouncing and pushing against his strokes, and he wanted nothing more than to unleash all the weeks of sexual frustration on her. He wanted to make her scream, but he was still getting reacquainted with how good it felt to be inside her, and if he didn't pace himself, this would all be over sooner than either of them wanted.

He wanted this moment to last. He wanted to commit

every position he had her in to memory. The last time he'd made love to her, he'd been embroiled with jealousy and pain, but this time felt different. He felt as if they were slowly making their way back to each other. It wasn't completely the way it used to be, but they were talking again. They were confiding again, and that's what he wanted from his wife, not just her body, but all of her.

"Eric, please. I want it all," she said, echoing his thoughts.

He slipped out of her and turned her back around to face him. Havilland's left leg instantly came up, and he held it with one hand while bracing the other hand above her. He pushed himself into her hot and tight center again and delighted cries and pleas came from her as she took in every inch he gave her. He inhaled the fragrant scent of her body wash and then bit and sucked gently on her earlobe, while whispering nasty shit in her ear. The words did what he expected them to do—exciting her and making her attempt to increase their rhythm. But he wasn't relinquishing control just yet. Her thigh was slick from a mix of soap and water, but he dug his fingers in and kept a firm grip while continuing to thrust into her and losing himself. He looked down at her plump breasts and watched as the water trickled down each one to drip from her erect nipples. The sight begged for his mouth. He bent his head and gently pulled one between his lips, lightly tugging it between his teeth and letting go. Havilland cried out, clutched at the back of his head and urged him to keep up with the torturous play. He tugged a few more times before moving his head to the other nipple, all the while keeping up his slow stroke. He could feel what it was all doing to her, and he'd missed not having every inch of her body to himself. For too long, he'd been walking around, battling between his blinding anger and sexual frustration. Even at the height of his distrust for her, even when that image of another man kissing her replayed over and over in his mind, he never stopped wanting her. Whether she knew it or not, she had him.

"Faster baby," she cried, clutching his ass and shoving him so deep into her, he nearly came. "Please!"

Eric released her breast, brought his head to the crook of her neck and finally gave into her demands. The walls of the shower and bathroom echoed with their loud and erotic cries as he slammed in and out of her with abandon, until that glorious moment when they found release together. By the time the hot water turned to lukewarm and then cold, they hardly noticed it.

CHAPTER FORTY-EIGHT

Havilland lay beside Eric, watching his chest rise and fall with sleep. It had been a long time since he'd shared this bed with her and now that he was there, lying beside her, she took full advantage by watching him sleep peacefully. She couldn't tear her eyes away from him, but she also couldn't stop the racing thoughts that plagued her ever since they ended their lovemaking and lay in bed together in silence.

Eric had been in that mansion before her. But how much longer had he been there? What was Maya doing there? Did they meet there together? No, they couldn't have, because then Eric would know who her killer was. Unless...

She kept her eyes on his closed lids. Maya was a threat to Havilland's career, and she'd constantly gone to Eric to show him proof of her alleged corruption. But not for the first time, Eric protected Havilland. Did Maya finally grow tired of him sweeping everything under the rug? Maybe she was going after his job, which meant she was a threat to him too. Did he kill Maya before Havilland got there and then let her go so he could finish covering up his crime? Did he kill her to protect his family?

It was a full moon and its bright light seeped in through the curtains, bathing Eric's body. Havilland was able to clearly see his powerful thighs and legs resting atop the duvet cover, his muscular torso, and the corded veins on his arms and hands. He was indeed a strong man, but was he a killer? Her heart adamantly said no, that this was Eric and he would never entertain the idea. But when it came to protecting his family, who was to say what he wouldn't do? A week ago, she'd been willing to kill Terrence to protect the ones she loved. Could Eric have succumbed to the same thoughts?

Her cell phone chimed, startling her, and she quickly stretched over Eric's body toward the nightstand and grabbed for it. She saw who it was on the call display and looked over at Eric who was now wide-eyed and looking back at her.

"Who is it?" he asked.

Without responding, she swiped the call button to answer and immediately put it on speaker for Eric to hear.

"Where are you?" she asked.

"Call your boys at the DEA and be at Pier 96 in an hour."

"Where have you been?"

"Don't worry about that," Terrence said. "Just be there."

She hung up and turned to Eric who had now sat up in bed. "I have to go, and I'm going to need you to trust me."

He immediately hopped out of bed and went to his bureau for some clean and dry jeans.

"You're not going anywhere without me. Just explain everything to me on the way."

CHAPTER FORTY-NINE

During the day, Pier 96 was bustling with industrial activity as container ships moved in and out of the bay, bringing goods. However, at midnight, what was once a throng of activity was now a quiet and desolate place, shrouded in mystery.

Eric parked the car one block away from the designated spot where Holladay said the DEA van would be parked. He turned the car off, and both he and Havilland checked their guns and tucked them away with an extra clip.

"You ready?" he asked her and then started to pull the handle to open the car door.

"Eric?"

Her voice stopped him, and he turned around to look at her.

"That night at Terrence and Devon's house, I never meant to accuse you of—"

"Don't worry about it," he said, turning to leave again.

She tugged at one long sleeve of his gray cotton shirt, stopping him again. "But I am worrying about it. I need to know. It's just me here, now, and you can talk to me. I need to know why you were there."

He stared for so long, and she noticed the deep blue of his eyes turning dull in the darkened car.

"I came there looking for you. After Maya told me you took the ledger from the evidence locker, I told her I would handle it. But I could hear in her voice she wasn't happy with that decision. Something told me she was going to go after you herself."

"How did you know I'd be there?"

He shrugged. "It was just a hunch. Your brother called to tell me he and Terrence had met with the buyers and that Terrence seemed nervous and looked to be ready to skip town. I didn't think he'd skip town without getting that ledger, so I went to his house on the off chance you were meeting him there."

"I didn't see your car, but I did see Maya's. I thought maybe I was too late. Maybe she'd caught you with the ledger, called it in and already had you in custody. The rest is just like I told IA. I knocked on the front door with no answer, went around to the back and found Maya in the den."

"Did you think I did it?" she asked.

"At first, I didn't know what to think, which is probably why I didn't immediately call it in. Then when I heard your voice, I was relieved because if you had done it, you wouldn't have returned to the scene. But then I got angry all over again because my original hunch had been right. You were there to give Terrence the ledger."

She nodded and looked away. "And so, we're back to the same argument." She closed her eyes and then pounded her fist into her palm in frustration. "Dammit, Eric is this always going to be between us?"

He touched her elbow softly, and she turned back to look at him.

"You were right about me. I do have this need to be a perfect agent, and if my record is spotless, my wife's record has to be spotless too. When I overlooked all that stuff Maya found, it's because I didn't want to have to face it. I didn't want to admit that you were anything less than perfect, and that's not fair to you, especially when I'm nowhere near a perfect man." He paused. "You're Havilland, and that should be more than enough for me."

"But is it?" she asked, quietly.

He raised a hand and put it to the side of her face. "I want it to be."

She nodded and moved to cover his hand with hers, but he pulled it away just before she could and turned to get out of the car. Tears stung the backs of her eyes, but she tucked them back and also got out of the car. Together they walked the short distance up the block without another word said to each other. When they got to the non-descript van, Eric knocked twice and the doors immediately swung open. He ushered Havilland inside first and then followed after her.

"Agents Sawyer and Sawyer. Glad to see the both of you here, together," David said and motioned for one of the other DEA agents to hand them earpieces.

"Have we missed anything?" Havilland asked, fitting the earpiece into her ear.

"Nothing, yet," David said, looking down at his watch. "Everything's quiet out there, but it's still early."

Havilland watched as Eric fit his own earpiece in and tested the sound, and she thought back to the last time they were inside a van and prepping for a surveillance mission. Only then, she was being used as bait. They still had so much to work through. She wasn't foolish enough to think that one night of passionate sex would wash away months of distrust between them, but she had hoped it would have at least made a dent in that wall.

A text came through on her cell phone breaking up her self-pity party, and she looked down and saw it was from Terrence, telling her that he was there along with Stephen.

"Terrence and Stephen are here," she announced. "They're waiting on Robert."

"All agents stay alert," David said into his mic. "Miller and Currin have arrived."

"Copy that, sir, I have eyes on them," one of the agents responded.

In a few moments, Havilland saw Terrence and Stephen exit a car and walk along the pier. Seeing her brother caused fear to rise within her, but she had to remember he came into this on his own free will. He may be her little brother, but as her mother wisely stated, he was a grown man who made his own choices. She was just glad he was now cooperating and not digging himself deeper into a prison sentence.

Eric must have sensed her anxiety because he put a hand over hers and clutched it tightly. She looked down at his hand and then up at him, but his eyes remained focused on the camera.

"We have movement in the lot," one of the DEA agents said, coming loud and clear through her earpiece.

Havilland turned her attention back to the camera and soon caught sight of a black town car pulling into the lot. In another moment, a driver exited, moved to the back, and opened the rear door. Her heart sped up as soon as she saw Robert Foxworth get out of the car. After nearly a year, after so many lies and secrets, she was going to get him. Her investigation was finally coming to an end.

"Target in sight," David confirmed.

Terrence walked up to him and the two exchanged a few words. Several more minutes passed, and another car and van pulled up, and two men in suits approached, closely followed by several burly and imposing men who must've been their bodyguards.

"Buyers are in sight," David once again announced. "Nobody moves until we confirm Foxworth has received payment."

* * *

Something wasn't right.

Robert kept telling himself that from the moment he stepped out of the car and spotted not only Terrence but Stephen Currin as well. Terrence had brought the young man in on their deal because he was a brilliant chemist. But he was never supposed to know that Robert himself was involved in the drug scheme. He already noticed Stephen's curious frown when he pulled up to the pier, but he would have to worry about that later. This was about appeasing Cirillo long enough to get his money. Later, he'd have the CBI arrest them and unfortunately, also Stephen.

Robert was ready to burn it all down to the ground. He'd made a sizable amount of money these past seven years once he got into this illegal side of the business, but now he was ready to wash his hands of the whole thing and return his company to strictly legal operations. He was doing it for Devon. One day, when he was no longer capable of running things, she would step in as CEO, and he didn't want her walking into black market deals, pill mills, and cartels.

Thinking of Devon made him angry and worried all over again. Where the hell could she be? His gut told him, she was still alive somewhere, but he couldn't understand why she didn't just call him—unless she was unable to. They'd called the hospitals, morgues, even the jails and gave out her description and everywhere was a bust. He was relieved for that, but fear gripped him with the possibility that someone was holding her against her will, and if it wasn't Terrence, who could it be? So many questions and possibilities ran through his mind about his daughter's whereabouts, but for now he had to tuck it away and handle this one last deal.

Robert stepped up to Terrence and spoke under his breath as he watched Cirillo and his enforcers join them on the pier.

"For seven years I've been dealing with the Lupino cartel, and they've never had reason to complain. Now, for the first time, you tell me they're nervous about this buy and asked to see me? What the hell did you do?"

Terrence turned to him with indignation clouding his eyes. "I told you. It's this shit with the CBI. I thought we should have everyone here to make sure the product gets through without interruptions." He paused and winked at Robert. "And to make sure I get my money."

Robert nodded but still didn't like it. He'd made damn sure to keep himself as far away from the product and money as possible. That was why he brought in Terrence, but just this once, he would have to go against his rule to make sure there were no further problems. That feeling of uneasiness was growing with every minute they stood out there in the open. He needed to get his money, and after Rafael and his men left, he'd keep Terrence back to pretend to give him the money and then signal his driver, Gerard, to park a bullet in the back of his head. Maybe even Stephen, too, since he was already there and now knew about Robert's involvement. Collateral damage.

"Gentlemen, thank you for coming," Rafael said, stepping forward. "Robert, it's been a long time. I'm glad to see you could be here to ensure our business arrangement remains intact."

Robert nodded, stepping forward and shaking hands with

him. "It's good to see you again too. But if you don't mind, for all of our protection, I'd like to do this quickly and get out of here."

"Of course."

Rafael motioned for his men to bring the money, and Stephen pulled a large black duffel bag from beside him and handed it to Rafael's men to inspect. Terrence walked over to the bag and shined a flashlight over it while the men opened it and went through the sealed packs of raw materials, inspecting the quality and ensuring the count was correct.

Several moments later, one of Rafael's men gave him a subtle nod that everything was in order and Rafael smiled, handing another similar duffel bag of money to Robert.

"I'm sorry I had to waste your time coming down here, old friend," he said. "I heard your son-in-law here was being questioned, and he made some moves a few days ago that made me a little nervous."

Robert grabbed the bag of money and looked over at Terrence. "What moves? What happened?"

But before Rafael or Terrence could answer him, headlights all around them came on, blinding him, and then the deafening shouts of law enforcement could be heard.

"DEA! Drop your weapons and put your hands up!"

But Rafael and his men didn't heed warnings of law enforcement. They pulled their weapons from their backs, raised them, and as soon as the first bullet sounded, everyone started shooting.

CHAPTER FIFTY

"I should've known the deal was shady the moment Robert brought it to me. But my greed and desire for freedom blinded me to it all."

Terrence sat beside his own lawyer, not someone under Robert Foxworth's payroll, but his own personal lawyer. The two of them, along with a few DEA agents, including David Holladay as well as Carl Hewitt, and Havilland and Eric all gathered around a large table inside a secluded office in the federal building downtown.

The minute Rafael Cirillo and his colleagues were subdued, they were arrested and taken into federal custody, while Terrence and Stephen were both put into protective custody to get their statements. A few men from Rafael's organization were killed in the gun battle and headed to the morgue. Robert Foxworth was among them.

"I figured he always saw me as his eventual patsy," Terrence continued. Finally, after nearly a year, he was able to tell his side of the story.

"The man never liked me and he disliked it even more when I married his daughter. Bringing me into his business dealings was a way to cut ties with his buyers and also get rid of me."

"All right, back up." Agent Holladay spoke up. "Exactly how did he first approach you to start selling the raw materials illegally?"

"It was about a year after Devon and I married. We were living with her father in Georgia and just had a fight about the same thing we always fought about—I wanted her to stop putting a leash around me, and she refused. Well, obviously Robert heard us. He invited me into his den, poured me a glass of brandy, and told me all about the more lucrative side of his business. I was shocked at first. Robert always struck me as the straight and narrow type. I never would've guessed he was selling his own raw materials on the black market."

"Why are you bringing me into this?" Terrence asked.

"Because the business has expanded, and I need someone I can trust to help me with operations. Who better than my son-in-law?" Robert asked, swirling his glass of brandy.

"You mean someone just as corrupt?"

Robert snickered. "Look, Terrence, I sized you up from the moment I met you, and I can see that only one thing rules you: money. I'm offering you a chance to make some without my daughter's knowledge. She's well taken care of financially, so this will be all yours. Take it or leave it?"

"After I agreed to come in, he told me I was responsible for finding a new chemist, and the chemist would report only to me. He never did say what happened with the previous one." Terrence paused and looked over to Havilland. "That's when I brought in Stephen Currin. I told Robert about him, but per Robert's orders, Stephen never knew Robert was our "silent" partner."

Havilland spoke up. "But if his buyers were arrested, what's to stop them from giving Robert up?"

David shrugged. "They probably would've named him,

but Robert made sure there was never anything connecting him to the scheme."

"Except there was something that connected him," Eric said and looked directly at Terrence.

Terrence nodded slowly. "His accountant's ledger. After I realized what he was up to, and that I was a sitting duck, I snuck into his den one night, opened his wall safe, and took the ledger and replaced it with a forged copy I'd made weeks before. I had the combination memorized from watching him open it so many times. The next day, Devon and I were on a plane to San Francisco, and I had the only proof that Robert was the mastermind of his own scheme. After we left, he must've realized what I'd done."

"Did he confront you about it?" David asked.

"Nope. That would've shown his hand. He liked to sit back, analyze, and wait until the perfect opportunity."

Eric picked up the story from his viewpoint. "The night of the party, he used my team and the legal system to retrieve the real ledger, the one you took from his safe. I made photocopies of the pages and gave them to a colleague to look over. By the time I got them back from her, I realized my department now had the forged ledger."

Carl visibly reacted. "What the hell are you talking about? How did we go from having the real thing in evidence to something forged?"

Eric leveled him with a look. "Maya."

David lifted up an evidence bag containing a cell phone and a leather-bound book. "These were confiscated from Robert Foxworth's town car. The phone is registered to him, and there's a voicemail from Agent Maya Landon on it. She talks about demanding money for keeping him out of prison and her plans to arrest Agent Havilland Sawyer." He pointed to the book. "This is the actual ledger CBI confiscated from your office safe the night of the party. This is the ledger that ties Robert Foxworth to the entire scheme. We'll have our handwriting analysts confirm it was written by him."

"Maya must've stolen it out of evidence and replaced it with the fake," Eric said, picking the story back up and then spoke to Terrence. "But what you didn't know was that Robert added your account numbers to the fake ledger, which would have virtually assured an arrest and conviction. It was insurance, just in case he couldn't get the real ledger back."

"Christ," Carl muttered.

Terrence shook his head in disbelief. "He despised me that much, huh?"

"I wouldn't take it personally," David said. "Something tells me any man Devon brought home would've served his purpose. He wanted out, and the only way he could see doing it was giving his buyers and law enforcement someone else to focus on."

Terrence sighed. "Anyway, the rest is history. When I realized Robert was setting me up, I contacted Agent Sawyer, because I didn't know who else to go to about this, and she was the only one I trusted. I agreed to be her CI, and she would be my liaison with the DEA." He paused to look at Eric. "That's all there was between us."

"What about Devon?" Eric asked. "Did she know about the illegal side of the business?"

"No," Terrence said. "Whatever else he was, Robert Foxworth was at least a good father. He kept her far away from all of that. She didn't know a thing." He paused and turned to Agent Holladay. "Have you found her, yet?"

"She's officially listed as a missing person, and we've been working with SFPD to locate her. Any idea where she'd go?"

Terrence shrugged. "If she's not in Atlanta or by her father's side, then I'm all out of ideas. If she is hiding some-where, and for the life of me, I still can't figure out why she would be, I doubt she'll stay hidden for long when she hears about Robert's death."

David cleared his throat and started gathering up his notes. "I think I have as much as I need. All that's left is for Mr. Miller to sign this paperwork, agreeing to go into witness protection and testify in open court."

Terrence's attorney took the papers from Agent Holladay, read over them, and then handed them over to Terrence.

"This all looks to be in order."

"So, that's it?" Eric asked, his voice booming through the silence. "He gets protective custody and walks away from a murder charge?"

"Agent Sawyer, you need to stand down," Carl ordered.

Eric turned to him, bristling with animosity. "You forget we have a dead agent in the morgue, and he's not going to answer for it?"

"I didn't kill Agent Landon," Terrence said, shoving the papers away. "I saw her once, just before she went into a private office with Robert, and he didn't look happy to see her. She must've been working for him to get that ledger, and then things went bad. My guess is she was a loose end, and he killed her to keep her from talking."

"Agent Sawyer," David Holladay said. "We retrieved Robert Foxworth's phone and financial records at the approval of his attorney, who is now acting on behalf of his estate while Devon is missing. There are multiple calls from Agent Landon, as well as records of cash deposits from a shell corporation he owns to Agent Landon's private account. While we can't prove Robert Foxworth killed her, or even had her killed, these calls and cash deposits confirm she was on his payroll."

Terrence kept his eyes on Eric and could see the man was still not satisfied.

"I'd like everyone to leave the room, except Agent Eric Sawyer."

* * *

Everyone hesitated and looked oddly around the table at each other.

"Y'all heard me. I want everyone to get up and get out except for you, Sawyer."

Carl, David, the DEA agents, and Terrence's lawyer all rose and began to file out of the room. Havilland was slower to move and sat rooted to her seat, dividing an apprehensive look between Eric and Terrence.

Eric, who was standing off to the side with his arms and legs crossed, noticed her still there.

He nodded to her. "It's all right."

"You heard him," Terrence said. "Let me talk to your husband, Hav."

She finally stood, turned, and exited through the door David was holding open for her. When it closed behind her, Eric turned back to Terrence and shrugged.

"What can I do for you?"

"For starters, I'm going to help you remove that chip on your shoulder by apologizing for what happened last fall. I was wrong for kissing her. We were both married, but at that moment, I didn't care. That was selfish and stupid of me."

Eric didn't say anything, and Terrence chuckled to himself, seeing that the man wasn't going to dismiss everything so easily.

"I was also wrong for putting my hands on you when all you were doing was reacting to another man touching your wife. I guess I would've done the same thing."

"Tell me something I don't know."

Terrence sighed heavily. "I kissed her. She didn't return it.

She didn't love me anymore. She loves you, and she's loyal to you. I knew that, and maybe I was jealous. Here I was searching for an escape from my circumstances, and I walked my way into a controlling marriage, a drug trafficking case, and a frame job. Hav, on the other hand, stayed true to who she was. Sure, I may have more money than her, but she's got you, Kimberly, and a career she loves. From where I stand, that's a hell of a lot more than me. So, I wanted you to hear it from me. Quit punishing her for my bullshit."

Terrence could see he was slowly melting the ice off his features. So, he did what he did best and laid it on thick.

"I'm going to tell you the same thing I told you that night in my house when you came after me."

Eric frowned. "You said 'give my regards to your wife and daughter.'"

Terrence shrugged. "All right, maybe not exactly those words. I was being a prick. But this time, I'm going to say it with sincerity. Go home. Live your life and be happy with your wife—and *your* daughter."

* * *

When Eric came out of the conference room, Havilland rushed up to him.

"What did he say to you?"

He put an arm around her. "Only what I needed to hear."

David and Carl walked up to them.

"Congratulations to you both," David said.

"Listen, I don't want to hear any jurisdiction crap. Make sure

you give her all the credit,"

Eric said, nodding toward Havilland. "Make sure you give her all the credit. She did all the work and took all the risk."

"I was planning to," David said and held his hand out to

shake both of their hands. "Maybe next time we work together, everyone can be on board."

He walked off and Carl stepped forward. "Obviously, I'm going to need you both in the office for a debriefing."

"Monday is soon enough," Eric said, brushing him off, and then he turned back to Havilland. "Let's go get Kimmy from your mom's. I'm not spending another night without the two of you."

CHAPTER FIFTY-ONE

*O*ne week later...

Fisherman's Wharf was where she first met him when he moved to San Francisco. Now, they had come full circle, and she was meeting him in the same place, just days before he left the city for an undisclosed location. As Havilland walked up to the railing where Terrence stood looking out at the bay, she noted the difference in his stance from the first time they met. Gone was the cocky, self-assured air to be replaced by relief and exhaustion. The next two differences were that they weren't alone. He had his federal agents standing guard—and she had Kimmy walking beside her.

One of the agents spoke up. "Deputy Director Holladay approved this, but for the sake of Mr. Miller's safety, we can only allow you five minutes."

Havilland nodded and Terrence waved them away in agitation. He then looked down at Kimmy clutching Havilland's hand, and she was looking up at him with innocent curiosity.

"Kimmy, I want you to meet Terrence Miller," Havilland

said. "This is someone Mommy used to know a long time ago."

Terrence slowly knelt down and outstretched his hand. Kimmy let go of Havilland's hand and accepted Terrence's gesture only to have her small fingers swallowed up by his.

"Hey there, beautiful," he said.

"Hi. Mommy said I was going to meet you, so I drew you a picture."

She went into her jacket pocket and took out a folded piece of paper to hand to him. Terrence unfolded it, and for a long time, stared at the childlike crayon drawing of a little girl and the Golden Gate Bridge behind her.

"She said you would be going away, so I drew the bridge and me to help you remember."

He kept his eyes on the drawing and then finally looked up at her. "Thank you. This is the nicest thing anyone has ever given me."

"Really?" she asked.

"Really. I promise I won't ever forget you. You've got all the best parts of your mom. Her eyes, her smile"—he paused and softly pointed a finger at her chest—"and her heart."

Kimmy beamed, and for the first time in a long time, Havilland saw Terrence return it with a genuine smile of his own.

He stood and focused on Havilland. "Thank you again for bringing her. I want to apologize to you again for that day in my car when I…"

She put up a hand to stop him. "I know."

He nodded, but she could still see the look of shame in his eyes for using her daughter to manipulate her. Maybe one day he would forgive himself for it.

"Any news about Devon?" she asked. "My office hasn't heard anything."

He shrugged and shook his head. "No, but the feds are on

it. They traced her whereabouts to a diner just outside of the city the night Agent Landon died. After that, the trail has gone cold. The good news is, she was alive that night. I just don't understand why she hasn't made contact."

"I'm sure they'll find her."

"Oh, yeah, they'll find her just in time to serve me with divorce papers," he said, laughing sardonically.

"You really think she'll divorce you?"

"Devon and I never should've been together in the first place. Now to top it off, I had not only been plotting to put her father away for a very long time, but now, because of that plot, he's dead. Even with his crimes, she won't forgive me for that."

"His death wasn't your fault."

"No, but it's my greed that brought all of us to this point. Maybe it's a good thing that she's not here to deal with her father's death, a husband who's in witness protection, and a corrupt business."

"Speaking of disappearance, there's something I've been meaning to ask you," she said. "Where were you that night? I came to give you the ledger and…"

"And what?"

And in my moment of madness, to kill you, she thought to herself but decided to let that secret rest with her.

"And nothing. So, where were you?"

"I got held up with the buyers. I was trying to convince Rafael and his men to meet for the last deal. I wanted to leave town, but then I had a change of heart and realized that if I didn't take Robert down once and for all, I'd never stop running. Sorry. Did I miss anything?"

She gave him a withering look and soon, the DEA agents walked up to them.

"We need to get going," one of them said.

"Five minutes. You weren't kidding," Terrence said, dryly.

He knelt down and shook Kimmy's hand one last time. "It was very nice to meet you, young lady. You be good for your mom and dad."

"Okay," Kimmy said.

He stood again, and without warning pulled Havilland into his arms and hugged her. She hesitated and then finally wrapped her arms around him and returned the hug. When he let her go, he looked over her shoulder, gave a subtle nod, and turned to follow his DEA escorts away from Fisherman's Wharf.

Havilland knew who Terrence had silently acknowledged. She sensed him walking up behind her and breathed easily when she felt his hands touch the small of her back.

"You all right?" Eric asked.

"I'm good." She turned to him. "Thank you again for letting me do this."

"It was important."

She nodded and a momentary feeling of dizziness came over her, but she shook it off.

"Since you're higher up on the food chain than I am, any idea where they're taking him?"

He laughed. "I don't have that much clout. This is a high-profile case. No way the DEA is clueing us in on his future whereabouts. Even our acquaintance with Deputy Director Holladay doesn't warrant a smidgen of information..."

Havilland could see his lips moving, but his words became one garbled mess. The dizziness had returned, and this time she was powerless to fight it. She could see the concern on his face and him mouthing her name, but she couldn't answer. She couldn't do anything but close her eyes and submit to nothingness.

CHAPTER FIFTY-TWO

"I keep telling you, I'm fine," Havilland protested, waiting with Eric in the private emergency room while Kimmy sat outside in the waiting room with Lola, waiting to hear that she was okay.

"And I keep telling you we're not leaving until I hear the doctor say those exact words," Eric said and then paused to grin. "But it's always nice having a charming woman faint in my arms."

Havilland smiled. She didn't know what it was, but she never grew tired of receiving praise from him. Maybe because she loved and respected him so much as an agent, a father, a husband, and a man.

His smile slowly disappeared and his features turned to concern. "I hope you don't think I went with you to Fisherman's Wharf, because of anything from the past. I believe you when you say there's nothing between you two. I even believed him when he said the same thing." He paused to move a curly strand of hair behind her ears. "I just can't help but be protective of you."

"I didn't think that. I know you're just looking out for Kimmy and me."

She then looked away and he followed her gaze.

"What?" He asked. "What just happened?"

"Nothing."

He peered into her eyes, silently willing her to talk to him.

She set her eyes downcast and then slowly raised them to meet his. "I'm not the first woman you've felt the need to protect."

He leaned back and nodded his head. "Christina."

"We never really talked about her, and here I find out you met with her, twice."

"We ran into each other at the playground one weekend. I asked for her consultation with the ledger, and we met again at a diner to talk about what she found."

She looked away again, and he immediately took her chin in his forefinger and turned her back to face him. "That's all."

"I know, Eric. I believe you, but the two of you were in a pretty serious relationship," she said, "and with everything we were going through, I thought that maybe you'd remember how you used to love her and how things must've been much simpler with her."

"By simpler, you mean no criminal ex-boyfriend turned confidential informant in a drug trafficking case, a chemistry genius and recovering gambling addict for a brother, and a very adorable and precocious four-year-old daughter? When you put it that way…"

Havilland snorted with laughter and punched him in the arm. Eric leaned over and softly kissed her forehead.

"You're right. I used to be in love with her, but that was a long time ago. It's you who I love and who I want. You and Kimmy and everything else that comes with you."

He kissed her again, this time on the lips. "And I'm sorry if my behavior ever made you question that."

"I love you too," she said. "I've missed you so much, and I'm sorry I had to keep so much from you."

He pulled her into him for an embrace. "Stop apologizing. You know damn well this isn't all your fault. I've been a pig-headed jerk."

Havilland's laughter muffled against his chest. "Yeah, you have been."

"Damn, you didn't have to agree with me so quickly."

They were laughing when the doctor walked into the room. "Agent Sawyer?"

They looked toward the door and answered in unison. "Yes?"

"Agent Havilland Sawyer," he amended. "Thank you both for waiting. Everything looks good. Your vitals and blood work came back normal. However, the baby is the likely culprit of your fainting and dizziness, so I'm going to order a sonogram to ensure everything is okay, and then of course, you'll need to follow up with your OB."

He stopped talking when he looked up and must have seen the looks of utter shock on both Havilland's and Eric's faces.

"Oh," he hesitated, drawing out the word. "Did you not know you were pregnant?"

CHAPTER FIFTY-THREE

One month later...

Eric stared down at his wife in awe as she practically levitated off the bed. He had her legs spread wide and was using his thumb and forefinger to tease her opening. He reveled in the look of pleasure that flooded her face as she wildly undulated beneath him. But the love he felt for her intensified as he noticed the beginning of a barely noticeable bump where their child was growing inside her. They were finally at that place he'd wanted so desperately to get back to. They were there, in that moment, together with no secrets or lies resting between them.

He was also no longer her superior, which was even better for the health of their marriage. After the grand jury indicted Rafael Cirillo and his organization on charges of selling and trafficking controlled chemical substances, Haviland had come to him requesting a transfer out of CCSP and into White Collar Crimes instead. He hadn't argued with her.

With the CEO and Founder of Foxworth Pharmaceuticals deceased, and his daughter currently missing, the company was temporarily being run by the Board of Directors.

Stephen Currin chose that as his opportunity to resign and take on a lower level and lower stress job as a Pharmacist at San Francisco General. Currently, he's still attending meetings and seeing his sponsor weekly.

Kimmy, who was spending the afternoon with Jeanetta to give her parents some privacy, every now and then asked about the man Havilland took her to see at Fisherman's Wharf. Eric and Havilland decided that when she was much older, they'd tell her the identity of her biological father.

"Eric, please."

"Just a little more," he said. "I want you completely open for me."

He increased the pace as he circled his thumb on the ripe bud surrounding her warm center. She was so wet he needed to be inside of her, but he needed more to savor this moment with her. For so long, he'd been convinced she no longer wanted him or loved him, but now, having her in his arms, in their bed and completely surrendering to him, was doing wonders for his ego. She was still his woman.

He realized what a shitty husband he'd been. She easily believed his words, trusted in him to not betray her, but he himself spent the better part of three months not believing in her all over a kiss that had been innocent on her part. He'd chosen that one incident to believe the worst in her all because somewhere in the back of his mind was the fear that she was never truly his. That fear only magnified when she constantly went out of her way to protect Terrence from criminal prosecution and from him. He saw it as betrayal, but she wasn't betraying him. She was protecting her CI. She was being a good agent. His deep fears were something he needed to resolve within himself because in his heart, he knew Havilland loved him and was a deeply loyal woman.

"Now, Eric!"

She cried out as her body seemed to elevate even higher

off the bed from an impending orgasm. Eric released his fingers, gripped his hands on her spread thighs, and pushed himself inside of her. With the sweet sounds of her moans encouraging him on, he leaned down and flicked her erect nipples with his tongue and put his head between the crook of her neck, where he kissed her and inhaled her scent. He rocked in and out of her, coaxing the orgasm out and smiling devilishly when her sweet pleadings grew to thunderous moaning. She bit down on the fleshy part of his shoulder and began to chant his name over and over as she came. Yes, she was definitely all his, and as he felt himself being carried away by an unbelievable pleasure of his own, he testified he had always been—and would always be—hers.

EPILOGUE

*B*ack to that night...

Devon sat on the bare mattress of the king-sized bed with only a dimly lit lamp on the nightstand beside her and looked around the boxed-up bedroom. She didn't feel any nostalgia or remorse but was in fact glad to be leaving. It was a gorgeous mansion, but she missed her bedroom at her father's home in Georgia. Terrence would fight the leave of absence, but like it or not, she wasn't coming back to California. She was done playing the tagalong. He was coming back to Atlanta with her and from there, they could wait for this whole thing with the CBI, whatever it was, to blow over. She couldn't get a straight answer out of her father or Terrence as to what it was all about, but as far as she knew, they hadn't restricted Terrence from traveling, so she'd packed a bag for him and had the staff box up the rest of his things earlier.

Her cell phone buzzed from the dresser, and she got up and checked it to see that it was once again her father texting and offering to send his driver to pick her up. She put the phone down without responding. She wasn't leaving there without Terrence and telling her father that would only result in him calling to lecture her about what a big mistake she was making by investing all of her hopes and dreams in Terrence. But he had it all wrong. Terrence, like he'd accurately guessed earlier, was a consolation prize. No, she'd already put her hopes and dreams in one man, and that had ended in disaster.

She glanced down at her wristwatch and saw it was nearly ten minutes past eight. He'd left here an hour ago and said he would be back by then.

Jesus, if he causes us to miss our flight...

She thought about his words and actions earlier and wondered what had gotten into him to ask her to leave the country with him. Why the hell would he suggest such a thing when all this time he'd been fighting to move up there to launch the new pharmaceutical plant? Now suddenly, he wanted to go traipsing around the world? That wasn't going to happen.

She picked up her phone to call him but stopped when she heard a muffled voice coming from downstairs. Finally, Terrence was back, and it sounded like he was talking to someone. She grabbed her purse and phone from the bureau dresser, clicked off the bedroom lamp, and made her way down the carpeted stairs. When she came to the bottom step, she wound her way through their luggage and followed the voice. It was coming from the den in the rear of the house, but as she got closer, she realized two things: it wasn't Terrence's voice but a woman's, and she was talking on the phone.

Was it one of the housemaids? They had all been dismissed earlier that afternoon, so who could this be? Devon nearly entered, but what the woman said next had her stopping in her tracks and moving to a shadowed corner just outside of the den.

"I know what you're up to. You're trying to fuck me over, but it's not happening. I'm going to arrest that bitch Havilland, and then you're next."

What the hell? Who was this and who was she talking to? And what was all this about arresting Hav?

"Bastard," the woman muttered.

For a moment, there was nothing but silence, and Devon imagined the woman was impatiently waiting just as she'd been doing herself. But waiting for what? For whom? It couldn't be her father, because he was at San Francisco International waiting for Devon. Terrence, maybe?

Suddenly, a noise sounded somewhere off past the dining room. Devon looked in that direction but stayed hidden in the corner of the hall. She had the eerie feeling that something was horribly wrong with this entire situation, and it would be best for her to just stay out of sight.

"Is that you? I'm in here!" the woman called out. "I've been waiting long enough, and you'd better have the money I earned by keeping you out of prison!"

Heavy footsteps sounded on the wood floors leading from the dining area into the hall. Devon ducked farther back into the corner, as far as she could, but still made out two tall and very dangerous-looking men walking right past her. They were so close she closed her eyes and prayed for the shadows to keep her hidden.

"Who the hell are you two?" the woman asked. "Where's Robert?"

Devon opened her eyes at the mention of her father's name and dared to step out of the corner and peek into the den. The men were closing in on this woman, and Devon got her first clear look at her face. She recognized her as one of the agents she met when she visited Eric Sawyer at the CBI offices. Gone was the pleasant and carefree look she had that morning. Now, her features were laced with irritation and a trace of fear.

"I said who are you?" she asked again, but they didn't answer and continued to slowly advance on her.

Devon watched in horror as the men flanked her on both sides, and the woman—Maya, that was her name—started to go for the gun at her side.

But, one of the men anticipated the move and kicked it out of her hand just as she got a grip on it. It flew across the den as Maya grasped her injured hand and cried out in pain.

"You son of a bitch," she sneered and attacked the man who kicked her gun away with a stomp to his foot and a kick to his knee.

The man yelped in pain, but before she could turn and face her other attacker, the second man was already on her. He sent a backhanded slap across her face that stunned her long enough for him to wrap his large hands around her neck. She was a tall woman, but he was several inches taller and used his height to his advantage as he towered over her and squeezed. Maya kicked and scratched, but in her increasingly weakened state, her hands and legs didn't have much of an impact.

Devon slapped a hand across her mouth to keep from screaming. She had to do something, but what the hell could she do? These men had managed to subdue an agent with hand-to-hand combat and weapons training. What chance did she and her one self-defense class stand against them?

Maya's struggles began to slow, and a wheezing sound came from her mouth as her body tried one last ditch effort to get air. Suddenly, Devon heard a distinct sickening sound of the woman's neck being broken.

The man dropped her lifeless body to the floor in a crumpled heap and looked over at his partner.

"You all right?"

"Yeah," the other spat, rubbing his knee. "Goddamned cunt."

"Well, get yourself together. The other one may still be in the house. The client said she hadn't arrived at the airport, yet."

"Maybe we just missed her on our way over here."

"Maybe, but if so, we'll just get her in Atlanta. We can do her the same way as this one. By the way, break the glass and damage the lock on those doors. I want it to look like a sloppy break in, and it looks like she cut the feed to the cameras before she came in."

His partner chuckled. "What the hell was she up to?"

"Some bullshit, which is probably why our client wanted her dead. We'll turn them back on when we leave."

"Remind me why we're going after an heiress, when she obviously has more money than our client?" one of them asked over the sound of breaking glass.

"It's over for Robert Foxworth. He's going to prison for a long time. I was assured that if we get rid of his daughter, the client will inherit everything."

"You're sure this one's on the level?"

"I haven't been disappointed yet. Now, come on. Shake that shit off and let's go find our heiress."

Devon kept her hand over her mouth, willing herself to keep from uttering a single cry. She closed her eyes and breathed silently in and out, shutting her frightened tears away. This was no time to lose it. She had to get out of there. She had to get to the police. No, she had to get to the airport. Her father would know what to do. He'd protect her from whomever these men were and even more importantly, whoever had hired them.

She slowly opened her eyes just in time to see them walk by her again. She dared to step out of the shadows only far enough to see where they were going. One was heading up the stairs to check the bedrooms while the other retreated to another wing of the house.

When she was alone in the hall, Devon clutched her purse in her arm, slipped off her shoes, and hurried across the marble floor to the kitchen, opposite from where the man had gone. She slipped into the darkened kitchen and crossed to one of the small picture windows over the sink. She opened it, winced at the loud creaking sound it made and chanced a look behind her. Seeing no one, she quickly put her shoes back on, lifted herself onto the counter and tossed her purse out first. She began to climb out, pulling herself through the window, and then terror seized her when she felt someone grab her ankles.

"Where do you think you're going, bitch?"

Devon screamed and kicked with everything she was worth. He was so strong and was pulling her back into the house, but she renewed her strength and gripped the window frame to keep from being pulled in and kicked and kicked. One of her stilettos finally struck him in the face, and he instantly released her. The sound of his enraged roar gave her the motivation to propel herself through the window and tumble to the grass below.

Fear gripped her heart as she jumped to her feet, snatched her purse and ran as fast and as far away as she could, seeking shelter under the night sky.

* * *

Thank you for reading EXPOSED! If you enjoyed Eric and Havilland's exciting love story, you'll love the next book in the EX FILES series, EXECUTION.

When Devon hears the plot of her own murder, the only

one she can turn to is a man who's very good at hiding. Too bad he's also good at breaking her heart.

ONE-CLICK EXECUTION NOW >
"A very suspenseful and intriguing story."

SIGN UP FOR LISA'S NEWSLETTER:
www.lisaryancampbell.com/newsletter

And if you love a springtime romance with suspense, make sure you check out EX APPEAL, an EX FILES novella.

Ava never thought she'd return to Gypsy Bay, but she did and her job is to investigate the unsolved murder of Michelle Meyer. But all the evidence is pointing to one person and the reason Ava left town in the first place…Michelle's husband.

"Loved, loved, loved this book!"

"Loved the suspense, danger, twists and turns!"

"I haven't been this intrigued by a book for awhile…this was phenomenal!"

ONE-CLICK EX APPEAL for a steamy and suspenseful read.

The Ex Files

Exiled

Exchange

Explosive

Exposed

Ex Files Box Set

Execution

Extortion

The Ex Files Novellas

Explicit

Ex Factor

Ex O Ex O

Ex Appeal

Historical Romance

Deceit and Seduction

ABOUT THE AUTHOR

Award-winning Author, Lisa Ryan Campbell began writing as a small child using her mother's pink typewriting paper. Years later, she decided it was important to get a "real job" and attended Arizona State University to major in English with the goal of continuing on for both a Master's and Doctorate degrees in English and teach at the college level.

In 2002, Lisa graduated with a Bachelor's degree in English Literature and an Ancient Egyptian romance novel she wrote in her spare time. She decided then she would not be continuing on to graduate school, but instead joined Romance Writers of America and focused on her true love.

Lisa is an avid traveler and has seen many of the world's treasures in Egypt, Peru, Spain, France, Morocco, England, Mexico and the Caribbean. She spends her time mostly at her home in Colorado writing, reading and watching 1940's noir movies. She also loves to laugh, so you may frequently catch her watching reruns of Archer, Veep and The Office.

Sign up for Lisa's newsletter and find out more about her books at www.Lisaryancampbell.com and connect with her on social media.